I0610498

KNOCKRAMORE

by

Valerie Hansard

Grosvenor House
Publishing Limited

All rights reserved
Copyright © Valerie Hansard, 2018

The right of Valerie Hansard to be identified as the author of this
work has been asserted in accordance with Section 78
of the Copyright, Designs and Patents Act 1988

The book cover picture is copyright to Bella Hansard

This book is published by
Grosvenor House Publishing Ltd
Link House
140 The Broadway, Tolworth, Surrey, KT6 7HT.
www.grosvenorhousepublishing.co.uk

This book is sold subject to the conditions that it shall not, by way of
trade or otherwise, be lent, resold, hired out or otherwise circulated
without the author's or publisher's prior consent in any form of binding or
cover other than that in which it is published and
without a similar condition including this condition being imposed
on the subsequent purchaser.

This book is a work of fiction. Any resemblance to
people or events, past or present, is purely coincidental.

A CIP record for this book
is available from the British Library

ISBN 978-1-78623-129-1

Contents

Chapter One

Rhoisin held on to her mother's hand as they waited to cross the road.

'Mum, why haven't I got a dad?'

Linda's grip on her small daughter's hand tightened. The question she had always been dreading. And what a time to choose! Just as they were lining up with several of her school friends waiting for the lollipop lady on the other side to stop the traffic. Linda looked down at Rhoisin's serious little upturned face; the fine arched eyebrows meeting in a frown over the wide-set grey eyes; the mouth puckered, poised with another question.

'Everyone's got a dad, love,' she began. The fat woman next to them inclined her head a little closer. 'It's just that some dads stick around and other dads...'

The pelican crossing bleeped and the man on the sign turned from red to green, changing his posture, now striding out, encouraging the waiting pedestrians to do the same. The lollipop lady, easily visible in her white coat, stepped out into the road, holding aloft the sign emblazoned with two children crossing. Two mums with toddlers in pushchairs led the way, followed by other mothers and young children straggling across the road in an untidy procession. From behind them Linda could hear the wail of a siren. As it increased in nerve-shattering decibels, there was a squeal of tyres as a battered black

Ford Cortina careered around the corner knocking over the lollipop lady and missing the two pushchairs by a hair's breadth. The lollipop lady lay quite still in the middle of the road, her crossing sign perched at a crazy angle on top of the two pushchairs. For a second there was a deadly hush, then, as the crying and screaming started, the screech of the siren surrounded them as a police car rounded the corner at an even more dangerous speed than the Ford Cortina, swerved round the inert body of the lollipop lady and drove on in hot pursuit.

Several hours later, slowly recovering from the shock, Linda realised that one day she would have to answer her daughter's question. That day had only been postponed.

It was over a year before Rhoisin again broached the question of the whereabouts of her father. In that time she did a great deal of thinking as she listened to her school friends comparing notes on what daddies did. At the time when she had first questioned her mother on the subject she was still unaware of human conception. Now, as her ninth birthday loomed, Rhoisin was beginning to put two and two together.

The callous death of the lollipop lady had shocked the community. It was clear that the driver of the Ford Cortina car had caused her death but as he had shortly afterwards killed himself by driving into a wall the matter never reached the courts.

For weeks following the horrific accident Linda and Rhoisin took an alternative route to school. Although ten minutes longer, which meant getting up earlier, they both agreed it was well worth it. Occasionally, as they walked to school by their new route, Rhoisin began to think about her father. By now the two issues had become inextricably linked: violent death and the disappearance of her father became confused in her childish mind. Perhaps her father had died a violent death? Or perhaps, worse still, he had caused the violent death of another? Rhoisin held on tightly to her mother's hand as they walked to and fro from school, careful not to stand at the front of those waiting to cross the road; to avoid, as it were, a ringside seat of another possible tragedy.

It was August. Four more weeks of the summer holidays still stretched ahead. For Linda it was the most difficult time of the year. It was the time, above all, when the phrase: 'single parent' acquired its full meaning. She felt deep pangs of guilt as she left for work each morning leaving Rhoisin alone for the day in the drab dingy flat. Until two years ago life during the summer holidays had been a great deal easier. She had worked in a small family owned newsagent and confectioners in the High Street. There was no problem having Rhoisin in tow in the holidays. Mr. Patel even encouraged it. He said it enhanced the family atmosphere. But Mr. Patel had sold out two years ago and moved to a better neighbourhood where he could educate his children privately. Now many of the small family concerns in the High Street were moving or closing down, forced out of business by the expansion of chain stores and supermarkets, encouraged by the late post war boom in the early 1960s. For a few months Linda took a job in Boots, but gradually the hierarchy in the assistants' pecking order got her down and she moved across the road to Posners, a small family fabric business, though as far as Rhoisin was concerned the change made no difference. There was a total ban on all employees bringing their children in to work.

As the hot and seemingly endless August wore into its third week, Linda received an unexpected invitation. For the past few months she had been going out on an irregular basis with a man called Jim Banks whom she had met at a St. Valentine's party. The difficulty of finding a babysitter in the evenings had rather curtailed their outings, but none the less Linda and Jim found each other's company quite congenial.

Jim owned a static caravan which he kept on a site near Margate. It was a very large caravan – more like a cottage really – with a spacious lounge/diner, small kitchenette, shower room and three bedrooms; one a reasonably sized double; the two smaller ones more like boxrooms. It was a well-kept caravan site. As Margate is within easy reach of London, many owners visited their caravans most weekends in the summer months, so the place had a tidy well-used look, with flowers adorning the small area in front of each caravan. Linda was pleased, flattered and rather excited when Jim invited her to the caravan for the last week of August.

'But I have a young daughter,' Linda sounded apologetic, almost as if it were her fault.

'That's fine,' Jim had replied. 'Bring her along. We'll have a great time, the three of us. I like little girls.'

Linda was relieved and very grateful. Rhoisin was excited. She had met Jim for the first time that morning when he had called for them in his car. He breezed in, loud and large, dwarfing the tiny flat, swinging Linda round, ruffling her carefully coiffed hair.

'You look a picture, Linda, you really do.'

Linda patted her hair self-consciously, murmuring: 'This is Rhoisin,' as she pushed the child forward.

Jim looked down at the small child, twisting her hands together awkwardly, rubbing one leg down the back of the other as she did when she was embarrassed.

'Rhoisin, eh? And how do you spell that?'

'R H O I S I N.' replied the child. 'But it's pronounced Roosheen.'

'And who thought that one up?' enquired Jim. 'I've never heard that name before.'

'My Mum likes it,' said Rhoisin. She liked it too. It was different, unusual and she enjoyed getting people to spell it correctly. She look up cautiously at Jim for the first time and didn't care too much for what she saw. A halo of red hair framed a pale freckled face. A squashed nose like a small turnip squatted uneasily in the middle. Glassy pale blue eyes set too closely together were fringed by almost white eyelashes, above which the off-white eyebrows were almost invisible. The lower part of his face was a slight improvement on the upper half. The mouth, shapely though insensitive, with lips curling upwards as if accustomed to laughter, the podgy chin deeply dimpled. He was a big man, and though not fat, aware now that in his mid-thirties, he had to keep a weather eye on his beer gut. It was his hands that particularly struck Rhoisin. They were hairy and covered with pale red freckles. Even the fingers had a sheen of downy red hair and squidgy, misshaped freckles. The hands reminded Rhoisin of an orang-utan.

Mother and daughter took to the caravan right away. It was lighter and more spacious than their council flat in Kilburn. It was only the second season that it had been in use so it was almost new; the paintwork, chintz upholstery and the curtains still looked fresh. Linda cooked a simple meal on the Calor Gas stove and the three of them passed the evening playing cards and chatting.

The next few days passed pleasantly in the pursuit of the usual beach activities. The weather was glorious so they swam several times a day, relishing the hot sun on their already sunburnt bodies as they came out of the chilly sea. They rubbed suntan lotion onto each other, Jim's hairy, prehensile hands lingering just too long as he neared the pubic area, fingers creeping ever so little underneath the bra. Rhoisin squirmed under his touch and rolled off her towel into the sand.

Jim laughed. 'I won't hurt you lass. Sure you're just like a daughter to me.'

Friday, the last day of their holiday dawned hot and still like all the others. The night before Jim had proposed taking them out for a meal on their last evening. The next day he drove Linda into Margate to the hairdresser, planning to return for her in about an hour and a half.

Rhoisin lay on her narrow bed, reading. It was already very warm and she still wore her nightie. She looked up as the door opened slowly and softly. Jim stood in the doorway, large and lumbering, bare-chested, his red body-hair gleaming in the sunlight. Rhoisin's heart beat faster.

'Hello,' said Jim. 'You not dressed yet?'

Rhoisin said nothing. Jim sat down on the edge of the bed.

'Enjoyed your holiday?'

Still Rhoisin said nothing.

Jim started to stroke her leg; slowly, gently, relishing the smooth, silky, pre-pubertal skin. Rhoisin froze. The sound of children's voices playing outside wafted in through the window. Jim continued to stroke, higher and higher, above her knee, over the top of her thigh, past the pubic area, now caressing her flat smooth child's stomach. Rhoisin lay inert, paralysed. With his free hand Jim unzipped his flies and took out his penis, hard, covered in downy red hairs. Shaking with excitement, he plunged his finger right inside the helpless little girl. Rhoisin screamed out in agony and fear. Carried away by lechery and stimulated by sheer sadism, he ripped off her nightie, mounted and raped her.

Rhoisin fainted.

'How did you get on, Roosh?' asked Julie.

'Badly,' replied Rhoisin.

'You can't have done badly – not in both of them. Not in either of them, in fact. You're much too good. Which one did you think was the worst?'

'Biology.'

'Really? Even worse than chemistry? I thought that was quite impossible. I couldn't even finish it.'

'There was too much choice on the biology paper. I spent simply ages just trying to decide which questions to do.'

'Which one did you do? The sexual reproduction of the lizard or the glow worm?'

'I didn't do either,' said Rhoisin shortly. 'I'm not into sexual reproduction of lizards or glowworms,' she added quickly.

'Just humans,' said Julie lightly.

'Yes... no, I... I...' she trailed off.

Julie looked at her curiously. It was strange how Rhoisin shied away from any conversation connected with sex. After all, at sixteen she couldn't think of anything more absorbing.

'Well,' said Rhoisin, 'at least we've got tomorrow off to revise for history. I bet that'll be a scary one.'

'Yes,' said Julie gloomily, 'that'll give us writer's cramp all right. Are you ready to go home, Roosh? If you are you can give me some tips on what to mug up on the way?'

Rhoisin laughed good-naturedly. 'OK. C'mon then. You've been picking my brains for the last four years. I can't really stop you now.'

'Hello, Mum. It's me. 'I'm back,' Rhoisin called, as she let herself into the flat and closed the door. Linda came into the hall, wearing a dressing-gown, her hair in curlers.

'Hello, love. How did it go?'

'Lousy.' Rhoisin dumped her heavy school bag on the floor and threw her blazer on top.

'What, both of them?' asked Linda, automatically bending over to retrieve the blazer from the floor.

'Oh, leave it there, Mum. It's only the 'school sack.' Christ! I'm hungry.'

'I'll put the kettle on,' said Linda, holding on firmly to the blazer. I'll hang this up first, though. I've paid for it. 'Now let's see. It was biology today and history? No, history tomorrow.'

Rhoisin smiled affectionately at her mother.

'Not bad, Mum. It was biology and chemistry today. We've got tomorrow off so we can revise for history on Thursday.'

'Tomorrow off, love? That's nice. Jim's got the day off tomorrow as well. He said he might pop in and have a go at that leaking tap while I'm out at work. It's only the washer I'm sure, but I find it awfully stiff even with...'

Rhoisin felt her stomach heave. She wanted, as she had on several occasions, to tell her mother about the rape but something stopped her. It wasn't that she felt her mother wouldn't believe her. It was more that Linda might stop believing in Jim. Rhoisin realised that by now her mother somehow needed Jim.

'Mum; can't Jim stay out of our flat during the day if you're out. I mean, he must have other things to do in his own flat.'

'Jim's a very kind, thoughtful man,' replied Linda. 'Really, if he offers to do us a favour I can't turn him down. He might be offended. And after all, it's not as if I have anyone else to do the little jobs around the house.'

'Well, that settles it,' said Rhoisin, gritting her teeth. 'I'll go round to Julie's for the day. Her mum won't mind. I'll take a bite of something for lunch so she won't think I'm trying to eat them out of house and home. Julie will be pleased. she'll do better if I cram her a bit.'

Linda frowned. 'Rhoisin, why is it that you always seem to be avoiding Jim? I mean, don't you like him?'

Rhoisin gathered up her tea things and put them in the sink.

'He's OK, Mum, he really is. But I need a bit of peace and quiet if I'm going to get good grades. Even the O Level grades go on the UCCA Form. I work better if people aren't around.' She looked at her watch. 'Five o'clock. Can you give me two hours to work before dinner?'

The afternoon sun streamed through the wide open kitchen window. The table was strewn with books: text books, study aids, notebooks, jotters, pens and pencils. Rhoisin was gradually making order out of chaos; distilling the notes taken in class, fleshing them out with tips from the Pan Study Aids. *Romeo and Juliet*. Pity they had to dissect it. She had enjoyed it before they had started picking it to pieces. Only one more exam after this; history. She was fairly confident of doing well in that; hopeful of an A. French had been the bugbear, but it was no use worrying about it now. She heaved a deep sigh and didn't hear the front door key turn quietly in the lock. Absorbed in her work with her back to the kitchen door she was unaware that the door opened slowly and Jim Banks crept into the room as silently as his large bulk allowed. He stood behind her for a full minute watching her at work. Her slim white hand sped deftly across the page, her dark shining hair obscured her face revealing the two soft curves at the back of her shapely neck. Jim felt lust stirring in his groin. His breath coming in short, shallow pants, he took a step towards her and reached out his hand to caress her neck. Now was his chance; the opportunity he had frequently been denied.

Rhoisin continued to write, totally oblivious of the man's presence; standing behind her, evil and menacing, ready to pounce on his prey. One more step, thought Jim, his excitement rising. Then he paused. She had a tendency to faint when frightened. Was there really any point in fucking a woman who was out cold? Part of the fun was their reaction. He wasn't a rapist – well, not entirely.

Jim stepped back and gave a gentle cough.

'Jesus Christ!'

Terrified, Rhoisin leapt out of her chair.

'What the bloody hell do you mean creeping in on me like that? This isn't even your flat! And who gave you the key?'

She was shaking, sweating with fear.

Jim walked calmly round to the other side of the table and stood facing her. 'We had to see how the clever little student was progressing, didn't we?' He gave her a lecherous smile, fingering his flies. He took a step towards her. 'I thought perhaps it was time the young lady took a break from geography and history and did a little study of a more practical nature.'

He reached out and tore the top button off her blouse.

Consumed with anger, Rhoisin momentarily forgot her terror. With one swift movement she stepped up to the table, picked up a pair of sharp pointers and drew them viciously across his face, just missing his left eye. Howling with pain, blood pouring down his face, Jim leapt around the room, rushed out of the front door and bounded down the stone staircase, taking the steps two at a time.

Shaking with terror, Rhoisin sat down and burst into tears.

'Mum, are you sure you're OK?' Rhoisin sounded anxious. She sat down at the kitchen table opposite her mother. Linda had clearly been crying. She looked up at her daughter, fresh tears welling up in her eyes.

'I went to the doctor's today,' said Linda slowly, 'because I found a lump. Here.' She touched her right breast nervously with her left hand. There was a long pause. Rhoisin looked up, frightened.

'Oh, Mum!'

'The doctor thinks it could be – could be cancer,' she whispered.

Rhoisin got up, went round to the other side of the table and put her arms round her mother. 'Oh, Mum!'

Linda put her head on her arms and sobbed. Rhoisin knelt down beside her mother and stroked her gently. Her thoughts were in a turmoil. Cancer! No! Surely not! Not her mother. Not at forty-one. People didn't get cancer at the age of forty-one. Old people got cancer. People in their eighties. Not young people. There must be a mistake. The doctors at the hospital would surely sort it out.

But what if there wasn't a mistake? What if her mother did have cancer? Would it be curable? She had heard of people who were cured of cancer. But say it wasn't curable and then her mother wasn't there any more? What would she do completely on her own? No brothers, sisters, or even aunts or uncles as far as she knew. And what about her father? Where was he? Was he still alive? Should she try and find him, especially if...

She tried to banish such dreadful thoughts from her mind. It was impossible to think of her mother not being there any more... She must try to be strong, supportive, cheerful if possible.

'Mum, it'll be OK. You'll see. Have they actually confirmed it yet? Said that there's anything – you know – malignant?'

Linda looked up. 'No. Nothing's been confirmed yet.'

'Well, then. Nothing's definite yet. It'll be OK. You'll see. Medicine has made enormous strides in the last ten years or so. Doctors can do wonderful things nowadays. Just look at all the people walking round with other peoples' hearts, livers and kidneys. Not to mention half the population over sixty-five with pacemakers, who are running marathons after open heart surgery. It'll be OK. They'll do microsurgery and you won't even notice the difference.'

Linda sobbed louder. 'They'll cut it off! You wait. Cancer's different. It's not clean and straightforward like a heart attack. It's a growth, malignant and deadly like a poisonous mushroom, slowly eating the body away.'

'Mum, it hasn't actually been confirmed yet, has it?'

'N – no. They haven't actually spelt it out yet. They're afraid to. They're afraid to tell me the real truth.'

'But, Mum, how far has the investigation got? Have you seen a specialist yet?'

'No,' said Linda, sitting up and brushing the tousled hair from her tear-stained face. I've an appointment at the hospital first thing on Monday.'

'Well,' said Rhoisin, trying to sound cheerful. 'You see? All isn't lost yet. The doctor will examine you and you'll have one of those mammogram things you were telling me about and we'll take it from there. Try and cheer up, Mum. Look, I'll make some tea and then I'll go out and get something special for our dinner.'

Chapter Two

'What can I get you, love?'

'Oh, I haven't ...' Rhoisin, lost in reverie, was suddenly jolted into the present. She quickly scanned the short menu. 'I'll have... egg mayonnaise and cress please.'

'White bread, rye bread, granary bread, French bread, pitta-bread, Nan-bread or pumpernickel,' intoned the waitress. 'Or you can have the whole lot toasted.'

'Even the Nan?' said Rhoisin, rather surprised.

'Egg and cress on toasted Nan.' The waitress wrote it down on the order pad.

'No, no,' said Rhoisin confused.

'No?' said the waitress, drawing a vicious line across her pad. 'Make up your mind, then. There's lots of other customers waiting.'

'Yes, sorry,' stammered Rhoisin. 'I only meant, well, toasted Nan does seem rather a contradiction in terms, doesn't it?'

'We don't go in for contradictions here,' replied the waitress tartly. 'We just try and give the customers what they want as quickly as possible.'

'Yes, of course. I am sorry.' Rhoisin could feel herself blushing. 'I'll have brown bread.'

'Granary or rye?' The waitress was a stickler for accuracy. She'd been sacked for less. 'Toasted or not?'

Rhoisin felt weary. The argument had sapped her appetite. 'I think I'll just have a coffee,' she said.

'Nothing to eat? You're wasting your money. There's a minimum charge of £3.50 at lunchtime. Otherwise we'd have every Tom, Dick and Harry, not to mention Sharon and Tracy, coming in here for a cup of coffee that's only 70p after all, and taking up the space where the boss could be making £3.50 or more. But it's up to you, love.' The waitress's aggression was slowly abating. 'Take my advice and have a nice sandwich.' She stared hard at Rhoisin. 'Looks to me as if you need a bit of feeding up. Have the granary. It's fresh today so it don't need toasting. And here –' she became almost confidential, 'have a cappuccino. They do 'em nice here.'

Rhoisin smiled gratefully. 'Thanks. That sounds lovely.'

The small coffee bar was cramped and noisy. Clouds of blue cigarette smoke hung in the air, making her throat prickle and her eyes smart. She sat at a table for two just inside the door. Each time the door opened to admit yet another person who would take up space, make a noise, and probably add to the pall of smoke, a blast of cold air vent its full spleen upon Rhoisin before wafting round the stuffy room, breaking up the dense coils of smoke into thin grey ribbons. She was undecided about whether or not to shed her thick duffle coat. Once the door was closed for more than a few minutes the room became unbearably hot. She decided to risk it, struggling out of the heavy coat with difficulty in the cramped space, feeling more comfortable in her thin black cotton skinny-rib sweater, which she wore with freshly laundered jeans.

'This seat taken?'

Rhoisin looked up to see a well dressed man of indeterminate age standing with his hand elegantly placed on the back of the opposite chair.

'N – no. Please do,' she murmured, indicating the seat.

Long tapered fingers, well-manicured nails, reached languidly for the menu. The waitress hovered, clucking impatiently.

'Yes, sir?'

'Egg and cress, please.'

Out of the corner of her eye Rhoisin noticed the finely chiselled profile.

'White bread, rye bread, granary bread, French bread, pitta-bread, Nan-bread or pumpernickel; plain or toasted,' droned the waitress. The man laughed.

'I didn't catch all that. Would you start again, please.'

The waitress leant towards him aggressively. Her voice became a hiss. 'White, rye, gran, Nan, French, pitta or pump-er-nick-el.'

Fine eyebrows arched above deep set brown eyes. Sensitive lips curled in amusement. The man spoke again in a resonant well-modulated voice.

'Granary, please.'

'Toasted?'

'I think not.'

'A good choice, sir. The granary's fresh today. Which is more as can be said for the rest of them. Coffee, sir?'

'Please. A cappuccino.'

The man glanced at his watch, then stood up and took off his overcoat, folding it across the back of his chair. His clothes were casually smart. Navy cashmere sweater exactly matching his trousers, crisp white shirt. He smiled across at Rhoisin.

'Warm in here. You come here often?'

Rhoisin looked startled. She hadn't expected to be addressed directly.

'No. It's the first time.'

'You work near here?'

'No. I just happened to be passing.'

The waitress arrived bearing two plates of sandwiches.

'Egg and cress on granary bread, sir, and the same for the young lady. Two cappuccinos coming up.' She set down the two plates of sandwiches, returning seconds later with the coffees.

Rhoisin glanced at her companion without moving her head. Although he was a complete stranger she felt some social constraint in starting on her food before he did. She eyed her plate. It was a substantial sandwich; a thick creamy filling, palely yellow, spotted with streaks of dark green cress, oozing out from between two moist slices of health-giving brown bread. A gourmet's delight, it was cut into four triangles, two of which were covered with a white paper napkin. Unsure whether to use the napkin to guide the unwieldy portion to her mouth, or use it to mop up the aftermath, Rhoisin glanced at her companion, more directly this time, to see how he was planning to tackle the operation.

The man smiled again, reassuring crows feet appearing around the eyes, lines of laughter deepening round the mouth.

'Looks a pretty hefty sandwich. Hope you're hungry.'

Almost as if she were his guest.

'Oh, yes,' murmured Rhoisin, still uncertain as to what to do next.

The man placed both hands on the first triangular portion; slim elegant fingers folding round the white paper napkin, smoothing the thin protective layer of paper round the succulent morsel, raising it to his lips. He took the first bite; his even, shapely teeth making a smooth semi-circle in the triangle away from the crust, in the part of the sandwich where the bread is at its best; moist, damp and soft. A large glob of egg oozed out and fell with a plop onto the plate, gleaming, translucent with mayonnaise. The man passed his tongue round his lips and glanced down at his plate.

Rhoisin watched, fascinated.

The doctors hadn't told Linda how ill she was. Instead they had placed the burden on Rhoisin's frail and inexperienced shoulders. Rhoisin, twenty-one, vulnerable and insecure, now had to grapple with the fear of being orphaned in the very near future. She had no one to turn to. No one with whom she could discuss her fears, for her mother or for herself. She had never watched anyone die before and she felt totally unequal to the enormity of it all. She couldn't actually imagine death itself. What happened? Where did the deceased go? Was there any pain? She was afraid to ask her mother if she suffered pain or if she was frightened. She felt unable to give comfort or even adequate sympathy. She could only feel her own fear at her approaching bereavement, and she did not as yet possess the experience and maturity to deal with it.

Rhoisin left the ward as the bell sounded for the end of visiting hour. The mournful hand bell sounded as if it were tolling for the dead. Linda had become weaker, even in the last twenty-four hours. She had been in hospital now since the end of October. Nearly two months. Soon it would be Christmas. Usually Rhoisin looked forward to Christmas, despite the regulation visit from lecherous Jim. Now she was dreading it. She felt she could even put up with Jim; for the day if necessary, just to have her mother home and well for Christmas.

As the bell jangled on, Rhoisin stood up and bent over her mother to kiss her good night. Linda lay limp on the fresh pillows, her skin shrivelled and yellow; eyes lack-lustre; her body emaciated. Rhoisin smelt her fetid breath coming in short shallow gasps. She felt frightened and very alone.

'Night, Mum,' she said, trying to sound cheerful. 'Sleep well.'

'Night, love,' said Linda weakly. 'I'll see you tomorrow, won't I?'

Will you? thought Rhoisin desperately. 'Yes, Mum. Of course you'll see me tomorrow.'

She walked slowly down the ward towards the exit, her feet heavy as lead. Coming briskly towards her down the corridor was a young female doctor; supremely confident, her white coat open, revealing a well-cut navy blue dress beneath. As she played with her stethoscope she emanated an aura of omnipotence. She nodded as she passed and gave Rhoisin a brief smile. Then she walked on and turned into the ward next to the one where Linda lay. Rhoisin suddenly had an enormous urge to speak to the doctor; to confide all her fears: to ask her about death; whether it was painful or whether one just slipped away into blissful oblivion. She wanted to ask the doctor if there was anything positive she could do; if she should stay with Linda till the end. But she lacked the courage and confidence to follow the doctor into the other ward. She was afraid to see more suffering and afraid, too, to confide in the doctor who had made a profession of alleviating suffering; whose whole life was involved with seeing people die and who possibly could no longer understand what it felt like for those who were inevitably left behind.

So Rhoisin went home quietly, full of loneliness and despair, leaving Linda to die all alone.

There were over fifty people in The Church of The Holy Child Jesus in Kilburn. Rhoisin was surprised. She hadn't realised her mother knew so many people. She had put an announcement in *The Daily Telegraph* and another one in *Hibernia,* the Catholic weekly read by many of the Catholics in London, British as well as Irish. It always struck her as odd that her mother had been a Catholic. Especially nowadays when most people in England weren't really anything at all.

I did well to steer clear of religion, she thought. Pure superstition, and so divisive. Still, there must be some force for good in the world otherwise there would only be war, murder and greed. There must surely be something or someone to oversee the wonders of nature, literature and beautiful music. The choir was singing now:

'Abide with me; fast falls the eventide:
The darkness deepens; Lord with me abide!
When other helpers fail, and comforts flee,
Help of the helpless, O abide with me.'

Rhoisin choked back a sob. She was helpless now. Was there a God to come to her rescue? Had He deserted her because she had never done anything for Him? Maybe she should have taken the whole religious bit more seriously. Learnt her catechism; gone to confession; taken communion. But it was too late now. Or was it too late? Some say it's never too late. Maybe she could try saying a prayer or two. She was entirely on her own now. She had no one. Not even a distant relative. And what about her friends? At first she had kept up with a few friends from her school days but as the years went by there seemed to be less and less reason to keep up the contact. There had been Julie, of course. Julie had been a real brick and a great laugh. They had shared most things at school. But Julie had mucked up her A Levels twice. Her Dad had paid through the nose for a crammer the second time and she had done even worse. He had told her in no uncertain terms to go out and get a job, so unable to find anything suitable in England, she had gone off to live in Australia. Her talent for letter-writing barely came up to her A Level attainment, so Rhoisin had felt quite bereft.

For some reason she had made few really close friends at university. She thought it was possibly because she had gone to university in London and, like many of the other students who also lived in London, she just went home at night. Also, even if she really had wanted to be more part of the student scene, she didn't have a great deal of spare cash to spend on drinks in pubs and in the Students' Union.

Then there was life at the flat. Linda had not encouraged her to bring friends home. In her teens Rhoisin would occasionally ask her mother if she could bring a friend back to tea after school. After all, other girls invited their friends and quite often invited Rhoisin, for although rather shy, she was certainly not unpopular.

'No,' Linda would say, 'not today, love. Maybe next week.' But when next week came Linda always had an excuse. 'It'll be a tiring day at the shop tomorrow,' she would say, or 'I can't really run to the extra expense this week after splashing out on those new curtains.'

So in the end no one came at all. Except Jim.

Jim. Nervously Rhoisin half looked round. Surely he was here. At Linda's funeral. Rhoisin wondered with a shudder if he still had the scar she had inflicted on him that day when he had just walked into the flat when she was studying. She was so terrified he was going to rape her again that she had just picked up the first weapon that came to hand. She had almost blinded him. Her mother was so shocked and upset that Rhoisin had nearly told her about the rape, but she wasn't convinced her mother would believe her. After all, it was just her word against Jim's.

They had been together for about twelve years, her mother and Jim. On and off. Sometimes Jim would disappear for months on end and Rhoisin would feel relieved and very thankful. She knew her mother saw other men during these periods for sometimes she would answer the phone to a number of different male voices, all of whom spoke of Linda in quite familiar terms. But as far as she knew they didn't visit the flat. Then Jim would return unexpectedly, lecherous, more gross and groping than ever. On the one hand Rhoisin found it difficult to understand why her mother was so pleased to see him; on the other, as she grew older, she began to see that Linda needed some permanent male support.

And then, where were the relatives? Didn't she have any? Most people did. You had to be related to someone. Of course not knowing who one's father was didn't help. Strange that Linda never wanted to talk about him. On several occasions Rhoisin had tried to draw her mother out but she had refused to be drawn. Once in the hospital, nearing the end, Linda had made an attempt to talk to her daughter.

'Love, there's something you ought to know about your father.'

'Yes, Mum,' Rhoisin said, all eagerness, drawing the chair up closer to the bed.

'Your father was a good man,' Linda went on. 'You mustn't blame him for going off the way he did. You mustn't hold it against him.'

'No, Mum,' said Rhoisin obediently, hoping for some concrete information.

'Your father wasn't really irresponsible. It was just that his responsibilities lay in other directions.'

Rhoisin felt it would be cruel to remark that she thought a man's first responsibility was jointly to the mother and his child before looking around in other directions.

'His name was Thomas O'Hare,' continued Linda, 'and he was tall and very good looking.'

He would be, thought Rhoisin. Those sort of men usually are.

'He was Irish,' said Linda. 'He said he lived on a large estate in the West of Ireland and that one day... one day... He said that one day he would come back... come back... and...'

Linda drifted off into one of her increasingly frequent sleeps and that was the end of the matter. She never referred to the question of Thomas O'Hare again and Rhoisin was afraid to allude to it.

The organ was playing soft, sad, slow music. The members of the congregation were crossing themselves and genuflecting before the altar, then filing out slowly and sombrely as befits a funeral. The priest stood at the door shaking hands. Rhoisin hardly knew him.

'Ah, Rhoisin, Rhoisin, what a terrible thing, to loose your mother so young like that. Our prayers and thoughts are with you,' he went on, pumping her arm repeatedly, Irish accent thickening through the smell of whisky. Rhoisin tried to smile, to say something, but her jaw stuck. She passed out of the church with the small band of mourners into the chill December air.

Out in the bleak churchyard they stood in small groups, some conversing quietly, others looking around, searching for a familiar face. On the periphery Rhoisin noticed four of the girls who had worked with her mother in the shop. One of them saw her and smiled. Otherwise she recognised no one. Although, wasn't that a horribly familiar shock of red hair by the furthest gravestones? Her stomach heaved as she hurried towards the gate, hoping he wouldn't see her and try to follow her.

Outside on the pavement she felt a hand on her arm. A male voice said: 'Rhoisin?' Turning round she saw a man in his forties who looked remarkably like her mother. Her heart thumped. Blood rushed to her face. Surely not? It couldn't be. Linda had never mentioned a brother. Could she have an uncle?

'Rhoisin?' The eyebrows raised over quizzical, wide-set grey eyes just like her own, a faint smile playing round the mouth.

'Yes,' she said, uncertain of what to say next.

'I'm Jack Hobbs,' came the not entirely unexpected reply. 'Linda's brother. Your Uncle Jack. I saw your announcement in *The Daily Telegraph*. This is my wife, Liz. Can we give you a lift to the crematorium?'

Chapter Three

Miread Devlin blew up her small travel pillow, placed it on the headrest behind her and settled down to try and get some sleep. The bus could hardly be described as a luxury coach but Miread had become used to it over the years. The best thing that could be said about it was the low cost; less than half that of the train. Though she had travelled by train a few times at the beginning, when she had been as yet unaware of the existence of the coach; trundling across Ireland, cha-cha, cha-chum; cha-cha, cha-chum, in about half the time it took the coach, revelling in the comfort. It was a friend at the bank, another of the clerks, who told her about the coach. Miread was amazed at the low cost.

'But it's no luxury ride,' her friend had warned her.

'Beggars can't be choosers,' said Miread.

'Sure it's only temporary,' replied her friend. 'You'll be a manager one day. You'll see. You'll be one of them high-flyers.'

In four years Miread had flown no higher than a desk in the inside office dealing with customers letters and phone calls, mostly complaints. However, it made a change from dealing with complaints over the counter.

After leaving school Miread had been determined to get out of Killalee. She had obtained honours in her Leaving Certificate, giving her the confidence to try for a job outside the confines of that small, parochial town. By the time she was seventeen and a half she had grown to loathe the place; grey, drab and sunless. A place where nothing ever happened, where everyone knew everyone else; where you couldn't go anywhere or do anything without the entire countryside, never mind the town, knowing exactly what you were up to. She had spent the summer after leaving school serving snacks in The Laughing Goat. It was great gas at times, specially in the evenings when the men would have a few jars too many and pinch her bottom or stroke her bare leg. She enjoyed that. But when the summer ended all the interesting people seemed to melt away: people from Galway and Donegal and even County Fermanagh across the border, visiting relatives and friends. There were tourists from Dublin and England too; posh toffs with smart clothes and refined accents, showing off and throwing their money around. But they were all good for a laugh and most were good for a healthy tip as well. Come the end of September there were only the locals left. Looking round at them Miread didn't care a great deal for what she saw. Even to a country girl with her limited experience they all seemed to lack taste, style or any interest whatsoever.

It was not, at this early stage in her young life, that Miread was remotely contemplating marriage, or even sex. She had been brought up a strict Catholic to believe that sex outside marriage was a mortal sin. And while she still lived in Killalee she went along with this belief. After all, no temptation had come her way as yet; and there is nothing like temptation for altering one's beliefs. It was more a need to stretch her wings; to see other places; to experience a different way of life. There were times when she felt she would just up and off and go to England. Lots of young Irish people were going to England. You read about it in the papers all the time. Some went for good, to get a better job. Some, the girls, went because they had to. Miread didn't want anyone to think that she had had to do such a scandalous thing. Not that there was any young man she could be linked with. But it was amazing how people could invent stories when they wanted to. Especially in a small place like Killalee, where nothing much ever went on; in winter above all.

So by the end of September she decided to go to Dublin and try for a job; a better job than just serving snacks in a pub. At first her mother had been against it. Miread had known she would be. Since her father had died of cirrhosis of the liver when she was seven, her mother had become increasingly dependant on Miread, both practically and emotionally. After all, poor Eamon wasn't up to much, but Miread tried to tell herself that it wasn't his fault he had always been backward and wasn't she the lucky one to have all the gifts and the looks. All the same, she couldn't look at Eamon without feeling guilty.

It took Miread only about a week to break down her mother's resistance to the idea of her going off to Dublin to look for a job.

'It'll be great, Mam,' she said persuasively, 'I'll be earning good money so I'll be able to help you out and I'll come back weekends, especially at first.'

So at the beginning of October, just eighteen, Miread went bravely off to Dublin on her own to seek her fortune. That was nearly four years ago.

She had been lucky. There was no doubt about it. In retrospect she had to admit that she had been most apprehensive about the whole venture. In one sense she had nothing to lose because she hadn't got a decent job in Killalee anyway, but what she had dreaded, without even admitting it to herself at the time, was that she wouldn't be able to find a job in Dublin either and she would be forced to return to Killalee with her tail between her legs to face the humiliation of everyone gossiping behind her back.

'There goes Miread Devlin. The one what went off to Dublin because she thought Killalee wasn't good enough for her.'

'That's Miread Devlin, what left her poor widowed mother to go off and enjoy herself in Dublin.'

But luckily that hadn't happened, not yet, anyway. Although there was so much talk of redundancies, especially in the financial sector, she was keeping her fingers crossed that her job would be safe. She had had a few promotions, been sent on a few training courses, and although she wasn't among 'the graduate intake', a new phrase to her, she was smart, good at maths and most attractive looking.

At the Convent of The Immaculate Conception in Killalee the girls' interest in their personal appearance was not encouraged. The Mother Superior was plain to the point of being ugly; wrinkled, lumpily fat and having reached that particular age which produces unwanted facial hair, was sporting a full moustache and straggling beard by the time Miread was ready to leave her spiritual care. None of the other nuns was anything to look at either, and as it was a very strict order still requiring them to wear the full-length habit and wimple, not much of them was discernible anyhow.

So it wasn't until Miread went off to Dublin and met, for the first time, rather more sophisticated girls in her peer group than she had had the opportunity to meet before, that she began to notice her own appearance. Her new found friends advised her on clothes, make-up, shampoo, hair spray and a completely different range of exciting toiletries that she had no idea existed. They took her to parties and here she met the young men of the day. A whole new world opened up before her. A world of laughter, parties, drink, men and sex.

The bus jolted and the grinding of gears woke Miread up. She'd been dreaming and having sexual fantasies. It was happening more and more. Sometimes she would fantasise at work, just sitting in her glass cubicle at the bank, reading customers' letters, studying their statements. The letters from women didn't turn her on at all. She dealt with these speedily and efficiently, seeking advice where it was needed, typing suitable replies and leaving the letters unfolded in the OUT tray ready to be checked and signed by her superior. Then she could afford to take a little longer over the letters from the male customers. The names meant a lot to her: Patrick, Michael, Dermot, had a ringing sound to them. She was less attracted to Gerard, Eoghan, Sean, and of course Eamon was a complete turn off.

The Dublin party scene of the particular set in which she found herself was a complete revelation to Miread. Her previously sheltered life at the Convent and in the narrow confines of Killalee had left her completely unprepared for the social and sexual freedom of life in the Big Town.

Her luck in finding a good job so soon after her arrival in Dublin extended to finding, almost immediately, a room in a flat shared with three other girls in Ely Place, just round the corner from Baggot Street, where the bank was. Baggot Street was a swinging place, full of coffee bars and little bistros, and five minutes walk from St. Stephen's Green, which many people considered to be Dublin's natural centre.

At weekends there were parties all around. Most were within walking distance of where she lived, in flats in the tall elegant Georgian houses of Fitzwilliam and Merrion Squares or in similar houses towards the southern end of Baggot Street. There were other parties too, in the smart, more suburban style houses of Ballsbridge, Sandymount and Blackrock. And sometimes several of them would pile into cars and drive out to the wealthy Howth peninsular on the north side of the city where the parties took place at the luxurious homes of students from Trinity College or University College Dublin, whose parents were inevitably away on holiday. These Howth parties, being so far from the city centre, led to most of the guests staying the night, and unavoidably, through lack of space, sharing beds or floor space in very close proximity.

Miread had been quite unprepared for her first sexual encounter. It was nearly Christmas and she had been in Dublin for only three months. She had been determined to fit in all the parties going before being forced to spend the rest of the festive season in the sanctity and isolation of Killalee. She and her flatmate had gone to a party in Baggot Street, at the flat of a bank colleague. The place was packed with people; smoking, drinking, joking, hugging, stroking, kissing. Miread had no idea whether those engaged in more intimate embraces were old friends or virtual strangers. She and her friend had a quick snack before they arrived but she was still quite hungry and there didn't appear to be anything to eat. So they drank instead.

By the time the tall young man, whose name was Ryan, came to chat up Miread she was beyond the point of taking in very clearly what he said. He brought her another drink and managed to squeeze them both onto a sofa. He put his arm around her and began to stroke her gently. She responded readily, moving closer to him, allowing him to unbutton her blouse and caress her breast. He drew her closer towards him, searching for her mouth. They joined in a long kiss, tonguing, relishing each other. Miread gave a little moan of pleasure. Suddenly the young man stopped kissing her, buttoned up her blouse, said: 'thanks a lot,' and went off to the other side of the room, leaving Miread a little hurt, rather puzzled and extremely frustrated.

She said nothing to her friend but waited impatiently for the next party invitation. The pattern was similar. Gerald was personable, extremely amorous, but never forced his attentions. It was Miread who then began to lead the way in these brief encounters, always a step ahead, careful what she had to drink, noticing the many other young couples similarly engaged around the room. By now Miread's sexual appetite had been whetted. She didn't consider the morals of it at all. As far as she was concerned her rigorous moral indoctrination at the Convent had absolutely nothing whatsoever to do with 'real life.' She saw no connection between religion and sexual desire. For her, young, lovely to behold, on the threshold of womanhood, nothing could be more natural than the urge to go to bed with a man and have full sex.

It was at a party in Howth that she met Tony. She was going home to Killalee in two days so she supposed she was feeling particularly reckless. They went quite far on the floor in a corner of the room. He got her bra off and was doing wonders with her breasts. He found her vagina and discovered to his joy that she put up no resistance. Miread felt she had now reached the point of no return and if she was going to have full pre-marital sex, the time had now arrived

'Do you want it all the way?' he murmured in her ear.

'Here?' Her eyes widened.

'No, there's a bedroom for that.'

He took her hand and led her upstairs. They were by now, both pretty frantic for each other. He opened a door at the top of the stairs. As expected, it was a bedroom, with another naked couple already on the bed. They moved over when Miread and Tony came in. He laid her gently on the bed and continued stroking her breasts. She moaned, insatiable, her vagina expanding. Quickly he stripped naked and mounted her and they came to their climax together in a physical ecstasy completely devoid of emotion.

Miread moaned softly in her sleep and went into a sexual spasm. Her travelling companion sitting beside her gave her a curious glance. The bus jolted violently and slowed to a halt.

'Killalee!' called the driver. 'Would all those for Killalee please descend now. And remember your luggage!'

Killalee. Killalee. Miread felt numb with sleep and weariness. Two whole days in Killalee. Well, there wouldn't be any sex, that was for sure.

She stood up stiffly, got out of the bus and made her way slowly, without much enthusiasm to her mother's whitewashed, rose-covered cottage.

Chapter Four

It was mid-March. One of those early English spring days so full of promise that it was virtually impossible to believe that the present weather would not continue at least until well into September. Already, in the middle of the day, the heat of the sun could be felt, sent to chase away the rain clouds, chill winds and winter snow. The whole of London seemed to be on holiday. Office workers took their sandwiches into the parks, filling up the benches, over-spilling onto the damp spring grass. Men in business suits loosened their ties, and removed their jackets, throwing them casually over their shoulders, to join the secretaries and bank clerks outside. Shoppers with carrier bags bulging with purchases, swarmed en masse out of the Oxford Street and Regent Street department stores, crowding the few available benches, looking in vain for a pavement street café. Round Leicester Square students lolled in the small park, sprawling on the grass, strolling around the pedestrian area outside, even sitting on the pavement. Young couples walked arm in arm, cinema queues abandoned for the sake of enjoying the warm spring weather. Rhoisin hurried along Charing Cross Road from the Duke of York's Theatre as fast as the crowds would allow, hoping to find a sunny seat in one of the Leicester Square sandwich bars. Since becoming a pedestrianised zone, Leicester Square and many of the small surrounding streets had begun to develop the pavement style cafés so popular abroad. She was fortunate enough to find a vacant seat at a table for two at the edge of the pavement.

The waitress arrived almost before she had time to study the menu.

'Yes, love?'

'Egg mayonnaise and cress, please,' replied Rhoisin almost automatically.

'White bread, rye bread, granary bread, French bread, pitta-bread...'

'... Nan-bread or pumpernickel,' said a laughing, well-educated male voice, as a shapely hand was placed on the vacant chair opposite.

'May I join you?' the voice enquired.

Looking up Rhoisin recognised the gentleman with whom she had shared a table a few months ago. It must, of course, be the same sandwich bar but it looked quite different from the outside in the bright spring sunlight.

The man placed the jacket, which he had carried nonchalantly over his shoulder, on the back of the chair and sat down.

'Have you ordered?' he asked.

'Just the filling, not the bread,' replied Rhoisin.

'Egg mayonnaise?' he enquired, teasing.

'Well – yes, actually.'

Their previous meeting flashed across Rhoisin's mind. The hot, smoky, crowded coffee bar – she looked across at it, now silent and almost empty inside. The cold blast of air that hit her face as each new customer entered contrasting sharply with the warm, sunny spring day. The egg mayonnaise oozing out of the thick, succulent sandwich, falling gently onto the plate, translucent, palely yellow, speckled with dark green cress...

'In granary bread?' His well-modulated voice broke across her thoughts.

'Yes, lovely.'

'And two cappuccinos,' he said, half to her and half to the hovering waitress.

'This is indeed a coincidence,' he said as he sat down.

'Yes,' said Rhoisin.

'Have you been here since our last meeting?' he enquired.

'No,' said Rhoisin. 'Have you?'

'Yes. Quite often. I work quite near here.'

'So do I,' said Rhoisin. 'But only since last week.'

'Oh,' he replied. 'What do you do?'

'I work at the Duke of York's Theatre in St. Martin's Lane selling tickets at the box office.'

'Really? What made you want to do that?'

'Desperation,' replied Rhoisin. 'I couldn't find anything better.'

'I see.'

The sandwiches arrived, appearing even larger than before. They both laughed.

'Last time I waited to see what you would do,' said Rhoisin.

'Yes. I noticed that. This time I'll think I'll watch you.'

Rhoisin smiled across at him, not sure whether to take him seriously. But he sat opposite her, quite still, one hand resting on his lap, the other gracefully, casually poised at the edge of the table, watching her. Rhoisin looked down at the hunky, convex sandwich, cut in triangles, half wrapped in a white paper napkin as before. No knife and fork to help with the operation. I'll have to get it right, she thought. She wrapped the napkin gingerly round one of the portions and lifted it slowly to her mouth. She felt his eyes on her but somehow she wasn't embarrassed. After all, it was just a sandwich. And she'd only met him once – very briefly. She didn't even know his name. She bit quickly into the damp triangle, hoping that speed would be the essence of success. It was a large bite. She felt the soft, cohesive egg glide slowly round her tongue, the crispy morsels of cress adding another dimension to the texture. The rich, smooth Hellmann's Mayonnaise soothed her taste-buds. None of your Heinz Salad Cream, thank goodness. How she detested Heinz Salad Cream! The way to ruin a good sandwich. The bread was fresh, too. She remembered last time the waitress said it was fresh and it didn't need toasting.

The crusts were still left. Normally, if she had been on her own she would have left the crusts, probably all of them, lying on the plate like lamb chop bones or spent spare ribs. She felt that crusts spoilt the sandwich; took away from the succulence that was its very essence. She always cut them off at home. But now she felt obliged to leave a clean plate, watched as she was by this man who was still a stranger.

He laughed. 'Very neat. Now it's my turn.'

She wasn't sure whether to take him seriously as he reverently wrapped the white paper slip round the curvaceous triangle, lifted it elegantly to his lips and took a bite. She noticed his even white teeth and strong pink tongue; then his lips closed together and his finely chiselled, smoothly shaven jaw moved as he chewed.

'Good, aren't they? That's why I come here. The prawn and lettuce are good too. It's the mayonnaise that makes it.'

'Oh, yes,' she said. 'It's Hellmann's. 'I always think Heinz Salad Cream ruins a good sandwich.'

He laughed. 'You seem to be an expert. We do have something in common. We'll have to try the prawn next time.'

They ate the second triangle at the same time, munching in silence, giving the food their fullest concentration.

Then the coffee arrived, two cappuccinos, topped with thick creamy froth, sprinkled with chocolate. Rhoisin took a cautious sip. It was very hot.

'Good?' he asked.

'Delicious. Especially the chocolate on top.'

'Me, too. In fact, I like chocolate on almost anything.'

'So do I,' agreed Rhoisin.

The sandwiches were finished, though some of their coffee still remained. The man raised himself slightly off his chair and extended his hand across the table. 'Stephen Piper,' he said. 'How do you do?' His hand shake was strong and firm.

'I'm Rhoisin Hobbs,' said Rhoisin, a little surprised. She hadn't expected such a formal introduction.

'Rhoisin? That's Irish, and very pretty too, if I may say so.'

'My father was Irish,' said Rhoisin recklessly, immediately regretting her remark. After all, she had no proof whatsoever of who her father was. But such a comment to a stranger could hardly be classed as an error. In case he showed any further interest in her spurious Irish background she looked at her watch.

'Oh, just look at the time!' she said, feigning concern. 'I've got to be back at work in ten minutes!'

'No problem,' replied Stephen. 'So do I.' He signalled to the waitress to bring him the bill. 'I'll walk back with you.'

Brr-brr, brr-brr. The sound Rhoisin had started dreading. She was afraid it might be the council, or, worse still, Jim. She had been expecting the council to ring ever since her mother's death. While Linda was still in hospital the rent collector had called round one evening for the arrears. Rhoisin had assumed her mother paid the rent by banker's order but she had been unable to find the rent book.

'My mother has been seriously ill,' she explained. I've been trying to find where she put the rent book.'

'What's the problem?' enquired the rent collector.

'Breast cancer.'

'Had it off, has she?' he asked, with breath-taking lack of sensitivity.

'No,' said Rhoisin curtly, 'it was too late.'

The man's eyes widened. 'I see,' he said. 'Well, if anything should happen, you know... I mean, if she don't ever come out of hospital or anything like that, then I should look to your accommodation.'

Rhoisin was stunned by his callousness.

'What on earth do you mean?' she gasped.

'What I mean is, love,' the man was obviously a cad of the first order, 'what I mean is, this is a two-bedroom flat. If the powers that be discover that you was the only one in it... well they might...'

Rhoisin burst into tears and threw the man out.

Now she constantly awaited the 'powers that be' to evict her.

She lifted the receiver in trepidation. 'Hello.'

'That Rhoisin? It's your Uncle Jack here.'

'Oh, hello, Uncle Jack.' Rhoisin felt a surge of relief. 'How are you? How's Auntie Liz?'

'We're both fine, love,' came Jack's warm, friendly voice along the wire. 'We were just wondering how you were getting on and if you'd like to come up here for the weekend as it's such lovely weather.'

'I'd love to, thank you, Uncle Jack. The weather's gorgeous in London too.'

'I'll meet you off the eleven o'clock train, then. Just as I did last time. Liz sends her love. 'Bye, then.'

"Bye, Uncle Jack – and thank you.'

Rhoisin put the phone down feeling a warm glow. Uncle Jack and Auntie Liz had been so kind since they had met at the funeral. She insisted on the Uncle and Auntie. It gave her a sense of belonging and gave her some sort of identity. She couldn't believe that she had found some relatives after twenty-one years. There was still such a lot to catch up on and a lot to sort out. For instance, why had Linda and Jack lost touch for so long?

She was pleased to be going away for the weekend: pleased to have a reason to get out of the flat. Despite having two bedrooms, it was cramped, dingy, dark and very lonely. Sometimes she felt the walls were closing in around her. They had never been on friendly terms with the neighbours. Linda had never appeared snobbish, but she did give the impression that she had nothing in common with people who lived in a council flat. After all, her daughter was a university graduate, which was a great deal more than could be said for any of the others. Now look at the university graduate! thought Rhoisin.

Selling tickets in a pokey little box office. 'Box' was the operative word. There was no doubt about it.

From time to time she thought of finding someone with whom to share the flat. Apart from the company it would help with the rent, as even council flats didn't come cheap. But she didn't know who to ask. She was still quite friendly with a couple of girls from university but they came from leafy homes in the shires. They would hardly want to live in a council flat in Kilburn. There was Janice, her relief at the box office, who was always friendly and had even mentioned recently that she was looking for a room. But she was fat and had BO. Rhoisin wasn't sure she would be able to handle it. She could always put an ad. in the *Evening Standard*. She had seen lots of requests in the 'Accommodation Wanted' column: 'Tidy, quiet girl seeks similar to share. Any location. But she might get hundreds of replies. How would she make the choice? Then once the girl had actually moved in who was to say that they would get on? Imagine sharing a kitchen, and above all the bathroom, with someone you didn't know.

And finally there was the question of the contents of the flat: her mother's things that Rhoisin didn't want to share with anyone. Then there were all those letters she had recently started to go through.

The evenings were the worst. Although she was tired when she got home, three days a week she stayed at the theatre till the performance started at 8.00 pm so she wasn't home till nearly 9.30. She had a snack in front of the telly and although she was in bed by 11.00, completely exhausted, she still found it difficult to sleep. It was the time of the day when she missed her mother most. There was no one else around to supply the little comforts of life. No one with whom to share the gossip and the trivial events of the day. Her main dread was that Jim should follow her home from work and force his way into the flat. Or that he had a key and would be awaiting her return. Or even that he would break in during the night; climbing up the drain pipe onto the balcony of the flat next door. This last supposition she dismissed almost immediately, as Jim's build and lack of athletic prowess were hardly cut out for shinning up drain pipes.

She imagined she saw his face everywhere: in the street near the flat, in the tube, around Leicester Square; near the coffee bar. She had seen him at the funeral in the distance. She was just leaving the churchyard with Uncle Jack and Auntie Liz when he seemed to pop up from behind a gravestone, gross, pulpy, pale orange, leering at her lecherously. She hadn't spoken of him to anyone. She was hopefully assuming that since Linda was no longer around there would be no need for Jim's presence either.

Rhoisin and Stephen met frequently for lunch, often in the same coffee bar. By now they had tried an extensive combination of different breads and fillings, even sampling some of the sandwiches toasted; usually on the advice of the waitress who always let them know if the bread wasn't fresh. Rhoisin wondered how many other customers were allowed such intimate knowledge of the workings of the establishment, and whether this resulted in a stock-pile of stale bread. But as she and Stephen lunched there almost every day, they were established regulars and should definitely expect some preferential treatment.

Rhoisin took an increasing delight in Stephen's companionship. He was kind, gentle and extremely courteous. They had now been seeing each other for nearly three weeks, meeting mostly at lunchtime. As Stephen was a theatrical agent he was usually tied up in the evenings, seeing shows and often dining with clients afterwards. The lack of evening outings was a relief to Rhoisin. Up till now any young men she had dated had become, to her reserved tastes, unpleasantly amorous after dark. So far, perhaps because they only met during daylight hours, Stephen had shown the utmost physical restraint. The most intimate gesture he had ever made was to take her elbow gently in order to guide her safely through the swirling traffic on Charing Cross Road.

Towards the end of the third week of their acquaintance Stephen asked her if she would like to go to the theatre with him the following evening. It was a new play by Tom Stoppard and he was particularly interested in seeing the performance by a young actor recently out of drama school. Rhoisin was delighted, albeit a little surprised. They were in their favourite coffee bar, half way through egg mayonnaise sandwiches in granary bread; an experience which always added extra intimacy to the occasion. Stephen smiled at Rhoisin across the table. She thought he looked particularly handsome in a pale blue open neck shirt and well-cut beige jacket.

'What time do you finish tomorrow evening?' he asked.

'Seven,' replied Rhoisin.

'Good. I'll meet you outside the Duke of York's at seven sharp. We'll have time for a drink before the play starts at The Queen's at eight.

'No lunch tomorrow?' enquired Rhoisin, teasing a little.

'Lunch? Of course we'll have lunch tomorrow. See you here at one. Meanwhile, I've got to dash.'

He reached over and patted her arm. For one wild moment Rhoisin thought he was going to give her a peck on the cheek.

They both enjoyed the play. They had a glass of wine before the performance and another one in the interval. Unaccustomed as she was to drinking alcohol, Rhoisin felt her head spinning a little. During the second half Stephen took her hand. Rhoisin made no resistance. She sat very still, stiffening slightly as he entwined his fingers in hers, caressing the palm of her hand with his thumb. As he leaned towards her slightly she wondered whether he would put his arm around her shoulders. But he made no more advances, just continued to stroke the palm of her hand gently. Rhoisin was aware of a certain frisson. The skin prickled at the back of her neck and sent a tingling feeling down her spine. Her heart beat faster and she was aware of a completely new sensation; a mixture of excitement and desire. She wasn't sure whether this was due to Stephen's subdued caresses, the unaccustomed consumption of alcohol or the amorous antics which were gathering pace before their eyes on the stage. After the theatre they dined in splendid elegance at The Ivy, and before seeing her into a taxi, Stephen kissed her very gently on the lips.

'Thank you for making it such a wonderful evening. I do wish you could come with me to the theatre each time instead of my partner. She's such an unattractive old bore; and she's a dyke.'

From which remark Rhoisin gathered that his 'partner' was not of the bed-sharing kind but rather more in the manner of a business partner. It was not something she had thought of before: Stephen in bed.

The following evening Rhoisin worked at the theatre until eight o'clock. It was still daylight when she left and as it was another warm, still spring evening she decided to walk to Piccadilly Circus and take the tube to Kilburn from there, with only one change at Baker Street. The alternative was to take the train from nearby Leicester Square, change at Piccadilly and again at Baker Street. She had no set routine. It depended on the weather, and her mood. She walked slowly towards Leicester Square, past the coffee bar where she and Stephen had lunched again today. Crowds were milling around, coming and going from pubs, and restaurants, or just strolling, enjoying the buzz and hub-bub of life in the great capital city on a beautiful spring evening. Her thoughts went to Stephen and their evening out together. His charm, courteousness, sense of humour. His hand in hers, lightly caressing. So restrained and caring; no forcing, no insistence.

At Piccadilly Circus she struggled across the road with the milling, surging crowd. A large-girthed man with orange hair and pale freckles brushed past her, crossing the road in the opposite direction. Rhoisin shuddered with revulsion. Just like Jim, she thought. She hurried down the steps to the station, through the automatic ticket barrier and down the escalator amid the jostling, laughing, chattering crowds. She enjoyed crowds. She felt protected by so many people around: here was safety in numbers. She didn't like large empty spaces. A train came quickly and she was lucky to find a seat. Only two stops to Baker Street. Not long enough for a cat nap. After the change at Baker Street there were a further five stops before Kilburn. She had gone to sleep on this leg of the journey a couple of times. Once she had slept right through to the end of the line at Stanmore and had to go all the way back again. Now she tried to be more careful and opened her eyes each time the train stopped. She alighted at Kilburn Station without mishap and turned into Dartmouth Road, just behind the station. It was now nine thirty and quite dark but there were still plenty of people about. She walked briskly and as she reached the right fork for Exeter Road she heard footsteps behind her; a heavier tread, walking faster than she was. For some reason she was afraid to turn round but just walked on, quickening her pace. She was relieved when the sound of footsteps receded as they continued along Dartmouth Road. As she neared the end of Exeter Road she relaxed a little, though she could still feel her heart thumping. The block of flats where she lived loomed into view on the right and, once on the steps, she took her latch-key out of her hand-bag. Before she could get the key into the lock a large figure lumbered round the corner.

'Well, here's Rhoisin! What a nice surprise!'

Jim stood in the shadow of the doorway, larger, more lecherous than ever, his carroty hair framing his pale, plump face; the long scar she had inflicted gleaming as he moved into a shaft of light thrown by the street lamp. As he lifted his hand to touch her she saw again his prehensile hands, reminding her of an orang-utan. She tried to stifle her gasp of horror and fear.

'What are you doing here and what the hell do you want?' she snarled between clenched teeth.'

'I came to see how you were getting along, my darling. We must see that Linda's lovely daughter is being taken proper care of, mustn't we?'

'I can take care of myself perfectly, thank you,' replied Rhoisin, desperately trying to keep her nerve.

'I'm sure you could do with a little company now and again.' Jim leered, moving a bit closer. 'A bit of male company in particular. I wonder if the little girl has a boyfriend yet? Has she had a proper fuck, or is she still afraid of sex?'

Rhoisin felt herself go limp and cold and prayed she wasn't going to faint. She must get away and escape from him. At all costs he mustn't get into the flat. Four steps led to the entrance door of the flat from the tarmac driveway, flanked on either side by flower beds full of prickly shrubs. Just as Rhoisin was desperately thinking out her next move three very noisy jets flew overhead. Jim looked up, craning his neck, slightly off balance. Summoning up all her strength, Rhoisin gave him an almighty push and with a howl of pain he landed flat on his face in one of the largest, most prickly shrubs.

Clutching her hand-bag and latch-key Rhoisin turned and fled as fast as she could towards the main road. She ran in the opposite direction to that from which she had come; to the far end of Exeter Road, planning to turn right into Walm Lane to the end of Cricklewood Broadway where she hoped to find a bus stop. Even in her panic she realised it would be a fatal mistake to go back to the tube station. At this time of night there would be few, if any, passengers going into London. She would have a much greater chance of protection on a bus where at least there would be a driver, if no one else.

As she rounded the corner of Walm Lane she heard the thud of heavy footsteps following her. Her heart thumped louder, sweat poured down her face. It seemed to her that the owner of the heavy footsteps was making quicker progress than she was. She stumbled over an uneven paving stone and almost fell. Bloody council, not taking proper care of the pavements. She clutched her latch-key and hand-bag more tightly. It wouldn't do to drop them, especially the key. If Jim had access to the flat she was finished.

She ran on blindly, panting, exhausted, running for her life. Still the heavy footsteps thudded along behind her. She thought she heard Jim's heavy breathing, imagined he had grabbed her and pulled her to the ground, raping her on the pavement of a public street with no one around to come to her aid. She had almost no strength left but she knew at all costs that she had to reach the comparative safety of the main road. Luckily she was wearing flat shoes, although the bottoms of her trousers flapped against her legs, slowing her pace a little. Just as she reached the end of Walm Lane she saw a bus approaching the stop on the far side of the road. Without thinking, she ran across the road, raising her hand. The bus stopped, the doors opened and she scrambled on thankfully. The driver looked at her curiously as she produced her travel pass.

'You seem in a bit of a hurry, love.' His voice was gruff, kindly. 'You late for a date?'

'Yes,' panted Rhoisin, flopping limply into the nearest seat.

'I'll put me foot down then,' said the driver. 'I'm at the end of the run now. Could do with a bit of an early turn in. Terrible traffic today. Going somewhere nice, love?' He wasn't being impertinent, just friendly.

'Yes. N – no. I don't know.'

Rhoisin had no idea where she was going. She had no plans at all. She was just extremely grateful to be speeding along in a bus which was, hopefully, taking her as far away from Jim as possible. And even if she were the only passenger on the bus the driver would be much too busy negotiating the traffic to bother her. As the bus made its way south down the Edgware Road towards central London a few more passengers got on. By the time they'd reached Marble Arch Rhoisin had begun to formulate a plan.

She would go and see Stephen and tell him all about Jim; about the way he had always pestered her. About the rape. It would be a relief to talk to someone about the whole sordid business. She was sure that Stephen would be sympathetic and understanding. She was also sure that if she were to talk to someone about the horrific events of her childhood she would be able to lay the spectre of her sexual fears and repressions. She had felt a strong physical attraction to Stephen when he had caressed her hand so gently at the theatre the previous evening. Maybe if he were to help her lay Jim's ghost and all his monstrous practices: well, who knows what might happen.

Rhoisin knew where Stephen lived. He hadn't actually given her his address in so many words but he had happened to mention that he lived in Almeida Street, Islington, just off Upper Street. He was chatting about how lively Upper Street had become in recent years; in contrast to how quiet it had been when he had first bought his house some fifteen years ago. On another occasion he said in passing how much he liked black front doors, especially on early Victorian houses such as his. And after all, if one happened to live at Number 10, the front door had to be black. Number 10, Almeida Street. It wasn't very difficult to remember.

Rhoisin knew Islington quite well. She knew that the numbers 38 and 73 buses went along Essex Road. If she couldn't discover which bus went along Upper Street she could always get off at the Essex Road library and walk up Cross Street.

She stood at Cumberland Place near Marble Arch waiting for another bus. It was now just after ten thirty; a little cooler but a beautiful evening nevertheless for the end of April. As she waited her nervousness increased. She expected Jim to appear at any moment: off a bus, out of the tube; to emerge from the cinema or the pub round the corner. She even expected him to pop out of the sewers through the man-hole cover by the bus stop. But it seemed that he had lost her scent and was no longer on her trail. Even so, when the bus finally arrived poor Rhoisin was a nervous wreck.

At that time of night it took the number 73 bus less than half an hour to reach the Essex Road library. Rhoisin got off thankfully, relieved the chase was over; that she was no longer pursued, a hunted quarry, but merely a frightened young girl alone in London rather late at night, seeking refuge.

She made her way to Almeida Street without any difficulty. There were a few people about; plenty of noise and laughter came from the nearby pubs and restaurants. She hadn't thought what she would say to Stephen. It didn't seem necessary. She would probably appear a little upset, perhaps distraught would be a better word. He would put his arm around her and she would sob out the whole story. Her pace quickened as she walked up Almeida Street. There was Number Ten, the black door gleaming, seemingly newly painted. She went up the two shallow steps and rang the door bell. Help was coming at last. At first nothing came at all. It hadn't occurred to her that he might be out. That was quite unthinkable. She rang again and sharp even footsteps clicked along the tiled floor. But surely...? No. But yes. It was. A lady opened the front door. Rhoisin was too surprised to speak. She had, of course, expected Stephen to be at home alone.

'Yes?' enquired the lady.

'I - I was wondering if Stephen Piper...' faltered Rhoisin.

'Of course,' said the lady. 'Do come in. My name's Rosalind.'

Chapter Five

Rhoisin had the week off. Her boss had only told her on Thursday that she needn't come in the following Monday. 'Have a nice rest. You deserve it.'

She tried to sound grateful, but really it was a pity to be given the whole week off at such short notice. What should she do with a whole week on her own in London? Stephen was away. He had gone to New York for two weeks.

'What a pity you're not free to come as well,' he had said. 'New York is wonderful. You really must come with me next time.'

So Rhoisin phoned Auntie Liz. She had been up to Leeds to stay with them several times now; and quite often the three of them had discussed the question of clearing Linda's things out of the flat. Rhoisin told them she was planning to ask the council to rehouse her in a smaller flat.

'The present flat is too full of memories. I think I'd be far happier living somewhere else. It doesn't have to be in Kilburn either,' she added as a bitter after thought.

In fact, she loathed the place.

Auntie Liz had offered to come down to London and help her clear out all Linda's belongings.

'Any time you like, love. You just give me a ring,' said the kindly lady. 'After all I've now't else to do but look after your tiresome uncle here.' Rhoisin laughed. She couldn't think of anyone less tiresome than Uncle Jack.

She called Auntie Liz.

'I'd love to come and help you, dearie,' she said. 'I'll come down on Sunday evening and we'll spend a nice week together. We might even fit in a bit of sightseeing. 'I'd love to see the sights of London. Make a change from dreary old Leeds.'

They spent Monday and Tuesday clearing out all Linda's personal effects. It was a very emotional time for Rhoisin and she often dissolved into tears. Auntie Liz was very comforting and encouraging, never censorious. She had the utmost admiration for Rhoisin and felt that she herself could never have coped so magnificently under similar adverse circumstances. Little did she know that the circumstances were even more adverse than she realised, for Rhoisin had not mentioned Jim to either her uncle or aunt.

When Linda's clothes were all sorted out the two women had the knotty problem of what to do with them.

'Take them to Oxfam,' said Rhoisin firmly.

'What!' exclaimed Auntie Liz. 'All those beautiful dresses and suits and evening dresses! That would be a real shame, that would.'

'Why not? Who else is going to wear them? I'm certainly not, and with all due respect, Auntie Liz,' eyeing her plump, rounded aunt with some circumspection, 'I don't think you could either.'

'I suppose you're right, dearie,' replied the good lady. 'Your poor mother must have looked a right picture in all this finery. You must have been real proud of her when she was all dressed up to go out.' Rhoisin sank heavily into one of the deep armchairs. She felt drained.

'You know something, Auntie Liz,' she said, 'I never saw my mother wear any of these clothes.'

Auntie Liz sat down in the chair opposite.

'Really? It's not as though the garments are worn out or getting shabby or anything, but they're not brand new either. You can see they've been worn at some stage, either by your mother or...?'

'Or who?' questioned Rhoisin. 'Who else would wear my mother's clothes?'

'But are they your mother's clothes?'

'What do you mean?'

'Well, you don't think she could have been looking after them for someone else, do you?'

'Why would she do that? And anyway, if they weren't her own clothes surely the owner would have reclaimed them at some point.'

'Would the owner necessarily know your mother had died?'

'I don't see what difference that would make,' replied Rhoisin. 'And anyway, I'm pretty certain these clothes belonged to my mother. They're just her style and the sort of colours she always wore. And look,' she lifted up a particularly elegant navy dress with white polka dots, 'they're all a size ten. That was her size. Not many people are a size ten nowadays. Even I'm a twelve.'

'And I'm an eighteen,' said Auntie Liz, ruefully. 'So why do you think you never saw her wearing them?'

'I don't know but I'm determined to find out,' said Rhoisin doggedly. 'There's a hell of a lot I don't know about my family, but I'm not going to live on in total ignorance any longer. Auntie Liz...'

She was on the point of telling her aunt about Jim but decided it could wait. They would worry about her, her aunt and uncle. They were such kindly people. They had quite taken her to their hearts and helped her with so many of her problems. It would be unfair to burden them with even more. It was sufficient for the moment that Stephen knew about Jim. Though she hadn't told him that she'd actually been raped: just pestered. Better leave Jim out of the picture as far as her aunt and uncle were concerned.

It was during the first weekend she had spent with her aunt and uncle in Leeds that Rhoisin had brought up the question of who her father was. She had been extremely disappointed to learn that they were a childless couple. She would have loved a bevy of assorted cousins milling around, but once she saw how saddened they were she didn't dwell on the point too long.

'It's a question of identity,' she said earnestly. 'Everyone wants to know where they come from, who they belong to. I only know where half of me comes from. And sometimes I'm not even sure how well I know that half either. For instance, can you explain why I'd never met you before my mother's funeral? Why is it that you and she lost touch for so many years?'

There was a heavy, embarrassed silence in the room. Her aunt and uncle glanced at each other uneasily. Then her uncle spoke in a very serious, almost sad voice.

'I suppose you should really know the truth, Rhoisin, love.' He spoke slowly, weighing every word. 'Your mother was very badly let down by your father. He was dashing and handsome and she fell for him in a very big way. She said to me at the time: "Jack, he's the most wonderful man I've ever met and he's promised to marry me when he comes back to London." But your mother was always an impulsive woman; impulsive and over-sexed. She jumped into bed too quickly with almost every man who came her way. I could never make out whether it was just for the hell of it or whether she was really in love with them all.'

My mother over-sexed, thought Rhoisin wryly. With a daughter like me. That's really too ironic.

'I suppose she must have taken precautions with all the others,' her uncle continued, 'otherwise, well, you would have had plenty of brothers and sisters. But maybe she thought your father really was the one. Mr Right. And so she just went ahead, doing what comes naturally and, well there you are, and what a perfect result, if I may say so. Your aunt and I could do with several more like you around here.'

Feeling rather embarrassed Rhoisin said nothing for a moment.

'So then what happened?'

'Well, after they'd had their little fling – and it was quite a fling, let me tell you. Your man was not short of the readies and they painted the town red while he was in London. Shows, restaurants, pubs, shopping trips. I don't remember Linda ever having such a great time. He bought her jewellery, beautiful clothes, furniture and china for the house. That man must have spent a fortune on your mum, Rhoisin. Then one day he just disappeared.'

Rhoisin's eyes widened but she said nothing.

'He told your mother that he had to return to Ireland "to deal with matters arising from the management of the estate." I remember the phrase so well. Linda kept repeating it. She thought it was a wonderful turn of phrase. I thought it was right toffee-nosed.'

There was a long pause. Jack gave a deep sigh. 'So your man went back to Ireland "to deal with matters arising from the management of the estate" and was never seen again, by Linda, anyway. He had promised to marry her before he went off, of course he had, with a beautiful ring an' all.'

'What happened to the ring?' asked Rhoisin, for lack of anything more coherent to say.

'The ring? I think she sold it when times were hard.'

There was silence in the room; the three of them absorbed in their own private thoughts. Rhoisin was the first to speak.

'Can you remember his name, Uncle Jack?'

'I can indeed, love,' replied her uncle. 'His name was Tom O'Hare.'

'That's what Mother told me herself, near the end. But she drifted off to sleep without saying any more. There are some letters, though,' continued Rhoisin, 'all tied up with ribbons.'

'Oh, yes?' Jack expressed great interest. ' Have you looked at them?'

'Only one or two,' said Rhoisin. 'But they're not all from Tom O'Hare.'

'Are they not? And who are they from?'

'I've only looked at a couple,' confessed Rhoisin. 'It seemed a bit like spying really. Perhaps we could...?' She threw her aunt an appealing glance.

'Of course we could, love,' said her kindly aunt. 'You just give me the word when you've a minute free for me to come down and help you to get the letters sorted. It shouldn't take us long.'

The clothes were packed up in neat bundles ready to take to Oxfam. Encouraged by such good progress,

Rhoisin decided at last she could face looking at some of her mother's letters. Both she and her aunt were fairly sure the bulky parcel tied with a red ribbon might hold the vital clue that would help her to establish the identity of her father and hopefully, even track him down.

Auntie Liz made a pot of tea and arranged an assortment of biscuits attractively on a plate. Any little touch to supply a bit of courage, she thought. As she set down the tray on the small oak table at the end of the room, Rhoisin stood up slowly from the sofa, where she had been sitting with the box of still unexplored letters, picked up two bundles and placed them by the tea tray on the oak table. Sitting down at the table, Rhoisin looked at her aunt nervously. 'Tea first or a letter first?' she asked.

'Definitely tea,' replied her aunt, pouring out. Rhoisin took the cup and set it down by the bundle of letters. She took a sip of the hot tea and gingerly fingered the bundle before carefully untying the faded ribbon.

'Well, here goes.'

'Biscuit?' asked her aunt, hoping to diffuse the tension a little.

'Thanks. In a minute.'

Rhoisin picked up the letter from the top of the pile. Each letter was still in its envelope, which had been slit carefully across the top with a sharp knife. Most of the postmarks were clearly visible. The one in her hand bore an Irish stamp and was postmarked: Sligo, 20 September 1953. Her hands shaking, she drew the letter out of the envelope and unfolded it carefully. Her aunt flashed her another encouraging smile.

Rhoisin cleared her throat and started to read the letter:

'*Knockramore, Killalee County Sligo,*
20 September 1953
'*My dearest Linda,*
How I miss you so dreadfully and think of you constantly as I go about the estate business. I have been away far too long; nearly a year as I told you, and things have got quite out of hand. McGuire, our manager, is getting old and my younger brother, Sean, is an even bigger scoundrel than I thought. He's been selling sheep off his own bat without keeping any record, in order to cheat the Inland Revenue. Did you ever hear of such carry on! Farmers are notorious for trying to avoid paying income tax so we are always the first people to be picked on. I have a great deal to sort out, my darling, so do not expect me in London before mid-November at the earliest. But we shall spend Christmas together, I promise, wherever that will be.
'*I love you so much and think of you unceasingly.*
'*Yours ever, Tom.*'

Rhoisin put the letter down, open, on the table. For a few minutes neither of them spoke. Auntie Liz, uncertain of her niece's reaction, gave her a sympathetic glance. Rhoisin wanted to cry. She just wanted to sit and weep at the sadness of it all and the waste of her mother's death so young. But in the presence of her aunt she managed, heroically, to take control of herself. She was the first to speak.

'Well, that helps to put us in the picture, doesn't it?' She tried to sound practical rather than emotional.

'We've got his address and the exact date of the letter. We can easily work out the dates to confirm whether or not my mother was pregnant.'

'Yes,' agreed Auntie Liz, relieved that Rhoisin was taking such a calm and practical outlook. 'But she may not have realised it yet.'

'No,' agreed Rhoisin. 'But it wouldn't have been long before she did. Let's have a look at the next letter.'

She picked the next half dozen off the top of the pile and examined the postmarks. 'They all seem to be in order,' she said. 'Mum was more organised than I realised.' She smiled ruefully. 'About some things, anyway.'

She skimmed silently through the next letter.

'I won't read the whole lot out,' she explained to her aunt apologetically. 'It'll take far too long. I'll just read out the most important bits. The next one is dated 10 October and says just about the same thing as the first one. Such a lot to sort out on the estate. Worried about McGuire, the manager's increasing incapacitation – that's a good word – he must have been very literary. Doesn't sound like Mother's type at all, really. And he thinks his brother is a crook.'

Rhoisin folded up the second letter and returned it to its envelope. She opened up the third letter and skimmed through.

'No. Nothing new here either. He asks after Mother's welfare and hopes she isn't working too hard.' She put the letter away and glanced through the next three. 'I must say, he's amazingly unoriginal,' she remarked.

The seventh letter was dated 7 November and was in quite a different vein.

'Frankly, I am more concerned than excited at your news. Of course I can appreciate your joy and excitement in discovering that you are with child. It is every woman's desire, nay, biological function, to give birth. The world would come to a stop if women did not continue to fulfil this role. But I do feel there is a time and place for everything. We are not as yet married, and to be forced to marry under a pressure of this kind, I feel would be likely to place an intolerable strain on our future relationship. I beg you to consider carefully that a termination would definitely be in both our best interests. Please arrange this as speedily as possible before the matter becomes too far advanced. I shall of course, send you whatever funds you require.

'Yours as ever, Tom.'

Feeling rather shaken, Rhoisin took the next letter from its envelope and opened it.

'Knockramore, Killalee, Co: Sligo. 22 November,' she read.

' Dear Linda,

'I must confess that I am at a loss to understand your intractability regarding a termination. Taking into consideration the considerable advance of medicine in the last thirty years or so there would be absolutely no risk involved. As I understand it a simple termination does not preclude any future conception. Things are more difficult here than I originally realised and an early marriage is certainly unthinkable. I beg you to reconsider my proposal. Funds are not a problem.

'Yours, Tom.'

'There's only one more letter in the same hand writing, Auntie Liz.' Rhoisin hands were shaking uncontrollably as she slid it out of the envelope.

3 December,1953
Dear Linda,
I cannot understand your attitude. Although I realise that you would like a child – this is not the moment. At present marriage is out of the question and I do not feel it is responsible to bring a bastard child into the world. The human race is still too hidebound by convention to appreciate the difficulties of a single mother. I beg of you to be sensible. I enclose a cheque for £100.
'*Your Tom.*'

Rhoisin choked back a sob. 'That's the last one, Auntie Liz, from Tom O'Hare anyway. There are other letters though. They might be from other men. Maybe Tom O'Hare isn't my father after all. In fact, I almost hope he isn't. Shall I go on reading now or shall we get dinner?'

'Dinner,' said her aunt firmly. 'We'll go out for a curry and go to the pictures. Then we can carry on with the other letters tomorrow.'

Chapter Six

Stephen returned from New York full of his experiences in that great city.

'It's teeming with life,' he enthused. 'It's on the go twenty-four hours a day. Nothing ever seems to shut down. Only the subway stops in the earliest hours of the morning. But you wouldn't want to ride on it then anyway.'

He's using Americanisms already, thought Rhoisin with some amusement.

'It's full of thugs and drunks even during the day. I was well advised to take cabs after 7.00 pm.'

He went prattling on, full of enthusiasm tempered with criticism. The purpose of his visit was to follow up the fortunes of an actress who had landed a big role on Broadway only two years after finishing drama school.

'And how was Miranda?' enquired Rhoisin, 'or did you feel she was just too type-cast.' She was learning the jargon.

'Yes, rather type-cast,' replied Stephen. 'But then a very pretty girl is bound to audition for the part of a very pretty girl.'

'I suppose there were lots of pretty girls auditioning,' said Rhoisin, wondering, not for the first time why Stephen, so gallant and handsome and obviously surrounded by pretty girls, should spend so much time with her. Not that I'm ugly, thought Rhoisin ruefully, but all these actress types are so glamorous; like Rosalind. 'Just a good friend,' Stephen had said. Rhoisin had been in no position to argue. She had no permanent claim on Stephen. Perhaps he liked safety in numbers to pre-empt any commitment of a serious nature? Maybe I'm his lunch time companion, she told herself more than once.

'But you see, Miranda,' Stephen was saying, unaware of Rhoisin's lack of interest in his budding star. 'Miranda has something extra that can't be explained. Of course she's enchantingly pretty. She has a perfect figure, a well placed voice, moves like a gazelle, sings like a skylark and dances like an angel.'

Rhoisin felt rather nauseous.

'But you can't really describe those qualities in words.'

'I thought you'd done it rather well,' said Rhoisin, with a hint of sarcasm.

Oblivious, Stephen laughed and put his arm round her. 'You do say the nicest things.'

They had arrived at the box office entrance to the Duke of York's Theatre.

'Miranda has that rare attribute: star quality. She will rise high, shine bright and reign long,' he prophesied. 'And I'm very happy to have such an exceptional actress on my books.'

'And I'm very happy for you,' replied Rhoisin demurely.

'Thank you.' Stephen's grip tightened round her shoulders. With his free hand he stoked her cheek gently. 'How about dinner tomorrow night?' he asked.

'Dinner?' Rhoisin was surprised.

'Yes. Happily I'm free of commitments for one evening. I know an excellent Italian restaurant in the

Liverpool Road. Take a taxi and I'll settle it when you arrive. It's number 207. Would eight o'clock suit you or is that too early?'

'Take a taxi all the way to Islington?' Rhoisin was impressed by such extravagance. 'But I'll be coming from Kilburn,' she objected. 'I've got tomorrow off.'

'So much the better,' said Stephen. 'You can have a restful day and a nice taxi drive at the end of it. No, don't argue,' he said as Rhoisin tried to remonstrate. 'Just do as I say and enjoy it.'

'Just do as I say and enjoy it.' The words rang constantly in Rhoisin's ears throughout the day. What else would he make her do? And would she necessarily enjoy it?

As Stephen had suggested, Rhoisin had a restful day; rising late, tidying up the gloomy flat and doing some essential shopping. Although she had applied to the council for a transfer to a smaller flat some time ago, she had heard nothing as yet. Having more than it's fair share of the homeless, Brent was a difficult council to deal with. But most councils have their problems, thought Rhoisin, and I bet they're all just as difficult to deal with. So for the moment she just had to stay put.

About six o'clock she had a long relaxing bath and chose her outfit with great care. Stephen had said nothing about a taxi home. Liverpool Road was only a few minutes from Almeida Street by car. You could walk it in ten minutes. Rhoisin kept wondering if Stephen would suggest going back to his house afterwards. Would he ask her to stay the night? Would he expect her to stay the night?

She had only been to his house once. The evening Jim had surprised her so unpleasantly outside the flat. She had been so desperately frightened and confused by the time she had reached Number Ten Almeida Street that she had just wanted to cry and cry on Stephen's strong shoulder; tell him how lonely and afraid she was. Afraid of Jim raping her again; afraid of being so alone.

But Rosalind had been there. Elegant, smooth Rosalind. Rhoisin was jealous of Rosalind. She was jealous of Miranda. She was jealous of all of them. All those pretty young actresses who sang like skylarks, moved like gazelles and danced like angels. She wanted Stephen all to herself; for her use exclusively. But would Stephen give himself exclusively to her? Was that within his capabilities? Or was it completely foreign to his nature? What was his relationship with these other women: these 'good friends.' How 'good friends' were they, how far did the relationships go? Did he bed any of them: all of them?

Bed. That was the word that worried and frightened her. Sex. When she imagined two people engaged in the sexual act, visions of Jim assailed her brain. To Rhoisin sex was inseparable from his coarse, groping hands, forcing their way against her will into her most private and precious place. But then, when she thought about Stephen, when she looked at him; so handsome, debonair, she wanted him. Her soul ached for him, her body craved him; but she was afraid. She couldn't tell, until they were actually in bed together, if it would be kill or cure. She found it impossible to imagine making love and actually enjoying it.

The taxi dropped them outside Number Ten Almeida Street. They could have walked of course, Stephen said, but it was getting rather late, after half past eleven. Stephen poured two large brandies and put on a CD of one of his favourite Hayden string quartets. He settled down on the sofa beside Rhoisin and put his arm around her. This is it, thought Rhoisin. this is how it starts. This is how it should be; gentle, caring, soothing. A long slow introduction to making love, in bed or here on the hearth rug. This is what I want, she told herself. I love him. I want him. I hope he loves me but at least he cares for me and I'm sure I can make him love me given time.

They listened to the music in silence. When the first quartet on the disc had drawn to a close Stephen turned the volume down so that the sound of Haydn's lovely music was just a murmur in the background. He began to stroke Rhoisin's face, her cheek, her neck. She sat quite still, doing nothing. He stroked her lips, then kissed them, very gently at first. Her lips parted as he slowly, gently, inserted his tongue, searching for hers, exploring her mouth, tongues now entwining, yielding to each other in a long, satisfying kiss. His free hand moved down and unbuttoned the top of her dress. He slipped it off gently and undid her bra. He continued to stroke, first her breast, slowly encircling it, then continuing over her stomach and on down towards the pubic area. She shuddered and gave a little moan. She longed for him to enter her but she feared him too. She felt his erection hard against her leg and she knew now she had to decide whether to allow his passion to take its full course. As his hand worked its way a little lower Rhoisin stiffened, as memories of Jim's prehensile hands forcing its way into her childish body overwhelmed her. Stephen stopped stroking.

'Don't you want to?' he asked gently. 'I really thought you did, otherwise I wouldn't have let things get this far.'

Rhoisin burst into tears. 'Oh, yes, I want it terribly,' she said, 'but – but – I – I can't tell you. It's too awful!

I'm sorry. I'm really sorry! I'll try and explain – in a minute.'

Stephen folded her in his arms. 'That's all right. Just take your time.'

Eventually Rhoisin read all her mother's letters. It took some time, spread over several weeks. She felt extremely guilty in the process, as she had done on the first occasion with Auntie Liz. She felt like an intruder, a spy. But she knew she had no alternative. She was sure these letters were the only clue to her father's identity and would hopefully lead to his whereabouts. The letters were not all in chronological order. She had thought she had seen all the letters from Tom O'Hare but in fact there were several earlier ones; extolling Linda's qualities, affirming his undying passion for her, promising they would soon be reunited and shortly married. These passionate testimonies of devotion left Rhoisin feeling very sad; and when she read through the later correspondence again, cold and cruel in its insistence that Linda should have an abortion, she shed some bitter tears. But one thing was definitely established: Tom O'Hare was undoubtedly her father. Not only did the dates fit but there was no mention in any of the other letters of pregnancy, marriage or even courtship.

All the other letters were from Linda's 'clients'. This revelation came as something of a shock to Rhoisin. Although living in close proximity to her mother for twenty-one years in their small, cramped flat, she had no idea that while Linda was leading the life of devoted mother and respectable shop assistant, she had also set herself up in the rather lucrative business of courtesan. With hindsight Rhoisin could begin to piece things together: the late nights when their elderly neighbour downstairs was asked to 'keep an eye on Rhoisin for me.' The weekends away as Rhoisin grew older and could be left on her own. Of course Rhoisin imagined Linda was with lecherous Jim. The thought of the two of them in bed together made her feel physically sick, but common sense persuaded her that if her mother fancied Jim in bed then so be it. At least, if Jim was getting his just desserts from Linda there was less likelihood of his continuing to molest Rhoisin.

But it seemed that Jim was not the only man in Linda's life.

Even though her relationship with most of the others was of a more professional nature, it did appear that they had great esteem and affection for their 'escort.' Which was in fact, Linda's role. Many of the men were businessmen from the provinces, forced to spend lonely dreary nights in London apart from their loved ones. But there was also a significant sprinkling of foreigners; Belgian, French, German, Dutch, who made business visits to London on a fairly regular basis, and always wrote to Linda in advance to book her services. There were Swedes, Finns and Danes, and a Norwegian who wanted to marry her. The Scandinavians' letters were the most effusive of them all. In reading their gushing thanks and their hopes of an early future meeting, Rhoisin could hear their lilting accents through the small errors of syntax.

It appeared that Linda had been 'in business' for about twelve years. She had started by advertising in the right quarters and had kept the first advertisement which had appeared in the press. *'Linda offers companionship and comfort of all varieties. Expert in all positions.*

*All tastes catered for. Equipment no problem. Social
contact preferred at first. Tel 8372 0428.'*

That would explain all the phone calls. The male
voices who seemed on familiar terms with her mother
but were unknown to Rhoisin. It would also explain
the clothes she had never seen her mother wear. Too
good for the shop. Too good for Jim. Kept exclusively
for the well-heeled clients who wined and dined her at
their expense before paying her handsomely for sexual
favours; all positions, all tastes catered for, equipment
no problem.

Rhoisin was stunned by these revelations. She was
both shocked and surprised. Shocked to discover her
mother had been partly supporting her on immoral earn-
ings. Surprised that she had not twigged sooner what
had been going on under her very nose. She couldn't
help wondering what her reaction would have been if
she had discovered her mother's secret 'profession'
during her lifetime. But now that Linda was dead she
would never discover whether Linda pursued such activities purely out of financial necessity or out of – well –
sexual enjoyment. Not for the first time did Rhoisin
dwell ruefully on the totally different sexual attitudes of
her mother and herself.

It was mid-July. Rhoisin had been working at the Duke
of York's Theatre box office for over three months. She
had begun to feel that selling theatre tickets had no
future whatever and she started looking around for
more satisfying employment that might have some
career prospects as befitted a history graduate with a 2/1
from King's College London. But as the recession continued to bite, jobs, particularly for graduates, were thin on

the ground. She toyed with the idea of applying for a teachers' training course; but although the course itself sounded interesting, she couldn't really imagine herself in the role of policewoman in a large class of fourteen-year-old tearaways in a tough London comprehensive school. As her search for a more rewarding job failed to materialise, she thought more about going to look for a job abroad. Perhaps in Europe? She would learn a new language, which would be a great asset. But where? And is a foreign language necessarily an asset if one does not continue to live permanently in that particular country?

Then there was Stephen. She was in love with Stephen. But did he love her? She felt that he was constantly holding something back; keeping from her some intimacy, some essential part of his soul that lovers usually share. But they were not yet lovers. That was the crux of the problem. Rhoisin was as yet unable to give herself entirely to a man. Stephen was extremely patient and understanding. They kissed, they stroked, they indulged in extensive foreplay, but even after three weeks of such intimacy, Rhoisin was unable to allow him to enter her body. She still feared full penetration. Which brought her to her other reservation about their relationship. If Stephen was able to refrain from the full sexual act with her then he must be getting sexual satisfaction somewhere else. Where? All the original jealousies overwhelmed her: Rosalind, Miranda, Cordelia. All the names Stephen would casually, accidentally, let drop into the conversation. Should she allow the relationship to continue? Where was it going to lead? Was he likely to propose marriage? Would she accept him if he did? He was, after all, fifteen years older than she was. Would this pose a problem later on? He also came from a different strata of society. She was lower middle class. Stephen was definitely upper middle class. Would this pose a problem in a marital relationship?

Rhoisin pondered all the knotty problems as she answered endless job advertisements and trailed along to endless unsuccessful interviews. By the end of July 1976 she had reached a decision: she would sublet her flat, leave the London job hunting scene and do a spot of father hunting in the West of Ireland. After all, at twenty-two years of age she was quite old enough to travel on her own.

Chapter Seven

Rhoisin had never been abroad before. Not even to Scotland or Wales. Of course Ireland didn't really count as abroad. They all spoke English and there was no need for a passport. However, it was across the sea, which made it feel rather different from a visit to Leeds or Margate. She decided to go by train and boat rather than fly. For one thing it was considerably cheaper; for another, with plenty of time to spare, she was curious to experience 'travel'.

It was a long journey and she was completely exhausted on arrival. She took the train from Euston at five o'clock in the afternoon, linking up with the boat which sailed from Liverpool at ten pm. She arrived in Dublin at six o'clock in the morning after a wretched night in a cabin for four. Then she struggled across a strange city to the railway station for the West of Ireland. Half dead with sleep, she was appalled to discover that the next train to Killalee didn't leave till ten thirty am. Settling down in a deserted corner of the station in her sleeping bag, she eventually fell into a deep, dreamless sleep, awaking at mid-day to find she had missed the train and that the next one left at four p.m. By the time she arrived in Killalee after eight o'clock on the slowest train on which she had ever travelled, poor Rhoisin was a physical wreck.

Arriving late in the evening in a strange town is always a disconcerting experience. Rather than wander round aimlessly, unable to make a decision, Rhoisin decided to take the first vacant room available. She paused outside a tidy-looking whitewashed cottage, roses climbing up around the door, with a sign up saying: 'B. and B. Vacancies'. Mrs Devlin had showed her to a simple attractive attic room; the sloping ceiling with dormer window looking out on the panoramic view of Sligo Bay. White walls, bright chintz curtains and bedspread setting off the simple pine furniture, gave the whole room a welcoming homely atmosphere.

'Oh, its lovely!' Rhoisin cried, as Mrs Devlin beamed.

For some reason Rhoisin had given her name as Ruth Hobson. It was a decision made completely on the spur of the moment without any forethought whatsoever. Later she thought that for some reason concealing her identity would facilitate the search for her father. Rhoisin was an unusual name, and a particularly Irish one. People always queried its origin and she felt instinctively that greater progress might be made without unnecessary questions. Fortunately formal identification was not required to book a bed and breakfast in the West of Ireland.

Rhoisin's first shock came the following morning. She rose late after a deep, dreamless sleep. Although she had spent ten undisturbed hours in bed, she nevertheless didn't feel completely rested. She felt heavy and weary, as if her sleep had been drugged. It was already nine thirty and as she was as yet unaware of the morning routine, she decided to dress quickly and go down to breakfast and enquire about showers later. She made her way down the narrow oak staircase and into the kitchen in some trepidation. Although a paying guest, she was not quite sure how much of the arrangement constituted in being just a guest, therefore fitting in with the family routine, or taking the role of the paying client and making demands accordingly.

The shock came as she walked into the kitchen and saw, seated at the table eating breakfast, a callow youth of about eighteen or nineteen with bright orangey-red hair and a pale skin with blotchy freckles. He looked up, nodded to her casually and continued to eat his breakfast. The hand lifting the cereal spoon to his mouth, she noted with horror, was of a similar hue. Feeling limp and nauseous, Rhoisin forced herself to sit down opposite this horrendous apparition; this apparition from the past which had haunted her since she was nine years old. Looking at him through half closed lashes she wasn't surprised to notice the bush of pale downy red hairs appearing above his open-neck shirt. This was surely Jim's son, she thought, amid rising panic. Before she could steel herself and realise she was expected to consume food in such close proximity to this horror, Mrs Devlin came into the room.

'Good morning, Ruth, love,' said the kindly lady. 'I'm glad you've had a good long rest. I hope you've had a grand sleep with it. This is my son, Eamon,' she went on. 'Eamon's on nights at the moment so he'll be around during the day. Ruth's from London,' she explained to her son. 'She's come to visit Ireland and I suppose you'll be stopping awhile with us?' She looked doubtfully at Rhoisin as if uncertain whether her hospitality would be good enough for a visitor from London.

'Oh, yes, of course... oh, no... I'm not sure of my plans yet.' Rhoisin was desperately trying to pull herself together, to ensure she didn't offend this kindly lady with the appalling looking son. After all, she thought, calming down a little, not all red haired, freckled men are necessarily rapists. Apart from his colouring, this one looked fairly harmless. She looked up at Mrs Devlin and tried to force her lips into a smile. She looked for any trace of red hair or blotchy freckles but there were none. It'll be the dad then, thought Rhoisin, her stomach knotting. It's more often the men who have this colouring. I bet the dad's a right horror. She wondered how quickly she could move out and find somewhere else to stay in Killalee.

'Will you have rasher and egg?' enquired Mrs Devlin. 'I've lovely fresh eggs, just laid this morning.'

The room was by the week. So that settled it. Rhoisin would be forced to share a house with an orange haired monster. The week would probably reveal whether or not he constituted a physical threat. It was the appearance of dad that really bothered Rhoisin.

She decided to explore the town and get the feel of the place before drawing up a plan of action. July was half way through. The month above all that Rhoisin, a Londoner born and bred, associated with high summer. With Wimbledon just ended, London's streets and parks crammed with tourists, exams over and done with, it was for Rhoisin the highlight of the year. So it was with considerably high expectation that she went into Killalee for the first time.

Here a complete contrast met her eyes. Arriving at the railway station the previous evening after eight o'clock, having travelled for more than twenty-four hours, she had been in no fit state to take in the scenery. Some instinct had guided her towards Mrs Devlin's charming cottage, despite its repulsive occupant. She had taken in nothing else save the fact that here was a place to lay her weary head for the night. Now she looked about her with considerable interest but was not very cheered by what she saw. The overall impression was of a uniform greyness: the sky was grey, the sea was a darker, more menacing, leaden grey. As she walked towards the town centre she saw that the houses were grey too. The style was not unattractive, being mostly of the same two-storey Victorian variety. They were built of granite with grey slate roofs, probably during the latter half of the nineteenth century. But they were in a shabby condition. Even the ancient cream paint on the window frames appeared grey. Nearer the sea the houses had small, untidy front gardens, many filled with rubbish, dumped there some time ago. Approaching the town centre the small, front plots disappeared and the plainer, flat-fronted houses faced directly onto the street. There were no brightly coloured doors, no spanking new paint. All the houses appeared uncared for, unloved.

With sinking heart, following the sign for 'Town Centre', Rhoisin made her way along what appeared to be the main street. Shops appeared: small, drab and pokey, displaying goods that wouldn't even be seen in London's charity shops. How could people live here, thought Rhoisin in despair. At least she was only committed to a week. That was something. The poor sods who lived here were serving a life sentence. It didn't occur to Rhoisin that, blissfully unaware of any alternative, the inhabitants of Killalee probably thought they were very well off.

She came to a pub on the corner called The Laughing Goat. It was newly painted cream with a white door and black window frames. It made a pleasant contrast to the drab houses and tawdry shops. Rhoisin looked up at the brightly painted sign swinging gently in the cool breeze against the leaden, hostile grey sky. The goat's body was in profile but it's head was face on, grinning, leering down at all who passed, as if the keeper of some evil secret. Too early for lunch, mused Rhoisin as she walked on, uncertain whether to be attracted by the fresh paintwork or repelled by the grotesque sign.

She walked slowly to the far end of the town to discover the same process in reverse. The flat-fronted grey houses in the town centre were interspersed with shabby shops selling tat, giving way to slightly larger, bow-fronted grey houses with junk-filled front gardens. At this end of the town was the country. Dull green fields divided by grey dry stone walls stretching into infinity. Rhoisin shivered. She didn't know much about the country. Apart from the visits to Jim's caravan at Margate she and Linda had never visited the real country.

'Too empty and quiet,' Linda had said firmly.

Seeing pictures of it on television Rhoisin had thought it was a pity not to make the occasional trip. Now it was there before her very eyes, she saw her mother's point. It rolled away into the distance, grey-green, empty and quiet. Nothingness.

She turned round and walked back to the pub in search of some life.

Rhoisin stood timidly at the bar of The Laughing Goat wondering if she had enough courage to ask for an egg and cress sandwich with Hellmann's mayonnaise. The scene at the coffee bar just off Leicester Square flashed through her mind. That cold January day when Stephen had chanced to sit at her table. The next meeting, sitting outside in glorious spring sunshine, giving her order as

Stephen seemed to materialise out of nowhere; handsome, debonair, jacket slung casually over his shoulder like any yuppie business executive. Although Stephen was no yuppie. Stephen had arrived some time ago. He was definitely out of the top drawer. The waitress, taking their order; hissing at Stephen: 'White, rye, gran, Nan, French, pitta or pump-er-nick-el.' The thick, creamy filling, palely yellow, gleaming between the hunky slices of healthy bread. Stephen's tapered, well-manicured fingers curving round the triangular portion, half covered with a white napkin, lifting it elegantly to his lips. Stephen's lips; Stephen's white, regular teeth; Stephen's tongue searching for hers; their mouths clinging, tongues now entwining. Stephen's sensitive hands stroking her body, her breasts; feeling for her secret damp place; for her soul.

Stephen! Stephen! Stephen!

'Will yous have a pint of stout or draught bitter, miss?'

The barman brought Rhoisin back to the present with a rude shock. She had completely forgotten she was in a pub. Not that she had anything against pubs, on the contrary. Nevertheless, she was in a strange pub, in a strange town, in a strange country and she was really looking for something to eat.

'Do you do sandwiches?' she inquired timidly.

'And what kind of a sandwich would yous be looking for?'

Rhoisin took the plunge. 'Egg mayonnaise?'

The barman laughed, though not unkindly. 'Not a chance. Not enough eggs left by this time of the day to put them in a sandwich. It's the lodgers. They eat 'em all up at breakfast time. I could do you cheese and pickle. Would that suit?'

'That'll do fine, thank you.'

'Staying long in these parts?' asked the barman, taking a large sliced loaf from under the bar.

'I – I'm not sure at the moment. My plans are… well… fluid.'

'I see.' The barman took a lump of cheese and a jar of pickles out of an ancient, battered fridge at the back of the bar. Rhoisin wondered if he had understood what 'fluid' meant.

'You from England, then?' he asked, conversationally, without any real curiosity.

'Yes.'

As two locals joined them at the bar, the barman lifted a pickle out of the jar with his fingers and laid it on one of the slices of bread. He wiped his right hand on his apron and drew it across his nose. He unwrapped the lump of rather dry looking cheese and contemplated it for a moment. He picked up a knife from the counter, held it poised above the lump of cheese for a second, changed his mind, set it down again and pulled two pints. Without a word or a glance at the newly arrived customers he placed the two glasses of beer on the counter, spilling a substantial amount from each glass over the half made sandwich. With similar lack of communication, the two new arrivals picked up their pints and made off to the far corner of the room.

The barman contemplated the unfinished sandwich with mild surprise, as if it were an activity he didn't normally engage in. He wiped both hands on his apron and drew the left one across his nose several times. Then he placed it on the hunk of cheese. Taking up the knife in his right hand he cut the cheese carefully, very straight and thin, arranging the slices on the bread with both hands, negotiating the big fat pickle like a skittle. Then he picked up the second piece of bread and placed it on top, pressing down hard with both hands, as if afraid the contents would escape. Finally, looking around for something on which to place his creation, his hands lighted on a chipped plate with garish floral design, on which he put a soiled greasy paper doily, topped by the sandwich.

'There you are, love,' he said, handing it across the bar to Rhoisin. 'Get your chops into that now and yous'll feel grand. And what can I get yous to help wash it down?'

Mrs Devlin was extremely tidy and well organised. She ordered her day by the clock, rising at six thirty and allotting a precise time for each household task throughout the day. Considering she might have as many as six paying guests at any one time, this was no mean feat. She was a kindly, hospitable lady who genuinely enjoyed taking in her 'visitors', as she always called them; and although she set such exacting standards for herself, she was surprisingly tolerant at the often haphazard movements of the visitors themselves. Her secret, she often told herself, was to allow plenty of time for everything.

'No point in trying to race the clock,' she often said. 'Time won't stand still. You've just got to fill it as best you can.'

In fact, this attitude, as Rhoisin discovered fairly quickly, was typical of most people in Killalee, whether town or country dwellers. Although Mrs Devlin's meticulous housekeeping was not a trait necessarily shared by her fellow country folk, her attitude to the inevitable passing of time was most certainly shared by all. No one had any sense of urgency whatsoever. Service in the few shops, the hotel and the pub was extremely slow to the point of being sloppy; especially in The Laughing Goat. Rhoisin, having overcome her repugnance to the landlord's way of making a cheese and pickle sandwich, returned on several occasions to listen to the local gossip in an attempt to find out more about Tom O'Hare and his family.

Everyone had time to chat. Communication with their fellow human beings was what the good people of Killalee enjoyed the most. No matter if nothing was on time. What difference did it make if dry cleaning was not ready for collection when promised; if cars were not repaired on time; if meals were late; if the dish was cold on arrival. What mattered was the chat and the gossip; finding out exactly what was going on in the town and the surrounding countryside and passing all the information on to one's neighbours.

And how the people of Killalee gossiped! And how they were curious! Everyone wanted to know everything about everyone. Especially about newcomers to the town. Everyone was most curious about Rhoisin. She had set the tongues a-wagging.

In an ideal world Mrs Devlin liked her visitors to breakfast at eight. This would allow her to have all the dishes cleared away and washed up by nine thirty at the latest, leaving her the rest of the morning to do the bedrooms. But Mrs Devlin was of a pragmatic disposition and she realised that if she hassled her visitors word would get round and bookings might fall off. So instead she sat with them as they consumed her substantial breakfasts, consuming endless cups of tea and her own delicious 'cake' (called soda bread in England), liberally coated with butter.

In this way the good kindly Mrs Devlin was able to draw out her visitors in informal conversation, building up a picture of their lives, their activities and their families, which she had no hesitation in passing on to all and sundry.

Blissfully unaware that Mrs Devlin preferred her visitors to breakfast at 8.00 am, Rhoisin appeared at a different hour each morning, long after everyone else had departed. She hoped and prayed fervently that Eamon would already have retired to bed after the rigours of his night shift as the porter at The Sheaf and Sickle Hotel. Even after three days in the house she still found his appearance quite revolting and extremely disturbing, although she had come rather thankfully to the conclusion that he was so dim as to border on the idiotic.

Mrs Devlin cooked her a soft boiled egg, made fresh coffee and toast and sat down opposite her with a cup of tea. Rhoisin surveyed the empty table in mild concern.

'I'm really sorry if I'm late each morning,' she said apologetically. 'I didn't know if there was a set time for breakfast or if people just...'

'Most of my visitors have their breakfast around eight o'clock,' replied the good lady. 'They seem to find that suits them so they can make an early start and visit more of the pretty places around.'

Rhoisin made an embarrassed apology. 'I... I'm so sorry I...'

'Don't apologise, love,' said Mrs Devlin. 'You're here for a holiday and a good rest which I'm sure you deserve after all that hard work. It must be very tiring working in a big place like London with all the travel on top of a long day's work; and all the noise and the crowds to put up with as well.'

Rhoisin smiled. 'You soon get used to it. I've never lived anywhere else. And I rather like the noise and the crowds,' she added after a pause.

'So I suppose you find Killalee rather quiet after London?' remarked Mrs Devlin, giving her a long hard look.

'Yes, very quiet,' said Rhoisin without thinking.

'Very quiet for a pretty young girl of your age who should be dancing the nights away on her holiday.'

'Dancing? I never really thought...' Rhoisin was taken rather by surprise at the idea of her dancing. 'Don't think I've ever been dancing.'

'They've dances every Friday night at The Sheaf and Sickle,' said Mrs Devlin. 'My Eamon has a look in some nights but he's a bit clumsy on his feet is Eamon.' She decided to take a more direct approach. 'Killalee would seem a strange, remote place for a pretty young girl used to the sophistication of London to come to for her holiday. Especially on her own,' she added obliquely.

'Yes,' said Rhoisin, unsure of what she was expected to say.

'Are yous making a study of the area? Doing some research?' suggested Mrs Devlin brightly. 'Would you be a student?'

'Well, no. Not exactly. What I mean is...'

Suddenly she had a brilliant idea. Thank you, Mrs Devlin! She would never have thought of it without her, not in a month of Sundays. This should make her investigations much easier.

'I'm not a student exactly. That is to say I'm a history graduate, doing research into some of the people who live in the area. Particularly the well-established landowning families in the West of Ireland, rather than the Anglo-Irish

Protestant families within The Pale around Dublin,' she explained shamelessly. She really should have thought this out a bit better. 'The family that interests me particularly is the O'Hare family. Thomas O'Hare. Their house is called Knockramore. It's here in Killalee.'

'Thomas O'Hare?' Mrs Devlin sounded a bit shocked and was silent for a moment. 'They're a long established family, the O'Hares,' she continued. 'They've been a long time in these parts. Some say from the fourteenth or fifteenth century. It's rumoured they did well out of the potato famine, putting up the prices daily whilst all around them the poor peasants was dying like flies. Yes,' she heaved a deep sigh, 'them was hard times. We just don't know when we're well off.

'But the O'Hares. They're less well off now than what they were in the olden times. Some say it was the war that affected the rich landowners. Old Mr O'Hare, he joined the British Army. Not that he had to, mind you. Ireland was a neutral country for better or worse. Though some say there were those what harboured the Germans just to spite the Brits. It's a strange thing, a war. All the different sides it brings out in people.

'It's said the O'Hares had a long running feud with their neighbours at Glendoyle; that they even murdered each other. Then Liam O'Hare, the present owner's father, he bought the Glendoyle estate and turned the house into a hotel. He made a lot of money at first and then things seemed to go wrong. There was less tourists coming here by the end of the sixties than there was in the old days. I should know. I've suffered from it meself. All the English people what used to come here for the ten years or so after the war, they all stopped coming. They went off to Benidorm and Tenerife and Majorca and places like that. You can't blame them, can you, wanting sunshine and cheap wine. They say it's not that dear either, to go to them places in Spain. Sure and I'd go myself if I had the right person to go with.'

Rhoisin listened with rapt attention. Any background information on the O'Hares could be useful.

'So what happened to the Glendoyle house?'

'It was bought by developers. It's a housing estate now.'

'Well, people have to live somewhere. Was it a nice house? Glendoyle, I mean.'

'I remember it was quite an imposing place. People said it was Georgian. It looked Georgian right enough but it couldn't have been, could it? Built only sixty or seventy years ago.'

Rhoisin was losing interest in Glendoyle. She wanted to hear more about Knockramore. 'Tell me about Knockramore.'

'Ah, Knockramore. I don't know there's a lot more to say, love.'

Mrs Devlin heaved a deep sigh and looked out the window with a faraway expression. 'Knockramore.' She got up slowly, filled up the tea pot and poured each of them another cup. Then she cut herself another slice of her home made bread and spread it liberally with butter. She offered another slice to Rhoisin, who shook her head. Mrs Devlin took a large bite of bread and butter and a sip of tea. 'Knockramore. Where was I now?'

'I think you said the war changed a lot of things for the O'Hares.'

'Ah, yes. The war. But war affects most people in one way or another, doesn't it? I mean, things is bound to be different after a war.'

'So the O'Hares bought the Glendoyle estate after the war, like I said, and turned the house into a hotel. Then shortly after that they started selling off some of their own land, maybe to pay for the losses of Glendoyle. Just little bits here and there; then now and again the odd chunk. Farm prices were not what they were in Ireland, specially after we went into the Common Market. But people are always blaming politics for their own mismanagement, aren't they?

'Whatever the reason, either the loss of farming revenue or the cost of the Glendoyle Hotel, the O'Hare's now take in paying guests themselves. But they only get the posh tourists, being as they charge a great deal for it all; what with a golf course, indoor swimming pool, candlelit dining room and the like. I believe it's more like a country club up there now. They don't even call it a hotel. It's called Knockramore Country House in the glossy magazines.

'But I'd watch your step with the O'Hares, Ruth, love. They can be a bit of a funny crowd, by which I mean strange, not prone to making jokes. Young Tom O'Hare, he was a bit of a tearaway in his younger days; but his brother was a real bad egg. Then there was a son. But no one's quite sure what happened to the son after that terrible accident.'

'Accident?' Rhoisin suppressed a shudder. It was curious how discussions about her father seemed to be associated with accidents.

'Yes,' Mrs Devlin went on, 'the family had a terrible accident. It must have been some ten or eleven years back. The son was sent to a special hospital in Dublin for spinal injuries. It was all in the papers at first and then the silence descended like a blanket and no one heard any more. No one even knew whether the son survived or not. Mark my words, Ruth, love, and watch your step with the O'Hares.'

Then, apparently feeling she had said enough, or possibly too much, Mrs Devlin stood up and started to clear away the remains of breakfast.

Pleased with the progress she'd made in such a short time, Rhoisin stood up, pushed in her chair tidily and started on her way upstairs to take her morning shower. She stopped in the doorway and turned round, watching Mrs Devlin for a moment totally absorbed in stacking the dishes correctly.

'Mrs Devlin,' she began timidly.

Mrs Devlin straightened up from her chores. 'Yes, love?'

'How far is it to Knockramore from here? Can you tell me where the house is? Is it too far to walk?'

Mrs Devlin paused in arranging the cutlery neatly in the milk jug. ''Tis about three mile from here. Quite a bit of a walk, but on the other hand 'tis not too far if you enjoy a good bit of a stroll.' Then a thought occurred to her. 'There's Miread's bike out there in the shed with no one at all to ride it. Miread works in Dublin all the week. I'm sure she wouldn't mind if you took her bike off for the day. We can always explain to her when she comes home Friday for the weekend that you'd the need of a bicycle for the day. Miread's a grand girl. You'll like Miread. She wouldn't be too far off your age neither. Sure I've a grand daughter in Miread. Not that poor Eamon is too bad either,' she added by way of apology. 'Not with the father he had and his learning disability an' all. I thank God for my two children all the same. There's others a great deal worse off than meself and they've got lazy, drunken husbands to put up with, which is a sight worse, I always think, than having no husband at all.

'Now, off you go, love. Have your shower and when you're dressed and down we'll look out the bicycle and I'll put you on the right road to Knockramore.'

Chapter Eight

Br-br, br-br.

'Hello. The Bank of Ireland, Baggot Street Branch. Miread speaking. How can I help you? Yes. May I take your account number, please? Yes, all the numbers. Yes, that's correct. And now the sort code, please. Now for security, may I have the name of your maternal grand-mother, please, Mrs Dolan? You don't have a grand-mother any more? No? That's quite common. It's just for identification purposes, Mrs Dolan. Oh, yes. Most banks have a similar system. I do understand, Mrs Dolan. But please try and understand me – or the banking system, at least. No, I'm not being rude, Mrs Dolan. It's for your own protection entirely. You must please understand that. No. We can't have people enquiring about other customer's statements of account. If you have any further complaints, Mrs Dolan, then I suggest you write to the manager.

'Jes-us!'

Miread put the phone down in total exasperation. Her colleague at the next desk looked up and laughed.

'What was all that about?'

'Refused to give any ID.'

'Silly old bitch.'

'Exactly.'

Br-br. Br-br.

'Oh, shit. Here we go again.'

'Maybe you should ask for a transfer?'

'The Bank of Ireland, Baggot Street Branch. How can I help you? Maeve! Thank God for that. Makes a change from the complaining customers. What's that? I won't thank God when I hear what you have to say? Well, fire ahead then. Let's get it over. What! The bastards! How can they be so disorganised? Turkey in September? But I want to go to Benidorm next week! Oh, shit. Yes, yes. OK, then. Phone me back when you know what all the others think. Don't worry. I'll be here all day. Aren't I bloody well chained to this chair? No. I'll answer it. If not just ask for me. Nobody'll know you're not a customer.'

Miread replaced the receiver with a resounding thud.

'Better not smash it. It's bank property,' remarked her colleague tartly.

'Well, that's put the kybosh on my holiday.'

'Why's that?'

'We've been overbooked. The hotel's full.'

'That's bad organisation. You should sue them.'

'That won't give me a holiday next week.'

'No. Have they offered you compensation?'

'Yes. A holiday in Turkey in September.'

'Turkey! Sure that'd be great gas! I'd love to go to Turkey. All that belly dancing in the souks. Much better than Benidorm.'

'I suppose so,' said Miread doubtfully. 'But where do I go next week?'

'Home to Killalee? It can't be that bad.'

'It is.'

Home to Killalee. Home to Killalee. Home to…

'Killalee! Killalee!' called the driver. 'Would all those for Killalee please get off now – and remember your luggage.'

Woken from another sexy dream, Miread stood up stiffly, gathered up all her luggage and struggled wearily out of the coach. A whole week in Killalee.

'Just stack them all up neatly, love. I'll do them in me own time later. I don't want you spoiling your precious holiday washing dishes all day.'

Mrs Devlin smiled at her daughter. Miread smiled back.

'It's nothing, Mam. Honest. Much better than arguing with difficult bank customers over the telephone.'

'You're not getting fed up with the bank, are you, love?'

'Well,' Miread hesitated. She didn't want to grumble to her mother whose life was, after all, a great deal worse than hers was. 'I've been there nearly four years now. I suppose I just feel like a bit of a change.'

'Restless after less than four years?' Mrs Devlin's voice sounded a little sharp.

Miread laughed. 'Mam, four years is a long time in one job. Lots of people move on after six months.'

'But not in a bank, surely?'

'What's so special about a bank?'

'Well, it's a great deal better than being in a shop, or taking in visitors.'

'Yes, I realise that.'

'And you're earning good money and you've had a few promotions.'

'Yes, I know. But I'll only get so far and no further because I'm not a graduate.'

'A graduate of what?'

'University.'

'But you could have gone to university with all those honours in your Leaving Certificate!'

'University costs money.'

Mrs Devlin sighed. 'I wish I could have afforded university. A bright girl like you should have gone to university. But you were only seven when your dad died and it wasn't that easy with Eamon like he is...'

Miread gave her mother a hug. 'Don't worry, Mam. Sure haven't you done wonders with the two of us and you being a single parent and all. Look, I'll just do these dishes quickly and then I'll go off out and see if I can stir up Killalee and have a bit of gas...'

'OK, love. Aren't I the lucky one to have such a grand daughter.'

Miread washed the dishes feeling guilty. She always felt guilty when she came back to Killalee and found how nothing had changed. How her mother's work load seemed to increase; how Eamon had become more imbecilic and more revolting to look at; and also how Killalee had become greyer, more silent and even more dead.

She tried not to think about Eamon but he was inclined to intrude upon her thoughts, especially as they had just spent half an hour or so having breakfast at the same table. Eamon disturbed her. It wasn't just his pathetic stupidity and total lack of interest in girls, though of course his appearance was hardly a turn on. On the other hand, there were plenty of red-headed lasses around; Ireland positively abounded in them, who might fall for a similar type; but Eamon actually blushed and turned away at the sight of any female other than her mother and herself. She couldn't believe that Eamon was her brother. In fact, she couldn't believe they were actually related in anyway at all. It wasn't just a question of colouring and the fact that poor Eamon was so stupid as to be bordering on the sub-normal. It wasn't just that. It was more – well – she did wonder more and more whether they actually were brother and sister. And her father too, come to think of it. There had been the same void there too. The same feeling of not belonging, of not being related. She did wonder...

Miread decided to take it easy till lunchtime and then wander into Killalee and look in at The Laughing Goat. It was a dull, overcast day. As she walked slowly past the dreary, grey stone Victorian houses with their rubbish-filled front gardens, she couldn't help imagining what it must be like in Benidorm at that moment. The photo in the glossy brochure appeared vividly in her mind's eye: the brilliant hot sun shining on the shimmering blue Mediterranean sea; the cloudless azure blue sky, the tourists milling around, heaving, swimming, sunbathing, eating exotic food, drinking delicious chilled white wine. The desirable young men; sunburnt torsos, rippling muscles, randy, rearing to go, wanting to go with willing girls like her... sun, sea and sex...

God damn it! The tears welled up in her eyes, her throat felt constricted. Oh, God damn it and blast it to hell! Turkey in September! She wanted Benidorm now, or Turkey now, or even Dublin. Anywhere would be better than bloody Killalee.

Miread went into The Laughing Goat and ordered a port and lemon at the bar. The pub wasn't crowded. Nowhere in Killalee was crowded because nobody wanted to be there. The barman passed the time of day with her.

'Hello, Miread. It's good to see you back. You here for long?'

Miread picked up her drink and handed over a five pound note. 'Just a week.'

The barman handed her the change. 'I suppose that's long enough for you in a quiet place like this.'

Miread managed a faint smile. 'Killalee's not so bad. The peace makes a change from the noise of Dublin.'

The barman raised his eyebrows. 'Is Dublin that noisy?'

'Haven't you been to Dublin recently?'

'Sure and I've never been to Dublin at all. 'Tis too far. I went to Galway a few times, though,' he said as an afterthought. 'That were far enough.'

Feeling even more despondent after this insular conversation, Miread took her drink to the furthest corner of the saloon away from the bar. She looked around the room. At the far end were two middle-aged male locals whom she had served regularly during her one summer as a barmaid. She had enjoyed it at the time when they had pinched her bottom and stroked her leg. She felt contemptuous of them now. She no longer needed their paltry overtures. She knew now where to seek, and obtain, far more serious sexual involvement. She scanned the room for unattached males. Unfortunately they all seemed to be pretty much attached, mostly young couples with rucksacks, obviously touring Ireland.

She looked away and stared down into her drink. She didn't even notice when the young man sat down beside her. She looked up with a start when he offered her a drink.

'Oh, I didn't notice...'

He laughed, flashing white teeth in an unusually sunburnt face. 'You're very deep in thought. I asked if I could join you but you didn't reply.'

'Oh, I'm so sorry...' Miread felt quite confused.

'Please don't apologise.' He held out his hand. 'My name's Dermot Malone.'

The small rowing boat listed dangerously and then tipped suddenly in the other direction. It pitched violently, quivered and then shuddered as if spent, like its two occupants, who lay satiated in its hold. Lying on an old mattress covered with rugs, completely naked, Miread and Dermot had just come to their climax together. Panting, perspiring, Dermot leaned over and caressed Miread's pretty oval face. Nuzzling into her damp, clean hair he kissed her gently, on the lips, chin, neck, finding her breasts, smooth, round and firm, the nipples standing erect, taut and rubbery. He felt his penis stirring for a second time, growing, swelling, filled with passion for this lovely woman who came to him so readily, damp and receptive, giving herself completely in joy and ecstasy. Quickly he raised himself up and mounted her again, entering her body, feeling her completely surrounding him as he drew himself back and forth as they came together as one. They lay entwined in silence for a while.

Miread stared up at the pale blue sky with the light clouds scudding past.

'That was even better than in the bushes,' she said at last. 'With the added excitement that we might end up in the lake.'

'Can you swim?'

'Of course! Come and get me!'

Miread dived gracefully into the lake, her slim, shapely body gliding smoothly through the water like a mermaid. Though happily, thought Dermot, following her into the water, her lower body, unlike the mermaid, is gloriously, wonderfully human.

They swam to a small island, walked ashore and lay down again together on the soft, grassy bank.

'I go back to work again in two days,' said Miread.

'In Dublin?'

'Yes.'

'Why did you go off to Dublin to work?'

'There wasn't much going on in Killalee and I didn't want to spend the rest of my life serving at the bar in The Laughing Goat.'

'Glad you were there when I came along, anyway.'

'If you'd come along sooner maybe I wouldn't have gone off to Dublin,' said Miread laughing. 'Where were you before I left?'

'How long ago was that?'

'Must be near four years.'

'I suppose I was out on the Lough with my dad learning the ropes of being a ghillie.'

'Is it difficult?'

'No. Not really. It's more born in you than learnt.'

'Is there money in it?'

'Not much, except if you work for the posh hotels. I spent a summer a few years back on Lough Cong working for Ashford Castle. It's said to be one of Ireland's most prestigious hotels. It's packed with rich English and Americans all summer. I got well paid and great tips into the bargain.' Miread looked at him in amazement. 'And why on earth did you return to crummy Killalee?'

Dermot laughed. 'Crummy Killalee? It's not too bad. I had to come back. My dad had a bad accident and I had to look after me mam and the rest of the family.'

Miread was silent. Then she stood up slowly. Dermot looked up at her, standing naked, slim, beautiful and totally desirable. He felt a deep stirring within him, bigger, stronger than any physical passion. He wanted her utterly, exclusively, for ever. He reached up and took her hand and pulled her gently down beside him.

'Miread, I love you. Will you marry me?'

Miread was astonished 'Marry you? But I've barely known you a week!'

'That's no matter. We can think about it for another few weeks.'

'Another few weeks! Marry you and live in Killalee?'

Chapter Nine

Rhoisin followed Mrs Devlin's directions to Knockramore without any problem. It was straight through the centre of the town, taking the left fork at The Laughing Goat and then straight on and into the country until the northern shore of Lough Gill came into sight. It was an unusually nice day, as summery a day as can ever be expected in this rather sunless corner of the globe. The one advantage of this anaemic brand of sunshine is that it is rarely, if ever, too hot. So Rhoisin, bowling along the narrow country lanes on Miread's battered old bicycle didn't have to worry about either sunstroke or sunburn on her bare head and arms.

But what she did begin to worry about was what was going to happen next.

She was beginning to realise, as she tried to manoeuvre the unco-operative gears and find the optimum place to perch on the lumpy, uneven saddle, that it was all very well having travelled all this way to Killalee in search of her father, but what should she do now she had arrived? It was all very well knowing his name and his address, but what should she say when she arrived at his house in about ten minutes? Should she ring the front door bell, give her real name and say she believed that Thomas O'Hare was her father? It sounded preposterous! For all she knew he had no idea she existed. He hadn't wanted

Linda's baby. That much was quite clear but the reason was not. Either he had had no intention of ever marrying Linda, or he had gone off the idea after returning to Ireland. Or perhaps he was just not into the idea of being a father. Since reading her mother's letters Rhoisin had turned these possibilities over and over in her mind but was never able to come to any definite conclusion. If her father hadn't wanted her in the first place, which did seem a stark and indisputable fact, he was hardly likely to want to have much to do with her now: a young woman of twenty-two, with no past in which they could share except her conception; which was hardly her fault and apparently not his wish.

She cycled on in the pale, gentle sunshine, trying to appreciate the scenery as a means of helping to alleviate her problem. She had left Killalee about a mile behind, its drab, pathetic little suburb trying to encroach into the countryside in the shape of characterless, modern cottages all built to the same design. The countryside was neither hilly nor flat but gently undulating; a formation which had its advantages for cyclists, as she could pick up speed going downhill which helped to ease considerably the inevitable climb which followed.

The last hill was a steep one. Sweat broke out on Rhoisin's forehead as she pedalled furiously. Half way up she nearly got off the wretched bicycle but the anticipation of the swirling descent gave her courage to persevere. One last hard struggle and she reached the brow of the hill. Here, the breathtaking panoramic view forced her to dismount and take in the scene below. Green fields divided by grey dry stone walls sloped gently down to Lough Gill, shimmering, unusually blue, bordered by clumps of trees and small sandy bays.

On the far shore to the south was the tiny island of Innisfree, immortalised by W.B. Yeats' beautiful poem: *'I will arise and go now, and go to Innisfree.'* Here the lakeside was more rugged, rising in stark, stony slopes to further craggy hills beyond. Further to the west she could just see the grey stone of Parke Castle, with its round tower at the far end.

As she drank in the beauty of the scene below, Rhoisin momentarily felt a strange sense of belonging; as if this were her country. If circumstances had been different she might have been born and brought up here. She imagined herself as a child, cycling round the country lanes, swimming in the lake, walking the stark hills and clambering over the loosely built dry stone walls.

But in reality she was a stranger in this place, seeing it all for the first time like any visitor, any tourist. She remounted the battered old bicycle and sailed down the hill, her dark, shoulder length hair flying out behind like a banner. Before she reached the edge of the lake she came to a small wood; more of a copse. Here on the right, just as Mrs Devlin had described them, was a pair of tall, handsome, wrought-iron gates. On the right hand side was a bell with a sign above saying: PLEASE RING. This gate, which Rhoisin guessed correctly was intended for motorists, could only be opened from the house once the bell had been rung. The much smaller single gate on the left hand side had no bell above it, was unlocked, and was obviously intended for the free and unannounced entrance of pedestrians. Rhoisin leant the bicycle against the stone pillar, pushed open the gate which, although small in comparison to the main gate, was heavy and opened reluctantly with a loud protesting squeak. She pushed the bicycle through, leant it against the pillar on the inside and closed the gate.

Now she was in! Now she had arrived in the place where, except for the merest accident, she might have been born and brought up. She might still have lived here, in this remote and beautiful place. Doing what? It was no good contemplating what might have been. The moment had arrived for action. It was decision-making time. Should she arrive on a bicycle? Or should she dump it in the bushes and walk? Should she stick to her story of being a research student, or would this arouse suspicion? Would the O'Hares want to be the subject of research or would it make them distrustful and likely to clam up, rather as if they were being investigated by the CID? On the other hand, if she changed tack, would she get confused when reporting progress to Mrs Devlin? Would Mrs Devlin necessarily want a progress report? The answer to that one was definitely yes. Even so, it didn't mean she had to stick to the same story for each situation. Mrs Devlin might be quite impressed by her method of detective work if she did invent a new story. Rhoisin had a feeling that somehow Mrs Devlin was already a part of her life in County Sligo. She wasn't going to go away that easily; not for the moment, anyhow.

Rhoisin decided to arrive on foot. Miread's battered old bike was hardly a status symbol, so she concealed it in a large bush and walked slowly up the drive bordered on either side by massive rhododendrons, which she thought must look magnificent in full bloom. After a short distance she heard voices: the male voices rough and jarring, the female timbre a droning high-pitched whine; all undoubtedly American. Rounding the corner the rhododendrons ceased and on either side of the drive stretched a magnificent golf course; green, undulating, immaculately kept, the greens short and smooth like billiard tables. Two couples, dressed in garish golfing clothes were engaged in some sort of argument about the state of play, their rising voices twanging and grating, spoiling the peace and beauty of the magical surroundings. However unwelcome their intrusion into the silence, these vulgar Americans nevertheless gave Rhoisin an idea.

To hell with research, she thought. I've done enough. I might enquire about a holiday in this splendid place. I might even book it. Stephen said he was ready for a holiday; that he'd like to visit Ireland and see where half of her came from: the better half, he sometimes said, to tease her. He played golf too. He said he'd teach her. And as for the indoor swimming pool and the candlelit restaurant: well, it all sounded too good to be true and was certainly worth investigating.

She rounded another bend in the drive and the house finally loomed into view: large, impressive, Georgian and extremely elegant. It was built of granite, the grey stones perfectly matched in size, colour and shape. The central part of the house was roughly square, three stories high, the windows on each higher floor slightly smaller than the previous ones, each window-sill resplendent with boxes overflowing with scarlet geraniums. On either side were extra wings, only two stories high, giving the house a tapered effect. In the centre a magnificent double front door stood open on one side, revealing a small entrance hallway, panelled waist high in dark oak and decorated above with beautiful pale blue plaster work. As the glass door to the main entrance hall opened, a lady appeared, sweeping down the York stone staircase, at least twenty

steps high. Rhoisin wondered whether she was sufficiently well-dressed to dare enquire about staying in such
a magnificent place.

The lady, wearing a well-cut tweed skirt, Liberty print
blouse and sensible shoes, reached the driveway and
stared unsmilingly at Rhoisin.

'Come about the post of chambermaid, have you?'

Rhoisin came too with a jolt.

'Oh, y-yes. Yes, of course.'

'Better come inside then and we'll see if you're
suitable.'

Silently Rhoisin followed the rather forbidding figure
up the impressive staircase and into the elegant hall.

Chapter Ten

The elegant Georgian house on the Knockramore estate had changed very little in the last fifty years. When Rhoisin followed Lindsay O'Hare up the graceful curving stone staircase into the oak panelled entrance hall, she was seeing for the first time exactly the same fittings and furniture that had been there when Tom O'Hare was a boy. A little redecorating had been done to freshen the place up when it had been turned into a hotel, but the original colours had been carefully copied. Bathrooms had been added to all the bedrooms used by the guests, but this had been done so discreetly and tastefully that only the most discerning eye would have noticed the additions. Even the new beds were in the same style as the old ones and the reproduction lamps on the antique bedside tables were almost undistinguishable from the genuine ones in the drawing room downstairs.

The O'Hares never referred to Knockramore as a hotel. It was advertised as a Country House, offering comfortable accommodation in an elegant family home. This, to a certain extent, avoided the necessity for too many fire retardant doors. Where the fire regulations had insisted that some were installed, this was done with the utmost discretion. The space and elegance, the very essence of Georgian architecture, still remained.

Tom and Sean O'Hare had had an idyllic childhood. Although their father, Liam Thomas O'Hare was considered rather a reprobate, particularly in his younger days, he was in fact, a doting father and left his two young sons in want of nothing in their childhood. Their mother, mousy unmemorable Mary O'Hare, was a slave to their every whim. Nothing was too arduous or too troublesome where the wishes and the welfare of her children were concerned. She gave in to their every petty desire.

Thomas Liam, known simply as Tom, was the elder by two years. His brother, Sean Thomas, was known as Sean. By now a tradition had long been established in the O'Hare family that each male child should bear the name Thomas; a custom which often led to considerable confusion. The two sons grew up to be very different from each other. Tom was hard working and conscientious, taking, no doubt, after his grandfather. However, he had inherited some of his father's traits too, particularly his love of luxury and his weakness for women.

On the other hand, Sean was a lazy cheat. He appeared to be the meaner, baser version of his older brother. Though they both had the same attractive, dark wavy hair and exceptionally fine clear skin, Tom presented a gentle appearance with kindly, wide-set grey eyes under delicately arched eyebrows and a generous laughing mouth. Sean, by contrast, had close-set, hard pale blue eyes under bushy tangled eyebrows and a mean thin-lipped mouth that was a stranger to laughter.

Where Tom was vivacious and out-going, Sean was taciturn and withdrawn. Even as children Tom seemed to be the luckier, more favoured brother. He excelled at school, both academically and on the sports field, whereas Sean, by comparison, appeared backward and clumsy. Sean grew up insanely jealous of his brother Tom, whom he resented for his greater gifts and better looks.

Liam O'Hare had come to realise that the estate of Knockramore was no longer worth as much as it had been in his father's time. His purchase of the Glendoyle estate had turned out to be rather unwise. He had spent a great deal of money turning the house into a hotel; money he could ill afford to spend at the time and which he was now finding impossible to recoup. He wanted to be sure that after his death Knockramore would prosper again under a thrifty, hard working manager, so he made it clear, some time before he died, that he would leave the entire estate and any money that was left to his elder, more hardworking son, Tom. Sean would get nothing.

After Liam O'Hare's death, when Sean and Tom O'Hare were in their mid-thirties, Tom inherited Knockramore. By then Sean had become so jealous and resentful of his older brother that he began to think of ways of disposing of him altogether. Tom, in total ignorance of his brother's dark thoughts, was beginning to enjoy life to the full. He had become very successful at running the Knockramore estate and now there was more money in the bank he made sure there was also plenty in his wallet. He made frequent trips abroad, particularly to London, where he found he could indulge freely in his penchant for what he described as 'lower class women.' They were not the sort of women whom he would ever consider marrying. They lacked the style and poise, the breeding, which he considered essential to any woman he would bring back to Knockramore as his bride.

On the other hand, these 'lower class women' had a warmth and generosity of spirit which he found very endearing. They were genuine, they had no side and above all they gave themselves freely, both physically and emotionally, without apparently expecting anything permanent in return. And most important of all, they seemed to know how to keep out of trouble. Tom liked to enjoy full sex with a woman without any unnatural physical restraints. He made no secret of the fact that he expected the woman to take any necessary precautions and to take the full consequences herself if her method failed to work. So far he had been lucky.

Until he met Linda Hobbs in 1953.

He now looked back on the 'Linda affair', as he described it to himself, with some feelings of guilt but absolutely no regrets. He knew from the beginning that marriage to someone like Linda was quite out of the question. It was not a thought he had ever seriously entertained. Though unfortunately he had mentioned it to Linda and in a wild moment he had even given her a ring.

'Linda, my darling, you are the most wonderful woman I've ever met. Will you marry me?'

It was a question popped in the heat of the moment. At the height of sublime carnal ecstasy what he really meant was: 'You are the most splendid fuck I've ever had! Please can we go on like this forever!'

Linda took his proposal of marriage seriously and stopped taking the pill, thinking that if she should become pregnant everything would be all right. Tom, when he heard the news of her pregnancy, was already back at Knockramore and involved with another woman. When he heard no more from Linda, he assumed the 'affair' to be closed. Absorbed in his new relationship and extremely busy running the Knockramore estate, Tom conveniently forgot about the whole episode.

Tom realised he would eventually have to marry and settle down. In a way it seemed a pity. It seemed a waste of the wealth of attractive, selfless, sexy young women who were prepared to throw themselves at him, prepared to tarnish their reputation and run the risk of an unwanted pregnancy just to give him their all in bed.

There were mistakes: two of them, anyway. There was the 'Linda affair' in London, to which he no longer gave a great deal of thought. He just hoped that when Linda received his cheque she had been sensible enough to have an abortion.

Then, only one year later, there was Brigid right here in Killalee! He had heard that she was sent to a convent to have the baby, parental pressure, no doubt. It seemed there were no lengths these Catholic peasants weren't prepared to go to keep on the right side of the priest. He was most relieved he wasn't a peasant. Quite bad enough being a Catholic – of sorts.

Finally there was Knockramore to think of. Not that he wasn't planning on a long and fruitful life, but at some stage he would need an heir, a son to whom he could entrust the future of Knockramore. So Tom started looking around for a suitable bride. He quickly ruled out the inhabitants of Killalee. They were all peasants, no doubt about it. There wasn't one marriageable young woman whom he felt he would be proud to install as his bride at Knockramore. They were no better either in Sligo Town or Galway. So Tom took some time off and went to Dublin.

Everyone's hopes in Killalee were high when Tom O'Hare brought his new bride back to Knockramore in 1955. She came from the Anglo-Irish landed gentry, minor aristocracy. Her father was a lord; a title dating back to the seventeenth century and her name was Margaret Russborough. She was a Protestant, a big plus point as far as Tom was concerned. For Tom was a snob and had always been determined to marry well. He felt he had made a good catch. Not only had he married into the aristocracy but also into the Church of Ireland. For as Tom understood only too well, to be a Protestant in Ireland meant not only an escape from the confines of medieval Popery, but it was also a status symbol. Tom wanted his children to be brought up in the Protestant faith. Sadly, the marriage turned out to be a great deal less than he desired. Margaret's religious leanings tended towards the prudish and self-righteous. Sex had, of course, been eschewed before marriage and Tom, lying in bed, randy and rearing to go in the dark beside his limp, pious and unresponsive wife, was assaulted by lascivious thoughts of past mistresses; women who, perhaps because of their lower birth, knew how to give their all in bed.

Two years after their marriage their son was born. Another tragedy. For Roderick was afflicted with cerebral palsy and condemned to life in a wheelchair, the lower half of his body wasted, limp and useless. Shortly after the birth Margaret developed a serious infection of the uterus which resulted in a hysterectomy. Tom was distraught. The lottery of life had dealt him a frigid, pious, infertile wife and one crippled son. He never recovered. He grew increasingly to dislike his wife and could barely bring himself to look at his son. Instead he threw all his frustration into running the estate, recouping the losses his father had incurred over the purchase and mismanagement of Glendoyle. Knockramore started to make money again – real money; to bank, invest, to spend and enjoy.

The most profitable side of Knockramore was definitely the paying guests. In a way it was a pity. He would have liked to have his ancestral home to himself and his sad little family, free from strangers, paying intruders. But he realised this was an impossibility, another unfulfilled dream to join the two already shattered: that of having a rich and satisfying marriage and a healthy son and heir. So Tom improved and expanded the facilities for his paying guests; his profitable intruders. He built two swimming pools, one indoor and one outdoor, in the faint hope that even in County Sligo there might be a few balmy days. He created an eighteen hole golf course and an arboretum. He redecorated the whole house and engaged a top chef. But he still refused to call the place a hotel. He thought Knockramore Country House sounded far more appealing. And the guests came in droves.

On their father Liam's death, Sean moved out. It had become clear that Tom, as was expected, had inherited everything and Sean found it impossible to come to terms with his lot in life: the monstrous unfairness of it all. He failed to understand why he had been deprived of his inheritance. He saw no reason why half the Knockramore estate shouldn't rightly be his. He was now forced to seek his living in Dublin as a solicitor's clerk while his spoilt rich brother lived in the lap of luxury in a hotel. To Sean it was injustice of the greatest magnitude. He was embittered, twisted, seething with jealousy. But he bided his time, plotting his revenge. The only answer was death to all of them: his brother, his feeble pious sister-in-law and their sickly crippled son. He would have to make a clean job of it. No half measures. If they didn't all die together then any one of them remaining would inherit Knockramore. Sean was sure his brother had already made a will. It would be totally out of character if he had not. The interesting point was: who would inherit Knockramore after the deaths of both Margaret and Roderick? Roderick, now nine years old, had not been expected to survive so long. His continuing existence was purely due to a combination of expert medical care and a great deal of money. Margaret, too, was delicate, but Sean had always thought her illnesses to be more in the mind. However, the indisputable fact was there: if Tom, Margaret and Roderick were to meet an untimely end, then he, Sean, would be the sole remaining O'Hare. He was the obvious choice to inherit Knockramore if Tom died intestate. But would he? Was there a will? If there was, where was it and who were the beneficiaries? Had Tom relented and regretted their father's unfairness in leaving nothing to Sean? Was Sean now, in fact, the sole benefactor, or had he, perish the thought, left the estate to one of his mistresses?

Sean was a frequent visitor at Knockramore. He came down from Dublin most weekends, usually staying in the family wing, a substantial part of the house which Tom had set aside for his family's exclusive use. Whenever possible Sean would search in the private wing for a copy of the will; in drawers, cupboards, behind the books, behind the paintings. He even took up some of the floorboards. But his search yielded nothing. He continued to plot and fantasise. He would annihilate Tom and his two pathetic, useless appendages. He would become the sole owner and master of Knockramore. He would do exactly as he wished with it. He would have plenty of money. He would call himself Thomas O'Hare. He would be Tom O'Hare. But what about his mother, mad as a hatter? No matter. If he could deal with the other three there should be no problem in getting his mother out of the way either.

The tricky part was getting rid of them all together.

Shooting? Too noisy. Smothering? Too cumbersome. A fire? A distinct possibility, especially as old Mrs O'Hare was becoming rather addicted to fire-raising herself. But that had it's drawbacks too. The fire might leave the humans unscathed and destroy the building instead. Then he'd be left with nothing.

A motor accident? As he turned all the possibilities over endlessly in his mind this seemed the best option. But how to make it look like an accident? How to make sure that all the passengers met their deaths? He would only have one chance.

It was in all the papers, even the *Irish Times*. Mr and Mrs Thomas O'Hare of Knockramore, Killalee. They were well known in the area. He was a substantial land-owner and reputed to be very wealthy. It was during the first week in December and Mr and Mrs O'Hare were driving up to Dublin to spend a few days Christmas shopping. They wanted to brighten up poor young Roderick's sad dull life by showing him the lights and the thronging bustling crowds of Dublin's busy city streets. They were also planning to take in a few shows. But they didn't get very far. They had only just come through Sligo Town onto the Boyle road when, on a sharp bend, the car crashed into a dry stone wall. It was a dull foggy morning and there wasn't another car in sight. Mr O'Hare was killed outright. Mrs O'Hare died later in hospital in Sligo without ever regaining consciousness. They both had to be cut out of the wreckage. Sitting in the back of the vehicle their nine-year-old son, Roderick survived, but only just. The irony of it was that the poor boy had been crippled from birth, never able to walk. They took him to the hospital in Sligo, but he was later transferred to the special accident unit in Dublin. He had received severe whiplash injuries which resulted in further spinal injuries to those he had already sustained at birth. They said he was unable to use his hands for a long while, though he made some progress through intensive therapy. And now here he was orphaned, in an even worse state than before. At first the doctors feared for his life, but although his poor body was wasted from the waist down, the legs foreshortened twisted and useless, his brain was sharp and clear and he possessed a phenomenal will to live.

After the accident the police examined the car and established there was a fault in the braking system. They followed this up with enquiries at the garage where Mr O'Hare always had his car serviced, but as the car hadn't been near this or any garage since the end of August no charges were brought and the file on the accident was closed.

Of course the will was found, locked up in Tom's desk to which Sean had formally had no access. It's contents were quite clear: Roderick would inherit Knockramore when he reached the age of twenty-one. In the meantime the estate was to be managed by Sean, who had been appointed Roderick's guardian. Sean moved back into Knockramore and began to run the estate in his own way. By the terms of the will Sean was not allowed to sell any of the land or shares, but he was free to use the profits from both for his own ends, which he didn't hesitate in doing. He installed his mistress in the private wing, called himself Tom O'Hare and made himself extremely comfortable.

Until Roderick attained the age of twenty-one Sean O'Hare had everything he wanted. There were just two small problems: what to do with Roderick and his now mad elderly mother. Sean hardly gave the question a moment's thought. The solution seemed too easy. He merely locked them away. He had a special suite of rooms renovated with an entrance through a secret panel from the drawing room of the private apartment, which he used on the rare occasions when he felt it was necessary to visit his mother and nephew. There was another entrance from the courtyard, also well-concealed, which could be used by the doctor or Mrs Brothers, the housekeeper, if required. It would be necessary to let Mrs Brothers into the secret, as she would be responsible for preparing their food.

He kept on Roderick's tutor until the boy was eighteen, sworn to secrecy and well-paid for his pains. Lastly, he engaged a professional nurse called Judith to care for both Roderick and the old lady, now showing signs of Alzheimer's Disease.

Chapter Eleven

Brigid Devlin peeled the onions under running water. Even so, two tears slid slowly down her face and joined the stream from the tap in the sink. It wasn't only the chemical reaction, which affects most people, that made her cry; it was the association. She had been peeling onions under running water when Tom had told her he was going to marry someone else. Tom O'Hare. The very name upset her so much that just on hearing it was all she could do not to bawl her eyes out.

Tom O'Hare. She had met him just before Christmas. It would be over twenty-two years ago now. She was young, slim and not unattractive. She was working in the post office and general store in Killalee. After the first two visits in about a week he came in every day; for nothing really: a couple of stamps, a bar of soap, a tube of toothpaste. Nothing you couldn't save up, as it were, for a more worthwhile trip. Of course she knew who he was. Everyone knew the O'Hares, at least by reputation. They were well-known in Killalee. It was also known that they were wealthy. The estate consisted of well over five thousand acres of fertile arable land, much of which they still farmed themselves at the time. It was also known that Thomas was the hard working respectable brother. Sean was the schemer, the cheat, the layabout. There were some who said Sean had done time for cheating the Inland Revenue, but no one seemed to have any proof.

Brigid was amazed and flattered when Tom O'Hare asked her to go out with him after two weeks of almost daily visits to the post office. He took her to the pictures and then out to dinner at a cosy little inn about ten miles distant from Killalee. They got on well, chatting away happily, she with increasing confidence as they made inroads into the second bottle of wine. He drove her home, kissed her restrainedly on the forehead and said he would see her around.

She waited daily with increasing impatience for him to come into the post office. Ten days went by and he still hadn't put in an appearance. Apparently he seemed to have a good supply of soap and toothpaste. Brigid had almost completely given up hope when he breezed in, apologised profusely for his absence but he'd been very busy, and would she be free for dinner this evening? He chose an even more attractive spot to dine in with candlelight, snow-white linen table cloth and discreet, elegant service. Brigid was entranced and was ready to give him anything in return. Which is exactly what she did. He took her back to his private apartment at Knockramore and proved himself such a wonderful seducer that she gave him her virginity. He deflowered her in a torrent of passion that flowed over her like a great waterfall. He also gave her Miread.

Brigid was an innocent then. At nineteen she had heard about sex but she didn't fully understand the implications. Her strict Catholic upbringing had taught her that fornication outside marriage was a sin and that carnal knowledge was for procreation only. But these were mere words, phrases, repeated by the nuns at school and by the priest in church. So far she hadn't connected such rather pompous words with physical closeness to a man, utterly desirable in his rippling nakedness, doing the most wonderful things to her body that no words could describe. But Brigid had no idea she was pregnant. She was now going out regularly with Tom O'Hare and whatever the early evening should bring their way they always ended up at Tom's apartment, in bed, in an orgy of carnal ecstasy. After about four weeks she started to throw up after breakfast. Not every morning, but often enough to wonder if she was sickening for something. Thinking it was just a passing phase she said nothing to anyone.

A week or so later she was preparing dinner for both of them in Tom's apartment. By now Brigid reckoned he must have spent a small fortune on dinners, so feeling she should do something in return, she offered to cook something herself. She was peeling onions under the tap when, as luck would have it, she threw up all over them. It was impossible to hide the unpleasant fact from Tom who was sitting at the table watching her.

She had rather expected his sympathy and was surprised and hurt to experience the reverse.

'How long has that being going on?'

'A few weeks.' She sounded vague.

Tom looked horrified. 'A few weeks! Are you with child?'

Crisis always made Tom sound pompous.

'With child?'

The truth slowly dawned on Brigid.

'You mean – I could be expecting a baby?'

'That is the usual end result of sexual activity,' said Tom coldly. 'Didn't you take any precautions?'

'Precautions? Is there – well – something you can do to prevent having a baby?'

'There certainly is.'

To Tom it was history repeating itself. Another woman from the lower echelons of society whom he couldn't possibly marry was attempting to trap him in the only way these wily women knew how. The idea that he could have taken precautions himself never occurred to him. From his point of view it was up to the woman to take the precautions. He felt it was not his responsibility at all.

'I'll arrange a termination,' he said shortly. 'You can have a holiday in England. I know someone in London who'll fix you up.'

At first Brigid was uncomprehending. 'You mean get rid of it?'

'Yes.'

'But that's murder!'

'It depends on how you see it.'

'I see it as murder.'

'You can't bring a bastard child into the world.'

'There are ways of legitimising a child,' said Brigid bravely, 'such as marriage.' Such a thought had never occurred to her before.

'Marriage is out of the question.'

'Why?'

'Because I am shortly to become engaged.'

Become engaged!

Brigid's world fell apart. Her narrow world of innocence, fun and sexual pleasure had exploded. Nothing, no one, had prepared her for an unwanted pregnancy. In the fifth month, as the evidence began to show, she was forced to tell her mother who was suitably distressed and outraged. Abortion was out of the question.

Catholic peasants in the West of Ireland would never consider such a thing and by now it was too late anyway.

Brigid was sent away to a convent in Connemara. It was a very strict order. The nuns had absolutely no sympathy with girls who transgressed in this way and they made their pregnancies as difficult and as unpleasant as possible by subjecting them to extremely hard work. But Brigid was young and healthy, by then being barely twenty, and she gave birth to a happy, healthy baby whom she called Miread.

Seeing how enchanting her grandchild was, Brigid's mother was slightly mollified and offered to look after her during the day so that Brigid could return to work. With one big practical problem out of the way Brigid now had to face the second one; namely, that the marriageable young men of Killalee now considered her second-hand goods, so her prospects in the marriage market were severely reduced.

It was with some considerable surprise, not to say relief, that less than a year after the birth of Miread she received a proposal of marriage from Seamus Devlin. Feeling she had no alternative, Brigid accepted him. A few years into their marriage Brigid was forced to admit to herself she had probably made a mistake. Seamus had inherited a small painting and decorating business from his father, which, with diligence and prudence should have continued to provide them both with a very comfortable living. But Seamus was neither diligent nor prudent. He spent most of the day in The Laughing Goat with cronies of the same ilk and soon Brigid was forced to open their house to 'visitors'.

The birth of Eamon was a further unfortunate result of their union. Not only did the child have his father's rather repulsive appearance but he was also mentally retarded. Brigid soldiered on despite her drawbacks. Fortunately she was of a reasonably phlegmatic disposition and she faced her many problems with courage and fortitude. But it was her daughter Miread who was the joy and the light of her life and without whom she would have found the world a greyer, duller place. Miread was lively, intelligent, charming and lovely to look at. In short, everything a mother could desire and everything her son Eamon was not.

But memories are short, and by the time Seamus had drunk himself to death when Miread was seven years old, most of the inhabitants of Killalee had forgotten that Miread was not his daughter and mused sadly on the fact that Brigid Devlin's two children were not both equally well-endowed.

As the years went, by Tom O'Hare began to have increasing pangs of guilt about having fathered two illegitimate offspring. Although initially angry at the news of Linda's pregnancy, after a year he was quite overwhelmed with guilt. He wrote to her several times but as she had moved shortly after Rhoisin's birth he never received a reply.

His reaction a year after Miread's birth was similar. Guilt engulfed him. He wrote to Brigid, apologising for his coldness and lack of understanding and explained why marriage was impossible. It was a question of social class, he said. People of the landowning classes could not marry into the peasantry, particularly in the West of Ireland. He sent Brigid money which at first she returned. She was incensed, her pride was deeply wounded. He wrote again, several times, sending more money. In the end she didn't reply but just tore up the cheques.

Chapter Twelve

'Ruth!'

'Yes, Mrs O'Hare, madam.'

'No need for Mrs O'Hare. Just call me madam.'

'Yes, Mrs O'Hare – madam.'

'Just madam, Ruth.'

'Yes, madam.'

'Have you done the blue room, Ruth?'

'Yes, madam.'

'And the green room and the pink room?'

'Yes, madam.'

'What about the Georgian room.'

'I've done that as well – madam.'

'My goodness, you're a very quick worker, girl. Much too quick. I thought you said you had little or no experience.'

'No, madam. That is to say I haven't had any hotel experience but I've had plenty of practice cleaning my own flat.'

'That's entirely different, Ruth. I must make that quite clear at the outset.'

'Yes, madam.'

'The skill needed to clean a first class Country House Hotel such as Knockramore is entirely different to the haphazard effort needed to maintain a small flat – in Kilburn.'

Rhoisin's eyes widened as the devil took possession of her for a moment.

'Indeed? I thought it was just a question of shoving the furniture around in either case and...'

'Shoving the furniture around?' Mrs O'Hare was wild with indignation. 'The furniture in this house is antique, girl. You don't shove it around. You move it with the greatest care and reverence. Most of it's extremely valuable. And quite irreplaceable. I shall have to keep a stricter eye on you, Ruth. I can see that. You're very young to have the responsibility for such valuables as we have here. I hope I shan't regret your appointment.'

'No. I'm sure you won't – madam.'

'We may have to review the situation in a month's time.'

'Yes, madam.'

A month's more than I could stand, thought Rhoisin. Hopefully I'll have found out all I need to know long before then.

'You could start on the Long Gallery, Ruth. But don't rush and no shoving the furniture around.'

'No, madam.'

'You must move it gently with the greatest of care.'

'Yes, madam.'

'Ah, good morning, young lady. It's most kind of you to bring the breakfast up to my bedroom.'

'Don't mention it, sir. It's not just kindness. It's part of the service and will be charged to your bill, sir.'

'I daresay it will. This place is full of extras.'

The twangy, Texan drawl grated on Rhoisin's ears.

'You been here long, young lady?'

'Almost a week, sir.'

'You from around these parts?'

'No. I'm from London.' The large American gentleman threw back the covers and gingerly slid his pyjama-clad legs off the bed, feeling the carpet cautiously with his toes, as if not quite trusting to the solidity of the floor.

'From London? And what would a pretty young girl from London be doing in such a God forsaken spot as this?'

As Rhoisin was thinking out a suitable reply, the man stood up and took a step towards her.

'Pretty young thing, aren't you? And what's your name, then?'

He held out his hand.

'Ruth, sir. Ruth Hobson.' Rhoisin took a step backwards. The man laughed.

'Don't worry. I shan't touch you against your will. I'm not dangerous. I'm not a rapist. I just thought – a pretty young girl like you, stuck out here in the sticks, might like a bit of – you know – I realise I'm no picture postcard, or not even that young any more for that matter. I just thought that perhaps – it's worked before you know. Some young girls just love it with older men, even those they don't know very well.' He hesitated. Not for nothing, of course.' He laughed. 'I'm sure your salary could do with a boost.

Rhoisin stood frozen to the spot. This obscene American tourist was actually proposing to pay her for sexual favours!

He lowered his hand and took a step backwards.

'Well, never mind. I'm not usually very lucky,' he said sadly, sitting down on the bed and putting his head on his hands.

Rhoisin, overwhelmed with relief, walked to the door and opened it.

'Enjoy your breakfast, sir.'

With that she thankfully closed his bedroom door and returned to the kitchen.

Mrs Brothers, the cook, was busy making the basic preparations for lunch assisted by Moira and Peggy. Moira was small, slight and dark; barely seventeen. She moved like quick silver and chatted incessantly about nothing of any particular importance. People who knew her well had long stopped listening to anything she said so she always made a point of latching on to any newcomer in order to get a little attention. She made a beeline for Rhoisin when she came into the kitchen.

'Shall we do the spuds together? Then I can tell you all about the film me and Darren saw the other night.'

Rhoisin was grateful. With Moira prattling on she would have a chance to compose herself after the rather nerve-racking experience upstairs. Despite all her irritating chat she actually preferred Moira to Peggy. Peggy was much older, probably in her mid-forties, unmarried and very conscious of it. She was somewhat saturnine and lacking in charm. But it was her colouring that really put Rhoisin off: the carroty-red hair, the too-pale skin with freckles. It appeared that a surprising number of Irish people had this particular colouring. This was something new to Rhoisin; something else she had to come to grips with in this foreign land.

Moira chatted on about the film she had seen, giving Rhoisin a detailed account of the plot and full description of all the main characters. Rhoisin switched off. Moira started on her boyfriend problems. Rhoisin was miles away. Neither of the other two women in the kitchen were listening either.

'And some people say there was another Tom O'Hare and there's a son still alive and hidden away in an asylum somewhere.'

'Oh, Moira, you shouldn't be telling such tales, especially to foreigners all the way from London. You don't know what Ruth is going to think of us simple people from Killalee in County Sligo, giving out stories about your employer that you don't even know are true. Isn't that so, Ruth?'

Mrs Brothers turned and faced Rhoisin, speaking to her directly, so Rhoisin felt obliged to say something.

'I haven't met Mr O'Hare yet,' she said lamely, not having followed anything Moira had said for at least fifteen minutes. 'But Mrs O'Hare is quite a dragon.'

'That's only because he bullies her,' said Moira. 'She wouldn't be nearly so bad if it weren't for him. That's what I was saying about there being another Mr O'Hare. Haven't you heard that story too, Mrs Brothers?'

Mrs Brothers pursed her lips and rolled out another piece of pastry with deft determination. 'I'm not saying nothing, love. I don't think it's my place to go round spreading gossip about my employers, even if some of it might be true.'

Even if some of it might be true. Rhoisin pricked up her ears and made a mental note to have a private chat with Mrs Brothers in the not too distant future.

'Ah, Ruth. What a nice surprise, indeed. I thought you were on bedroom duty? I do hope your appearance in the dining room at dinner doesn't mean that I'll be deprived of your company upstairs in the morning with my breakfast tray.'

The large Texan leered across at her from his single table in the corner of the dining room and blew his acrid cigar smoke straight in her face.

'No, sir. Unfortunately not, sir. Mrs O'Hare asked me to help out in the dining room tonight as someone is off sick.'

'Someone off sick?'

'Yes, sir. Deirdre, sir, the tall blonde. Said she had a migraine, so Mrs O'Hare let her go home early.'

'Ah, Deirdre. Yes, of course. She did have a rather busy morning. Do you think you could get me some more of the yellow stuff that's on the fish?'

'You mean the *sauce Béarnaise?*'

'Yes. The Bernard sauce. That's a good girl, Ruth.' He gave a lecherous chuckle as he reached out and pinched her bottom. Feeling rather nauseous, Rhoisin beat a hasty retreat to the kitchen.

Knockramore had been built in the mid-eighteenth century as an elegant family house. In those days buildings were not designed for convenience, only for their appearance, so the kitchen and dining room were some distance apart, separated by the large entrance hall. When it was adapted to take paying guests some forty years ago it was considered too difficult and too costly to install a kitchen nearer the dining room so all the servants were forced to suffer an arduous trek between the two rooms. It had also been thought inappropriate to the style of the building to install service swing doors, lifts, chrome cocktail bars, or even fire-retardant doors.

So Rhoisin's passage from the dining room to the kitchen led, of necessity, through the hall.

It was here that she met Mr O'Hare for the first time.

She was carrying a large pile of plates as she left the dining room. Moira's advice before her evening's trial was: 'Take something with you each time you go. Otherwise your legs will drop off with all the walking around.'

So with this seemingly good counsel in mind she had piled up almost more than she could carry. Dinner was half way through. Guests were expected to arrive punctually and partake of a fairly compulsory pre-dinner drink in the drawing room beforehand, which was of course added to the bill. As all the guests were at this moment tucking into their main course, Rhoisin was rather surprised to see a pair of legs in well-tailored trousers walking slowly across the immaculately tiled floor towards her.

'Ah, good evening, young lady. You must be the new chambermaid, Miss Hobson, I believe. I am Mr O'Hare.'

Rhoisin was so surprised that she nearly dropped her pile of plates. Mr O'Hare! Thomas O'Hare! The man she supposed, no was certain, must be her father. The man she had come to seek; the person who was half her being; who was partly responsible for her conception; for her very existence. Now that her mother was dead, Thomas O'Hare was her closest living relative. He was her human anchor, her identity.

It was a full minute before she dared look up at him over her pile of plates.

Rhoisin slept late on her first day off. It was Sunday and the previous day had been horrendously long and emotionally overcharged. She had no actual fear of the lewd Texan guest but she still felt extremely uneasy of any unforeseen sexual advances and was as yet not sufficiently expert to be able to laugh them off.

Her surprise encounter with Mr O'Hare was in a different category altogether. When she eventually plucked up sufficient courage to look at him directly she realised afterwards that what she was hoping to find in him was a mirror of herself. She was hoping to see in Thomas O'Hare a more mature, male version of her own delicate, finely-made features: the wide-set grey eyes under quizzically arched, dark eyebrows, the pale translucent skin and the shining thick mane of dark hair. So in searching for her own as yet unrecognised beauty in Mr O'Hare, she was disappointed to find it largely absent. The colouring was very similar. The dark hair, now greying at the temples, was slightly curly, the pale skin had the same fine texture; but the face was heavy and jowly, the dimpled chin curved inwards, giving the impression of a person who was weak and indecisive. But the eyes struck a chill into Rhoisin: they were pale, steely blue and set too closely together. They were the eyes of a schemer, of a man intent on getting exactly what he wanted; the eyes of a man who lacked warmth, sensitivity, or any compassion. They were eyes which could inspire fear and hatred.

Their meeting had been brief; fleeting. Mr O'Hare regarded his new employee with only the scantest of interest. Undoubtedly she was attractive; more, she had an inner quality which gave her a hidden beauty. But this was no concern of his. What mattered to him was that she was working hard and therefore justified her place on his staff. He opened the kitchen door for her and bade her good evening.

Cycling home, exhausted that evening after ten o'clock on Miread's battered old bicycle, Rhoisin was too tired to give the matter any thought. Back at Mrs Devlin's pretty cottage she went straight to bed and fell into a deep and dreamless sleep.

It was after nine thirty when she finally struggled downstairs the following morning. Mrs Devlin, well turned-out in her Sunday best, had just returned from early Mass, feeling uplifted after taking Holy Communion. Miread was seated at the kitchen table, her attention equally divided between a bowl of corn flakes and a woman's magazine. She looked up curiously and smiled as Rhoisin came in to the room.

'Hello,' she said. Her voice was warm and friendly.

'Hello,' said Rhoisin, coming to sit down at the table.

Mrs Devlin looked at the two girls. Her heart missed a beat when she saw them together for the first time.

That's it! she thought. Why didn't I see it the first time? Of course that's who she is! She's Tom O'Hare's daughter! There's no mistake about it at all. The eyes give it away completely: those dark grey, wide-set eyes under the beautifully marked eyebrows. Tom's laughing mocking eyes.

She had had a shock when she first saw Ruth, walking in gracefully like a young gazelle, an apparition from the past. Straight from London. Tom had said the woman was from London. He had laughed about it. That mocking laugh which she had loved at first. The woman thought he was going to marry her, he said. He had thought so too for a while. But not for long. Not once he had come back to Killalee, to his home at Knockramore where he was Somebody Important With Money. Then he had realised that he couldn't possibly marry a shop-assistant from London – from anywhere. He hadn't mentioned a child, but then he would have had no reason to, would he? It might have put her, Brigid Sheehan, off. So she had her own child anyway.

Brigid looked at the two girls again. How old would Ruth be? Twenty-two? Twenty-three? A week or a year would make no difference anyhow. Men could sire offspring at any interval, with any frequency.

'Ruth,' she said, 'this is my daughter, Miread. This is Ruth, all the way from London. She's stopping awhile with us.'

Chapter Thirteen

'Mrs B, the egg should be mashed up really small. Like this.' Rhoisin tipped up the bowl of mashed hard boiled egg and held it out for Mrs Brothers' inspection. 'You see how it's all become one colour. Just pale yellow. If you can see any lumps of white then the sandwich won't have the specially smooth texture.'

Mrs Brothers examined the bowl with great seriousness. Then she cautiously dipped in her little finger at the side and licked it.

'Yes. Lovely smooth texture. Though it doesn't taste quite sharp enough.'

'It will in a minute.' This is a bit like *Blue Peter*, thought Rhoisin, but she said nothing, thinking Mrs Brothers probably wouldn't understand.

'Salt, pepper, no problem. Now we come to the most important ingredient, Hellmann's mayonnaise. Do you have any Hellmann's mayonnaise, Mrs B?'

'Hellmann's? Sure and we do. Mrs O'Hare would never allow Heinz Salad Cream to be served to the type of guest we have staying here.'

She handed over the jar and Rhoisin mixed in a generous dollop.

'Now we're ready to construct the sandwich,' she said, moving the breadboard nearer.

'What kind of bread's the best?' enquired Mrs Brothers, taking an armful of assorted loaves out of the larder.

'It doesn't matter. It's really according to taste. It's the filling that's the most important,' replied Rhoisin, selecting a delectable homemade brown loaf from Mrs Brothers' appetising selection and deftly cutting two thin slices. 'I usually remove the crusts,' she explained as she placed the second slice on top, 'But this bread is so fresh and tasty it would be a shame to waste any of it.'

Mrs Brothers took two plates off the dresser, placed them on the table, watching in fascination as Rhoisin put the finishing touches to her culinary masterpiece. Hoping to anticipate Rhoisin's next move, she placed a white paper doily on each plate. Rhoisin smiled across at her. 'Lovely,' she said, cutting each sandwich into as even triangles as the fresh homemade bread would allow. She passed one of the plates across to Mrs Brothers and they bit into their portions together with silent relish.

'Mm, delicious,' said Mrs Brothers appreciatively, 'I do understand why you like them so much.'

'Sometimes I add cress as well, though that's not essential.'

As Rhoisin spoke a large blob of egg oozed out of her sandwich onto the plate, reminding her immediately of Stephen. Stephen! She was missing him dreadfully. In fact she was on the point of giving up this whole frustrating pointless search and returning to London to stake her claim on Stephen before Miranda or Rosalind or some other glamorous actress type did. The longer she was away from Stephen the more she missed him, the more she ached for him. Today was Wednesday. If she gave in her notice today she could finish on Saturday, leave Killalee on Sunday and be back in London some time on

Monday. But what would she say to Stephen? That she had failed in her mission? That she had become sick and tired of the whole project? That she had spent three weeks actually staying in her father's house without confronting him; without confirming the fact whether or not she was Tom O'Hare's daughter? What would Stephen think of her then? Would he despise her for lack of tenacity; for not even attempting to finish what had become one of the most important missions in her life? Could she say: 'Stephen, I missed you so desperately and I love you so much I just couldn't go on without you.' It sounded rather pathetic. It was enough to put any man off and might even finish their relationship. On the other hand, she could just admit failure as a stark, bleak fact and try to take the line that after all, she had managed to live for twenty-two years without knowing who her father was so there was no reason why she shouldn't live in ignorance for another twenty-two years, or more. But she knew this wasn't the truth; and Stephen knew it wasn't either. They had discussed the matter often enough before she had left for Killalee. How she felt so strongly that she only knew half of herself; how she lacked a complete identity.

Then she had to look at the future. Hopefully one day she would marry and have children. Perhaps not with Stephen – that seemed almost too high an expectation – but maybe some nice, kind, ordinary man, even if he were less glamorous than Stephen, would come along, and eventually there would be children who would want to know about their background as they grew older; who their grandparents were. No, she would have to stick it out; there was no going back.

They finished the sandwich, Mrs Brothers watching Rhoisin as she munched in silence, deep in thought.

Mrs Brothers took the plates away, put them in the dishwasher and then began to lay a dinner tray for one. Rhoisin got up and automatically began to help her. Then a thought struck her: a dinner tray for one? Surely all the guests dined downstairs? It was an unwritten house rule that everyone appeared in the dining room when the gong sounded. Perhaps someone was ill?

'Who's that for Mrs B?' she asked, trying to appear disinterested.

Mrs Brothers looked at Rhoisin sharply: this young lady from England. You could tell she was the educated type. She wasn't the sort of girl who would normally take a job as a chambermaid. She wasn't working class or from peasant stock. Why had she come to Killalee? Why had she taken the post of chambermaid at Knockramore? Was she looking for something; for someone? How much did she know already? Would there be any harm in telling her anything? Would it matter if she knew what was going on? Who would she discuss it with in faraway London? But perhaps she was a journalist and it would be in all the papers, English as well as Irish. On the other hand, wasn't that just what Mr O'Hare deserved? To have all his machinations printed in the newspapers. It was about time the world knew what was happening at Knockramore. But would she be implicated in any way? It was hardly her fault she had chanced to be there when it happened. In the wrong place at the wrong time, as they say. However, she couldn't be blamed for anything. It had absolutely nothing whatsoever to do with her. All she did was to send trays of food upstairs. Even so, she knew. Mrs Brothers looked hard at Rhoisin.

'That's the dinner tray for old Mrs O'Hare. She's just turned ninety-two and she's too frail now to make the stairs down for meals, so I do send her food up to her on a tray.'

Rhoisin's delicate, arched eyebrows went up. 'Old Mrs O'Hare? I didn't realise there's an old lady as well. So she stays in her room all the time?'

'Well, her being ninety-two and all...'

'Yes, yes. I quite realise that. Even so, it's strange Mrs O'Hare never mentioned her.'

Rhoisin decided to take the plunge and come clean with Mrs Brothers. After all, if she didn't get a move on she risked still being at Knockramore for Christmas; perish the thought. 'Mrs B, I'm a student doing research into the well-established, landowning families of the West of Ireland,' she explained. 'I have a particular interest in the O'Hares.'

A research student, mused Mrs Brothers. Well, there wouldn't be any harm then, in telling her just a little...

'It must have been about eleven years ago, when young Roderick was only nine, there was this terrible accident and Mr and Mrs O'Hare...'

Rhoisin froze. She knew it must have some connection with an accident...

Chapter Fourteen

Old Mrs O'Hare lit another candle. It looked so pretty, flickering in the twilight. It made the room look much more attractive. Electric light, even a table lamp with only a 40 watt bulb, made the room look harsh and unsympathetic. It showed up all the room's blemishes; the cobwebs lurking in the corners, the cracked, stained walls, the peeling paint on the doors and window frames and the large burn on one of the curtains. It had been a near thing last time. Even she had to admit she had been careless. Judith had come into the room in the nick of time as the fire had taken a hold on one of the curtains.

'Mrs O'Hare! What on earth! What are you thinking of! You'll have us all up in flames in a minute!'

Judith had rushed over to the curtain, pulled it off the rail and stamped on it hard.

'There now. It's out. Thank heavens for that!'

She rushed off to get a bucket of water, just to make sure.

'Maybe we should try living without candlelight, dear,' she suggested. 'Most of us make do with electric light.'

More table lamps were brought to Mrs O'Hare's room and a few very low wattage night lights were added for extra atmosphere. The candles and the matches were confiscated.

For a few months Mrs O'Hare lived without candle-light with no complaint. She had genuinely had a bad fright. She was still sane enough to realise that death by burning could be pretty unpleasant. She wondered if Joan of Arc had felt much pain tied to the stake in Orléans by the British. It was Queen Elizabeth I who had tied her up, wasn't it? In her generally confused state of mind Mrs O'Hare's history had become rather muddled. Martyrs at the stake. France or England. What difference did it make now? Anyway, in the olden days all they had was candlelight. Come to think of it, it was a miracle there weren't more deaths by burning; more buildings destroyed by fire.

Little by little Judith gave in. One candle, then two, then half a dozen. Judith realised that once the old lady had a box of matches in her possession it didn't really matter how many candles there were. But she made frequent safety checks, just the same.

Judith was sorry for old Mrs O'Hare. She was sorry for all three of them, for Roderick and herself as well as the old lady. They were in a tight situation, no doubt about it. And she didn't really see what she could do about it. Unless she just gave in her notice and left. Then she could go straight to the police. But would they, could they, do anything? Was it illegal to keep people confined to their rooms in their own house? Especially such disadvantaged people as Roderick and Mrs O'Hare. Then, if she did leave Knockramore, what would become of Roderick? And what would become of her without Roderick?

So Judith did nothing and just gave both her charges whatever they wanted, if it was within her power to do so. It wasn't as if either Roderick or Mrs O'Hare were exactly fit or capable of coping with the outside world on their own. Mrs O'Hare, at ninety-two, was well in the grips of Alzheimer's. Although the doctor hadn't mentioned it so far, Judith, as a professional nurse, recognised all the signs, foreseeing the day when she would no longer be able to manage the old lady on her own. But although ill and quirky, Mrs O'Hare had undeniable charm. She was never malicious, always contrite after her little misdemeanours and often very amusing. Except for the distinct possibility of another little fire, or even a major one, Judith felt she had old Mrs O'Hare under control, certainly for the present.

Roderick was a different proposition altogether. Roderick was twenty years old, a cripple and condemned to life in a wheelchair.

Rhoisin had now been working at Knockramore for over a week and was becoming more accustomed to her strange new life. It was very hard work and by the end of each day she was most grateful it was a temporary situation. Indeed, there were days when she felt so utterly exhausted that she felt like giving in her notice on the spot. Mrs O'Hare was an exigent employer. She was fair, she was never harsh or unkind, but she demanded the highest standard of work. As the hotel was short staffed, everyone at Knockramore was rushed off their feet from morning till night.

Rhoisin couldn't decide whether it was the difficulty of persuading people to work in such an isolated place or whether the O'Hares just wanted to save money. Because of staff shortages most of the employees were expected to undertake work outside their normal duties. Although Rhoisin had originally been engaged as a chambermaid, which she understood meant working in the bedrooms, she invariably found herself preparing vegetables in the kitchen, serving in the dining room and even in the bar. Dining room nights were late. Bar nights were even later. The journey back to Killalee on Miread's old bicycle was often made late at night in the dark. After the first two weeks Mrs O'Hare suggested that Rhoisin live in on a permanent basis, which at first Rhoisin was reluctant to do. Although it would undoubtedly be more convenient and far less tiring, she somehow felt she would be too overwhelmed, even engulfed, by the O'Hares. There was a strange atmosphere in the house, as if a momentous event, perhaps a disaster, was about to take place. Rhoisin wanted an escape route left open. Also, she had no wish to give up her cosy little room in Mrs Devlin's cottage. There were times when she wondered if Mrs Devlin knew more about the O'Hares than she had so far admitted. It would be just as well to keep in contact with Mrs Devlin.

As she went about her work in the house, hoovering, dusting, polishing, admiring the antiques, she took a particular interest in studying the paintings. The house was like a museum or an art gallery. There were antiques and paintings everywhere. Many of the paintings were of rural scenes. These bored her. The more time she spent in the country the more she disliked it. Yes, there were very beautiful parts, especially round Knockramore itself, but she felt disorientated by the space and the deafening silence. She began to feel almost relieved she had not been born and brought up here. And there were times too, feeling so alienated from the place, that she thought it an impossibility that she was Tom O'Hare's daughter or indeed even remotely related to any of them.

Nevertheless, she studied all the portraits. They were mostly of men and clearly of members of the O'Hare family, according to the brass plaque on each frame. But she failed to pick out any of Tom O'Hare, nor was she able to spot any strong likeness. She also looked for some resemblance to herself in this family portrait gallery but found none. She wondered if there were more portraits in the private wing. Maybe the more recent ones were kept there. Although kept locked, the staff were allowed to go there. After all, someone had to keep it clean. Rhoisin couldn't imagine Mrs O'Hare cleaning even her own bedroom. It was just a question of being the chosen cleaner. Her chance came two days later as she was dusting the Long Gallery. Mrs O'Hare came bustling along at the far end, her sensible rubber-soled shoes squeaking on the gleaming wooden floor that Rhoisin had just polished. She was, unusually, wearing a summer taffeta skirt which swished as she walked. Jewellery glinted at her throat and wrists, several rings adorned her fingers.

'Good morning, Ruth. I see you are hard at work this morning. This floor is certainly a credit to you. Perhaps we could see our way to a small rise at the end of the month. I shall have to discuss the matter first with Mr O'Hare, of course.'

'Yes, of course, madam. I do appreciate it – and thank you very much, madam.'

'That's quite all right, Ruth. It may not happen but I'll see what I can do.'

'Thank you, madam.'

'Now for the rest of the morning I would like you, please, to clean our private sitting room and then you may take the afternoon off.'

'Yes, madam. And thank you very much again, madam.'

'Don't mention it, Ruth. Here is the key to the private apartment. Put it on the table and pull the door to as you leave. I shall be up shortly.'

'Yes, madam.'

As Rhoisin took the proffered key her heart beat faster with anticipation. The private apartment at last! What luck! If Mrs Brothers was right then she should be able to find the secret panel and then...

But first she had to finish dusting the Long Gallery. The whole Gallery had to be dusted and polished every three days; the oak floor and all the antique furniture, some with intricate designs of scallops and curlicues. Mrs O'Hare ran her hand over the surfaces every three days and woe betide the cleaner who was responsible if the work was not up to standard. She would have to get a move on if she was going to get everything finished before lunch. It would be nice to have the afternoon off. She might cycle down to the lake and take a walk. She might even have a swim if the water was warm enough.

Rhoisin dusted and polished the furniture as quickly as she knew how and was through in twenty minutes flat. Gathering up all the cleaning equipment and fingering the key in her pocket she made her way along to the far side of the house where the private quarters were. She let herself in quietly and found herself in a large, airy, attractively furnished sitting room with two elegantly proportioned Georgian windows overlooking the park to the south side of the house. The view was magnificent. The well-kept emerald green lawn sloped gently down towards the golf course, dotted with fine, ancient trees, the greens appearing like a series of bowling greens. Beyond lay Lough Gill, pale blue and gleaming in the gentle sunshine, the shore an endless variation of tiny sandy coves, rocky outcrops and clumps of trees. On the farthest shore was Yeats' romantic Isle of Innisfree. She stood at the window looking at the beautiful scene below. But for fate, this could have been her birthplace. Cruel fate? It was hard to tell. If what Mrs Brothers had said was true, and there was no reason to suspect it wasn't, then things could turn out to be very interesting indeed. In the meantime, she had better get on with the cleaning and see if she could find the secret panel.

Rhoisin worked as fast as she could, hoovering, dusting, polishing, replacing trinkets, patting cushions. Anxious though she was to find the secret panel, there was no escaping Mrs O'Hare's anger if the cleaning hadn't been done properly. After about an hour she stood back and surveyed her work with satisfaction. Then she started her search. She began in the far corner of the room and worked her way along the wall opposite the two elegant Georgian windows. A thorough search entailed taking several of the paintings off the walls. Although no art connoisseur, she knew enough to realise they were oil paintings and probably originals. The contents of this place must be worth a fortune on their own, never mind the value of the house itself, she thought, as she carefully dusted a portrait of a rather handsome gentleman wearing a Charles II style wig. She was so engrossed in her task that she didn't hear the door open quietly. Mr O'Hare stood in the doorway. 'Well now, there's my pretty little Ruth all on her own in my private sitting-room. I wonder what she's up to, eh?'

And he strode into the room to stand right beside Rhoisin, glowering down at her threateningly. 'Is this a scheduled visit with permission from the lady of the house or is it just a little tour of exploration on her own initiative? Or maybe she's come to offer her master some very special service of a more intimate nature particularly suited to the private apartment. Well, Ruth? Pretty little thing, aren't you?

Chapter Fifteen

Mrs Brothers took the meringue cases carefully out of the fridge and laid them in a straight line on the kitchen table. Raspberry Pavlova. Mm, delicious. One of her favourite desserts. She imagined them filled with beautiful fruit from the estate freshly picked by Bert less than an hour ago, and then covered with swirls of rich whipped cream standing already prepared in the fridge. Desserts were her speciality. She looked at her watch. Five past six. It was time to get on with the rest of the dinner preparations. She might ask Ruth to finish off the Pavlovas for her. Ruth was far more intelligent and adept than the rest of the kitchen girls put together. Ruth and her egg mayonnaise sandwiches! There was something quite touching about her enthusiasm for them. She had quite an ecstatic expression on her pretty little face as she ate it. But where was Ruth? It was time for her to put in an appearance.

There was something about Ruth that jogged her memory. Something that reminded her of someone else, but she couldn't quite put her finger on it for the moment. She wondered if she had been wise to tell Ruth quite so much. A student doing research into the well-established landowning families in the West of Ireland? She had never heard of anyone doing such a thing before. But of course nowadays there were students of everything you could think of; just to give people something to do. As so many of the traditional jobs were replaced by machinery there had to be something in their place to keep people occupied. She heaved a deep sigh and shuffled into the larder as fast as her great bulk would allow. With her job for life she must be one of the lucky ones. At fifty-nine there was no way Mr O'Hare could replace her now before she drew her pension.

Mr O'Hare. Time was when there were two Mr O'Hares: Mr Tom and Mr Sean. And this one wasn't the real Mr Tom. This one was Mr Sean, the schemer, the layabout, the n'er-do-gooder. The one they said had done time for cheating the Inland Revenue. Sometimes she thought she should expose him. But she was never sure which move to make first. Should she go to the police? But she had no proof that he had caused the accident in the first place. Could she say anything to his wife? How much did she know already? After all, they had only been married seven or eight years. The accident had happened over eleven years ago. It was quite possible the new Mrs O'Hare knew nothing about it at all. Then there was old Mrs O'Hare, upstairs all day, taking her meals on a tray. It didn't seem right that she should be shut away like that. Mr Tom would never have allowed it. And poor little Mr Roderick! What a sad state that unfortunate child had been born in! Never able to walk, incontinent, no future prospects, especially in such a remote God forsaken spot such as Knockramore. If they lived in Dublin, or even Galway Town, maybe the doctors could have done more for him, but in Killalee! There wasn't much hope for the able-bodied, never mind the crippled, maimed and the mentally retarded.

She thought of Brigid Devlin's child, Eamon. That poor boy. Not only those dreadful looks, just like his father, but backward as well. He was lucky to have landed the job in The Sheaf and Sickle Hotel, even if it was just nights. As long as there was a hotel in Killalee they would need a porter.

But Miread now. There was a girl after your own heart. Miread was a lass with ability, with talent and stunning good looks into the bargain. Miread would go far, there was no doubt about it. Brigid Devlin was lucky to have Miread as a daughter. There were those who said, if their memories went back far enough, that Miread was Tom O'Hare's illegitimate daughter – or even one of several illegitimate offspring. Word spread around at the time that Tom O'Hare was a bit of a lad with the ladies, with a definite preference for those who were not out of the top drawer, so to speak, but rather more from the peasant class, as he would have put it himself. Well, Mr Tom certainly picked his bride out of the top drawer all right. Margaret Russborough, daughter of a lord and her being a Protestant and all. But she had failed to make him happy, or give him a healthy child. Mrs Brothers heaved another deep sigh. Poor Mr Roderick. It would have been kinder, really, if he had perished in the dreadful accident.

After months in hospital Roderick had finally returned to Knockramore and his uncle's care. Mr Sean couldn't face any more bills, I shouldn't wonder, thought Mrs Brothers, deftly decorating her pie crust before placing the pie in the oven. And then he had him shut away out of sight in a room beyond the private sitting room when he took over the private wing after his brother's death.

She had been sworn to secrecy.

'I don't want anyone to know Mr Roderick is here. Do you understand, Mrs Brothers?'

It was more than her job was worth to cross him. He made it quite clear. Her heart was in her job at Knockramore, although she had certainly been happier under the old regime with Mr Tom. But she was getting on now and since she had been widowed she felt she was no longer up to the hassle of finding a new post. She had her little car and enjoyed her weekly day off driving around Lough Gill and popping into The Laughing Goat for a jar or two.

So for the sake of a quiet life she kept mum and did what she was told. This consisted of preparing three daily meals for Mr Roderick and old Mrs O'Hare and sending them up to the private apartment in the service lift. Everyone in the kitchen thought the trays were for Mr O'Hare, as he rarely took his meals in the dining room with the guests, but she had to know the food was for Mr Roderick. As his intestines were congenitally deformed he could only hold down very plain, bland food, so he had always been on a special diet.

Then there was the will. She remembered the day Mr Tom had called her and dear Robert into his private sitting room.

'Mr and Mrs Brothers,' he said. 'I know I can take you both into my confidence. You have both been in my employ for some considerable time now, far longer than anyone else on the estate. I know I can trust you both completely and anything said will never go further than the four walls of this room.

'The position is this. For reasons of conscience I feel impelled to make a new will. The reasons, of course, are of no concern at the moment to anyone except myself and the new beneficiaries who will be informed in the usual way on the event of my death.

'The normal procedure in making a will, which you may or may not know, it to pay a visit to one's solicitor and let him arrange the whole matter. As it happens, my solicitor is in Dublin and a visit would necessitate a tiresome journey with the probability of a night away from Knockramore. As you are both fully aware, Mr Roderick's health is a cause for considerable concern at present, and added pressure is upon me due to the fact that Mrs O'Hare's nervous condition has worsened due to her son's declining health. Bearing these facts in mind you will both understand it is with the greatest reluctance that I would leave Knockramore at present, even for the shortest period.

'I have therefore decided to draw up my own will, which I have already prepared, and all it requires is the signatures of two independent witnesses, which is why I have asked you both to come here.'

After his rather lofty speech, (Mr Tom could sound so pompous on certain occasions,) he went to the large roll-topped desk between the two long Georgian windows and drew out an envelope. I remember the scene so clearly, thought Mrs Brothers. It was June, the sunshine on the plane trees made beautiful dappled shadows on the lawn outside. Mr Tom invited me and dear Robert to sit at the coffee table with him. I was a little over-awed as I had never sat down with Mr Tom before. Robert sat beside him on the sofa and I sat in an armchair. He unfolded this official-looking, hand-written sheet of paper. The hand writing was so wonderfully clear and neat, and Robert, being curious as he always was, said afterwards he had been able to read nearly all of it. Imagine reading a private will! But no matter, the secret was safe with him for Robert died not long afterwards. As for me, I know how to keep a secret.

So Mr Tom asked us to sign, which we did gladly, for him always being a good and generous employer. And we had to sign it twice, for there were two copies, giving dear Robert even more opportunity to study it all. Then Mr Tom signed it as well, wrote in the date and thanked us most gratefully.

'There are two copies,' explained Mr Tom. 'One which I will post to my solicitor in Dublin, for it is he who will be the executor, the person who will arrange all the details in the event of my death. The other copy will be kept in a safe place at Knockramore.'

As it turned out, it was Robert himself who posted the copy to the solicitor, who never acknowledged its receipt; though curiously enough Tom O'Hare took his solicitor's silence as tacit confirmation of its safe arrival.

Six months later Tom O'Hare was dead and as no copy of the will which Mr and Mrs Brothers had witnessed ever came to light at Knockramore, Robert finally phoned the solicitor to inform him that he knew of the existence of a later will which was substantially different to the one currently in operation.

Later on that day in the privacy of their own room, Robert told his wife what he had been able to read in Mr Tom's clear handwriting. Mrs Brothers was amazed at the revelation. Although she had suspected all along that pretty little Miread Devlin was the love-child of Thomas O'Hare, she was unaware there was definite proof. But of course she could never mention the subject to Brigid Devlin. Poor Brigid had quite enough to contend with, being widowed and having that appalling-looking idiotic son, Eamon. She was beginning to have her suspicions about Ruth Hobson. A history graduate doing research into the landowning families of the West of Ireland? You could take it or leave it; and Mrs Brothers was inclined to leave it. But there must be some definite reason why a well-educated English girl should come to Knockramore and take a post as a chambermaid: a situation well beneath her calling. Was she looking for something, or someone; perhaps her father? Did she realise that Tom O'Hare was dead and her uncle was posing as his brother? Mrs Brothers had a great deal to think about.

After Tom O'Hare's death the original will came into operation. This left everything to Roderick when he attained the age of twenty-one, to be administered for him entirely as he thought fit, by his uncle, Sean O'Hare, who would forfeit all his interest in the estate when Roderick reached his majority. So Sean lived on in the hope that there was another later will leaving the entire estate to him on Roderick's death. He searched Knockramore cease-lessly, intensifying his efforts as Roderick's twenty-first birthday loomed nearer and nearer.

Chapter Sixteen

As Mr O'Hare reached out his hand and touched her cheek Rhoisin put the painting she was about to replace on the wall down on the floor. It was a portrait of a gentleman in Edwardian dress; high stiff white collar, dark, buttoned-up waistcoat; fob watch on a gold chain just showing out of the pocket. The subject was looking straight out of the painting at the beholder; a direct challenging gaze; quizzical eyebrows raised above fine wide-set grey eyes; a sardonic smile barely playing round the shapely lips. The well-manicured hands with tapered fingers lay loosely, elegantly placed on his lap.

Mr O'Hare lowered his hand and looked down at the portrait.

'My paternal grandfather, Thomas Liam O'Hare, painted in 1902.'

He looked straight at Rhoisin. 'Don't you see the family resemblance?'

Rhoisin looked down at the portrait. Yes, she thought, but she said nothing. Her heart began to beat faster; the palms of her hands felt clammy and her mouth had suddenly gone very dry. What was he going to do to her, this Mr O'Hare, whom she assumed to be her father? Was he dangerous? Was he a rapist? Should she forestall a disaster and challenge him? How should she put it: 'sir,

I have reason to believe you are my father;' or, 'sir, are you aware you have an illegitimate daughter?

Both sounded equally absurd.

She looked down at the portrait again. It certainly reminded her of someone, but not Mr O'Hare. It was the wide-set grey eyes; and those eyebrows, mocking, teasing. Did she resemble the gentleman in the portrait? It was hard to recognise a likeness of oneself in another person. She supposed it was because she had become so used to looking at herself in a mirror over the years that she no longer paid much attention to the image that stared back. She stole another quick glance at Mr O'Hare without moving her head. No. He hardly resembled the portrait. Perhaps the colour of the hair and the fine skin texture? But it was virtually impossible to compare living human skin texture with an oil painting, however skilful the painter. The eyes were quite different. Pale steely blue and set too close together. Rhoisin had noticed them during their first meeting and they had struck a chill into her soul. The eyes of a schemer, of a man intent on getting exactly what he wanted; lacking in any warmth, compassion or sensitivity. They were eyes which could inspire fear and hatred.

Suddenly it struck Rhoisin in a flash. No! Surely not! She couldn't be right! But she knew she was. She knew now who the portrait reminded her of: Mrs Devlin's daughter. What was her name? Some Irish name; unusual, like hers. Quite pretty too. It had escaped her for the moment. But no matter. The name wasn't important. What was important was the fact that Thomas O'Hare had sired more than one illegitimate offspring. Maybe there were dozens? Which would make her task even more difficult. She was convinced she was right. There was no mistaking those eyes under the quizzical, delicately shaped eyebrows.

'Well, Ruth, What reason brings you to my private apartment?'

Rhoisin swallowed hard and tried to screw up her courage.

'Sir, Mrs O'Hare, your wife – I – I mean madam asked me to come and clean the sitting room, sir.'

'Just clean it, or spring clean it?'

'Well – clean it, sir.'

'And take the paintings off the walls?'

'Well, sir, I couldn't quite reach this one to dust it, sir...'

'So you took it off the wall.'

'Yes, sir.'

'Have you dusted all the other paintings?'

'Yes, sir.'

'Particularly the ones along this wall?'

'Well, yes, sir.'

He leaned closer towards her, threatening. 'Tell me, Ruth, what is a well-educated English girl like you doing in County Sligo? What really brought you to Knockramore? You can't pretend that chambermaid is your true vocation. There must be some other reason you came here.'

By now Rhoisin was completely on her guard. She was sure she was somehow related to the O'Hare family, but not through this man, who stood above her, glowering, ominous. She tried to compose herself.

'Well, sir, I was curious to see Ireland, sir, and so I thought...'

At that moment the door opened and Mrs O'Hare came into the room dressed to go out.

'Are you ready for lunch, dear?' she asked.

'Lunch?' Mr O'Hare looked at his watch. 'But it's only twelve o'clock!'

'Yes, but we're expected at the Munroe's at twelve-thirty and it's a good half hours' drive.'

'Oh, y – yes. Of course. I'd almost forgotten. I'll get ready right away.

Mrs O'Hare turned to Rhoisin.

'Still hard at work, Ruth?'

'Yes, madam.'

'Keep up the good work, then. Just pull the door to when you leave. It locks automatically. You can leave the key on the table.'

With that they were gone and Rhoisin was left on her own in the private apartment amid the family portraits.

Mrs O'Hare looked at her watch. 'If you don't get a move on, dear, we shall be late.'

Sean O'Hare stopped at the junction and turned left onto the main Boyle Road. He put his foot down and they drove on in silence for about ten minutes. The car slewed dangerously round a sharp bend and he pulled hard on the steering wheel, narrowly avoiding the ditch.

'Watch out, dear!' Mrs O'Hare's voice was shrill with fear. 'I didn't mean you should emulate the Formula One racing aces.'

Sean O'Hare slowed down a little and said nothing. Women were all the same. There was no pleasing them. They knew no happy medium. It was either too hot or too cold; too much or too little; too fast or too slow. Sometimes he thought Lindsay was no improvement on Elizabeth. At least Elizabeth was beautiful. The trouble was she had known it and all the other men had known it too. From that point of view Lindsay was definitely an improvement, and she was a supremely good organiser. Knockramore was now run much more smoothly and efficiently than it had been in Elizabeth's day.

The car tyres screeched as he took another corner too fast.

'Careful! I want to arrive alive.'

'Sorry.'

He slowed up again. Wasn't that the bend? Wasn't that the very dry stone wall which had claimed his brother's life? And Margaret's too? How had young Roderick managed to survive such a horrendous accident? It was unbelievable. He had just ended up in a worse mess than he had been in originally and was probably costing even more in medical care into the bargain. He thought he had done a really thorough job on the car, cutting the brake cable. As far as he knew no one had ever suspected him. The police had interviewed him, of course. As the deceased's younger and irresponsible brother he had been one of the first to be questioned, but they couldn't pin anything definite on him. He had known his brother's car hadn't been near a garage in months so the whole thing had just looked like careless neglect. The unfortunate part was Roderick's survival. It was amazingly bad luck. Usually Roderick sat in the front seat beside his father while Margaret suffered with her migraine in the back. Thomas O'Hare felt so guilty about his son's appalling quality of life that he did as many small things as he could to improve it, often at the expense of his wife's comfort. Perhaps, on that fateful day, Margaret had dug in her heels and complained more than usual about being stuck in the back all the way to Dublin, 'while my nine-year-old son rides in luxury in the front.'

Sean slewed dangerously round another bend and shot passed a driveway graced by a beautiful pair of wrought iron gates.

'You missed it,' said his wife tartly.

'Yes. Sorry.'

He reversed at speed and jerked sharply forward towards the elegant gates which opened with a graceful sweep as they approached. They were obviously expected.

You missed it. Yes. Sorry. Well, he wasn't going to miss it next time; and he didn't mean a pair of entrance gates. He meant Roderick's demise.

Roderick would be twenty-one in October. It was time to act.

'More coffee, Sean?' Alison held the coffee pot aloft.

'I wish you'd remember to call me Tom,' said Sean Thomas O'Hare, irritably.

His hostess sighed. 'It's difficult to remember when I've known you as Sean for so long. Why did you change it, anyway?'

'I've never liked the name Sean. It's a peasant's name.'

His hostess laughed. 'Well you could have chosen a different name from your brother's.' Her eyes narrowed and she gave him a hard look. 'It might have been more sensitive.'

'On the contrary, I wished to emulate him after his sudden and tragic death. Also, it's a tradition in the O'Hare family that the eldest son should be called Thomas. I am now the elder and only son in this branch of the O'Hare family.

'Is it your official name?' Alison didn't seem to be able to let go.

'Quite official; and anyway, it's my second name.'

'...And you could stay to dinner, spend the night and do that rather torturous drive when you're fresh in the morning,' Colin was saying to Lindsay O'Hare.

'Oh, yes, do, Lindsay,' Alison joined in, pleading. 'It'll do you good to get away. You hardly ever have a break from Knockramore. We could have a lovely boozy evening, the four of us, and then you could take your time in the morning...'

Get Lindsay away from Knockramore for the evening? That might be a very good solution, thought Sean. It was time for him to act now, this very night.

'That's a splendid idea, Colin. It'll do Lindsay no end of good to have a night away from Knockramore. She works much too hard. But I regret I must decline your lovely invitation. The lord of the manor, you know, has his little responsibilities which cannot be ignored.'

He gave a short, dry laugh. 'But I'm in no hurry to be back until later this evening.'

Rhoisin continued to dust the large roll-top desk between the two elegant Georgian windows. Looking out at the magnificent view of the rolling green lawns and the immaculate golf course sloping down towards the lake, she felt a strange sensation of having been there before. It was uncanny and not a little disturbing. It was Knockramore itself, the house and the grounds, that awakened in her this feeling of belonging. It didn't happen in Killalee. Perhaps it was because she was surrounded by the family portraits? Although on her first visit to Knockramore on Miread's battered old bicycle she had experienced a similar sensation when reaching the brow of the hill, gazing down at Lough Gill shimmering in the pale blue sunshine. Then she had imagined herself as a child in this place, walking, running, cycling, clambering over the rocky hillside, swimming in the lake and picnicking by the shore. She flicked the duster idly, with no sense of purpose, almost knocking a china ornament off the top of the desk. She heard a car starting up and, craning her head, she could just see Mr and Mrs O'Hare slip down the drive in their sleek, black BMW. This is it, thought Rhoisin. Now is the time for action. Now is the moment to discover if what Mrs Brothers said is really true. She threw down the duster and started to lift more paintings off the wall.

Chapter Seventeen

'Come on, Judith, let's have another game. You've improved so much you could even beat me next time.'

Roderick swivelled the wheelchair round with great expertise and began to replace the chess pieces on the board.

With a deep sigh Judith got up and walked slowly to the window, her stiffly starched uniform rustling gently, her sensible shoes squeaking on the highly polished wooden floor. She drew back the half closed curtain and looked down into the drive as the sleek BMW slid quietly away.

'Your parents have just gone out, Rodders.'

'How often have I told you they're not my parents.'

'Sorry, Rodders.'

'And you're supposed to call me Mr Roderick. But it's all right because I prefer Rodders from you. Come here, Judith.'

'Please.'

'Please, Judith.'

Judith walked over slowly and stood beside the wheelchair. Roderick held out his hand and with the other hand patted his knees, swathed in blankets. Obediently Judith knelt down and put her head in his lap. Roderick began to stroke her face, her eyes, her hair. With practiced skill she raised herself up and balanced expertly on his lap. His stiff fingers fumbled for the awkward buttons on her starched uniform. He finally managed to undo enough to find her over-ripe breasts. His hands slipped further down her body, searching for the gap at the top of her thigh between the suspender belt and her cami-knickers. Their mouths met and for a moment they clung to each other with the desperation of those who have no alternative. Two lonely, trapped human beings. Roderick, aged twenty, in the flower of youth, on the threshold of life, trapped in a wheelchair by a useless body which was only semi-functional. Judith, kind, plain, over forty, rejected by men, desperate for emotional and sexual release. Two tragic isolated people whose only solace was each other.

The bell rang by the service lift. Judith got up to answer it.

'Hello.'

'Hello, Judith.' Mrs Brothers' voice came over the intercom. 'I'm just sending up the lunches, dear. A nice bit of tripe in white sauce for Master Roderick and some fresh salmon with *Sauce Béarnaise* for you and Mrs O'H. Let me know when you're through with it and I'll have the puddings sent up directly.'

'Thanks, Mrs B.'

There was a creaking, cranking sound as Mrs Brothers pulled on the rope and the ancient lift moved slowly up the shaft. Judith walked across the room and knocked on one of the connecting doors.

'Mrs O'Hare! Lunch is on its way up! Are you ready? Want any help?'

'No, dear. I'm fine. I'll be with you in a moment.'

There was the sound of the toilet flushing, the scraping of furniture on the wooden floor and a falling metal object. After a few moments the door opened and Mrs O'Hare came into the room. She was petite and slight, with a beaked nose and a halo of fine, grey hair. She walked completely upright, making darting movements like a bird, turning her head rapidly from side to side so as to miss nothing. She wore a beautifully cut turquoise silk dress which shimmered in the light and camel bedroom slippers on her feet. She needed neither cane nor glasses and save for her staring eyes and manic laugh, she was quite remarkable for ninety-two. She came and sat at the table which was already laid with a snow white Irish linen tablecloth and table-napkins, well polished silver and Waterford cut glass. Old Mrs O'Hare demanded a high standard of presentation. Roderick was already at the table in his wheelchair, sipping a glass of champagne.

'Good morning, Gran. I hope I find you well today. I'm sorry I can't get up. May I pour you a glass of champers?'

'You certainly may, Roderick. I always look forward to my daily dose of champagne. Just what the doctor ordered.' Mrs O'Hare gave a cackle and sat down at the table opposite Roderick, elegant and straight-backed.

'And how are you, Roderick, my boy?'

'So-so is good, very good, very excellent good; and yet it is not, it is but so-so.'

'More of your Shakespeare?'

'Yes. Touchstone in *As You Like It*: Act V Scene 1. Shakespeare is one of the few things that keeps me going in this dismal prison.'

'And food and drink, and your old Gran and Judith,' said the old lady knowingly.

'Yes, Granny. I count my blessings every day,' replied Roderick sarcastically.

Judith brought over the lunch tray from the service lift and unloaded it onto the table. 'Something nice for everyone here,' she said in her jolly nursery-maid's voice. 'Everyone's got their favourite food.'

She served the meal and sat down. Roderick poured her a glass of champagne. Solemnly they raised their glasses in what had now become a daily ritual.

'Death to Sean O'Hare!'

'Death to Sean O'Hare!'

'Death to Sean O'Hare!'

They lowered their glasses and started eating their food in silence.

It was broken as usual by Roderick.

'I wonder how it's going to happen.'

'What, Rodders, dear?' Judith knew she sounded patronising. She couldn't help it. It seemed to go with the job.

'Uncle Sean's death.'

'How or when?'

'Both. First how.'

'Maybe another car accident?' Mrs O'Hare was carefully negotiating a salmon bone. Wouldn't do to get one stuck in her throat. Even more eminent old ladies than she, and she considered herself quite eminent, had had trouble with salmon bones lodging in the throat.

'They've just gone out,' she added.

'Which car?' asked Roderick, with scant interest.

'The BMW.'

'Too bad,' said Judith. 'That's the only reliable one.'

They ate on in silence, Roderick frequently replenishing their glasses. When Mrs Brothers rang to ask if they were ready for their pudding, Roderick was opening the fourth bottle of champagne. As Judith cleared away the first course and was serving the pudding, Roderick said: 'Better check on supplies, Jude.'

'Yes.'

She got up and went to a large cupboard in the corner. She opened it and counted up the remaining cases of champagne. 'Seventeen.'

'That should do for a couple of weeks.'

'Not at the rate you're downing it,' said Judith. 'And you're already drunk.'

'Not drunk enough,' said Roderick, refilling his own glass first. It's about the only thing to do in this place. I can't even fuck.'

Judith smiled at him. 'You do the next best thing.'

'For you, not for me.'

'Pudding, Mrs O'Hare?'

'Not too much, dear. I've got to watch my figure at my age.'

She gave another cackle of laughter.

Roderick drained his glass and poured himself another. 'I think we should try and formulate another plan.' His speech sounded slurred.

'A plan for what, dear?' asked his grandmother.

'Bumping off Uncle Sean, of course.'

'We tried once before without success, and he is my son.'

She sounded doubtful.

'Well, he's not treating you like one.'

'No.'

'The thing is,' said Roderick, half emptying his glass in one long gulp, 'the thing is, Uncle Sean seems convinced there's another will.'

'Another one?' Judith sounded surprised. Why should there be another one? You mean a later one?'

'Yes.'

Roderick fingered the stem of his glass, lifted it half way to his lips and then paused, resisting the temptation to finish it in one long draught.

'Yes. You see, the existing will – the only one anyone is aware of – was drawn up by my father when I was only two and a half, leaving the entire estate to me when I reach the age of twenty–one, to be administered by Uncle Sean, entirely as he sees fit. So he's running things exactly as he pleases and presumably siphoning off any funds he can for his own use later on.'

'Meaning that when you're twenty-one he will no longer have any control.'

'Exactly.'

'But what makes Uncle Sean think there could be another will?' Judith started gathering up the plates.

'Because Mrs Brothers' husband, Robert, told him so.'

'Robert Brothers? But he's been dead for years!'

'Yes. He died shortly after my parents.'

'Not another accident?'

'No, no. He had something awful – like – I can't remember, but it's not relevant.'

'No. But how do you know this?'

'My uncle told me in an unguided moment. Apparently Mr and Mrs Brothers witnessed the will.'

'Here at Knockramore?'

'Yes.'

'I thought all wills had to be drawn up by a solicitor.'

'No. Not necessarily, provided they are witnessed by two independent people who are not beneficiaries.'

'So your uncle knows that another will exists?'

'Yes.'

'What is he hoping to gain from it, if it's ever found?'

'I imagine he's hoping my father changed his mind...'

'And left some of the estate to him after all?'

'Yes. So periodically he turns the west wing upside down, hoping it will turn up.'

'And if he doesn't find it within the next three months, you'll be in control of the whole estate and he'll get nothing.'

'Unless I have a little accident first.'

'In which case...'

'In which case, as the only surviving relative, he stands to inherit the lot.'

'I see. A potentially nasty situation.'

'Yes.'

'It looks as if it's a question of who's going to have the first accident.'

'Jungle law. The survival of the fittest.'

'Exactly. Any ideas?'

Roderick drained his glass and looked across at his grandmother, who was having a little doze. 'Any ideas, Gran?'

Old Mrs O'Hare woke up with a start.

'What's that, Roderick, dear?'

'Any good ideas for bumping off Uncle Sean?'

'Bumping him off?'

'Yes. Before he bumps me off.'

'Oh? I see. How about a little fire? Just in his bedroom. I like a little fire.'

The old lady gave one of her manic cackles.

'A little fire?' Judith sounded rather alarmed. 'Even a little fire could take hold and...' She got up to clear away the plates, swaying slightly. Roderick refilled her glass.

'I think a fire's a bit extreme, Gran. It could get out of control and then we'd all go up in flames. No. We'll have to think of something more specific, like poison for instance?'

'First find your poison.'

'Couldn't you do that, Jude, with your medical connections?'

Judith picked up her glass and drained it and, swaying a bit, grabbed the back of Roderick's wheelchair.

'I don't know.'

Roderick grabbed her hand and giggled. 'Do a dance, Jude. Go on. Never mind Uncle Sean for the moment. You're just in the right state to do a dance.'

'OK. In a minute. I'll clear these away first.'

Judith piled the dishes onto the tray and zigzagged unsteadily across the room. She rang the lift bell.

'Mrs B-ee. Mrs B-ee!'

'Oh, good,' said Roderick with satisfaction. 'Jude's drunk. She always dances better when she's drunk. Have some more, Gran. Then you're more likely to want to dance too.'

He filled the old lady's glass to the brim.

'Steady on, Roderick. If I finish all that I'm more likely to fall over.' She laughed again.

'Yes, I know, Gran. That's why I do it. Because it amuses me. There's not a lot to amuse one in here.'

He wheeled his chair over to the stereo and put on some music, soft, slow, insinuating. After a few moments Judith got up and began to dance, gyrating slowly, sinuously, sensuously. She took off her starched cap, her shoes, her stockings. She peeled off her apron. Roderick wheeled his chair towards her, trying to keep in time to the rhythm of the music, and lifted up the hem of her starched dress. Mrs O'Hare stood up unsteadily and began to glide around the room, weaving in and out of the furniture, laughing.

Suddenly there was a most almighty crash. A picture fell off the wall as a concealed door in the wooden panelling opened and Rhoisin appeared through the gap in the wall. The two women stopped dancing. Roderick put down the hem of Judith's dress and looked up.

'You see! I told you they'd find us!' he cried triumphantly.

Rhoisin stood and looked at the scene in total amazement. It was surreal, like a play by Jean Cocteau. She was reminded of the Mad Hatter's Tea Party, except that instead of the debris of afternoon tea on the table there were five empty champagne bottles.

Chapter Eighteen

Miread couldn't sleep. She lay in bed, tossing and turning on her pillow, wakeful and wondering. What should she do next? Did she have to do anything? Did life require one to make decisions or was it possible to continue floating, as it were, on a sea of flotsam and jetsam? Though it didn't seem quite right to think of her life as flotsam and jetsam yet. It sounded as if too much had been discarded too soon, when she had, in fact, just started out on life's difficult course. But did one actually have to chart the course or just take down the sail and let the boat drift?

Dermot Malone had asked her to marry him. He said he loved her. But several other young men had said they loved her. But what they meant was that they loved making love to her. No other young man had actually asked her to marry him. Would she have accepted them if they had? Why did people get married anyway? To have children? Physically speaking that was quite unnecessary. She was quite sure that if she stopped taking the pill and continued with her amorous escapades, babies would follow as rapidly as nature intended. At the moment she had no plan to stop these amorous escapades. They were now an essential part of her life, as necessary as eating and drinking. She enjoyed making love with different men. Variety was the spice of life, so they said, and with someone as highly sexed as she was she actually found it much more stimulating to have several men on the go at once. Of course she hadn't mentioned this to any of them. She didn't want any jealous scenes and she didn't see why anyone, as yet, should have exclusive rights.

As yet. Maybe this was the crux of the matter. Was this why people got married? To have exclusive rights over each other? Was this desirable? Say one of them got bored? There was no divorce in Ireland. There was no divorce in the Catholic Church either. But was she still a Catholic? Fornication outside marriage was a sin, after all, and she had certainly sinned many, many times. If she were going to be married she would have to go to confession first, which might prove a lengthy and unpleasant business.

What other reasons were there for getting married? Economic? Her mother would certainly agree with that. But to a man of some economic substance, not to a twenty-two year old ghillie with a low income and poor prospects. She almost certainly earned more than Dermot did and something told her this was not how the happiest marriages worked. Was she in love with Dermot? In all honesty she wasn't sure what being in love meant. She realised she loved making love to a man whom she found physically attractive and encouraging him to do amazing things to her body. She also enjoyed doing wonderful things to his body in return, which only made her desire his attentions all the more. But what happened if this love-making ran out of steam; if he should stop desiring her, if she became fat and unattractive? Or if she should go off him? If she were actually married it might be far more difficult to go off and find a more suitable replacement.

If she married Dermot would she be condemned to a lifetime of living in Killalee? Could Dermot be persuaded to leave Killalee? If he did leave where would they go and what would Dermot do? He was only trained to be a ghillie so presumably they would have to live by a lake. What would she do when she wasn't bearing and rearing children? Did she want a lifetime of domesticity and child rearing? Would she pine for the bustle and bright lights of the Big Town? Would she miss the party scene and the wonderfully free and varied sex? Or did she really want a lifetime of parties and sexual freedom?

But what would happen if she didn't get married? Most women she knew who were not married were plain and unhappy. They had that air of having been rejected, washed up. They were pitied, referred to as spinsters, old maids. She wouldn't want people saying things like that about her.

So what if she said 'no' to Dermot and went back to Dublin to her job in the bank? He would probably be rather upset at first. They had certainly had a marvellous week together and he was without question the best lover she had ever had so far. But he would find another girl to marry in the neighbourhood for he was extremely attractive and if his financial prospects were not that great, well, nor were the expectations of most of the girls in Killalee.

Could she say, let's wait a bit? That would be the most sensible course. They had, after all, barely known each other a week. It would be rushing things to get engaged so soon. Tongues would start wagging in Killalee. And what would her mother say? But did it really matter what other people thought or said? Marriage, if it was to be, was just between her and Dermot. Yet, on the other hand, other people did count for something. No man is an island. So Dermot must mean something to her if his proposal was keeping her awake all night. Oh, hell, she thought, I'm going to feel dreadful in the morning. And I've got to be at the coach station before 9.00 am. I hope Dermot will be there to say goodbye...

She tossed restlessly, then sat up on the edge of the bed and plumped up her pillows. She looked at her bedside clock. It said ten past one. 'Oh, hell,' she said, out loud. She got out of bed and went over to the window. She drew back the curtains and looked out at the night sky, unusually clear, stars twinkling, an almost full moon illuminating Lough Gill with the stark, almost black lump of Parke Castle looming on the southern shore. To the eastern side of the lake towards Knockramore there was a dull red glow. Funny, she thought, it's the middle of the night. It can't possibly be the sunrise. More like a fire. But it couldn't be a fire, could it, at this time of night? Thinking no more about it she went back to bed exhausted and fell fast asleep until the alarm went.

Brigid was running across the golf course at Knockramore towards Lough Gill with Thomas O'Hare. They were barefoot and lightly clad. It was high summer and unusually for that part of the globe, the sun shone. But it was a pale gentle sun which rarely burnt or even tanned the skin. High, fluffy white cirrus clouds scudded across the sky, not a deep Mediterranean blue, but paler, more fragile. They reached the edge of the golf course and ran on towards the lake, the long grass tickling their bare legs. They were laughing. Tom reached out and picked her up in his arms. Still laughing, he carried her a few yards and laid her in a mossy hollow under a tree. He kissed her all over, first her face, her neck, and then, peeling off her scant summer shift dress, kissed her whole body, feeling with his fingers for those special places which aroused her the most. With well-practiced fingers she unbuttoned his shirt, unzipped his trousers and when they were both quite naked, he mounted her and came into her, spending all his passion in a torrent of overflowing love.

She was already pregnant, the bump beginning to show. They lay in the hollow, Tom continuing to caress her, stroking her swollen stomach, feeling for the movements of the child they had created together. She was Mrs O'Hare. She was married to Thomas O'Hare and soon she would have his child, his son. They would have many more children and would always be happy and always live together at Knockramore. Mr and Mrs O'Hare of Knockramore… Knockramore… Knockramore…

Brigid struggled awake; mouth dry, palms damp, sweat breaking out on her forehead and between her breasts. It wasn't the first time she had had this dream. It had recurred at irregular intervals ever since she became aware of her first pregnancy and Tom had told her he was going to marry someone else. It wasn't always exactly the same dream. Sometimes they were in Tom's private apartment at Knockramore, sometimes they were on a boat on the lake. He always made love to her; wonderful, passionate, exhilarating love which no man had ever done since, transporting her to what she could only describe as heaven. And in the dreams he always told her how much he loved her and how they would plan their lives together around having children and living in Knockramore.

And then she would wake, as she had done now, and realise it was all a dream. That it had all taken place in a nirvana of long ago. Also, it had only partly happened. They had made love, wonderful love, many times, but when she had become pregnant he had discarded her like an old rag and married another woman. And she was left to bear their child all alone in the chill confines of a convent surrounded by disapproving and unsympathetic nuns.

He had married an aristocrat, the daughter of a lord and a Protestant to boot. But all his wife could give him was a damaged heir, a sickly son who would probably not survive into adulthood.

But now Tom and his aristocratic wife were dead. Killed in a car crash which, it was rumoured, was engineered by his own brother. But no one could prove it. Rumour had it too, that the sickly son lived on, incarcerated in some asylum near Dublin, or somewhere in England, heir to the O'Hare estate, estimated at a large fortune. And her daughter Miread, pretty, talented Miread, was also Thomas O'Hare's child. But because she was born out of wedlock she would receive nothing at all from her father's estate.

Was there no justice in this world?

Awoken from one of these dreams, (the O'Hare series, she sometimes called them) Brigid always felt despondent and alone. Her initial reaction was to sob her eyes out, but instinct told her that this type of indulgence is harder to stop than to start, so common sense prevailed and her stronger self took over as she counted her blessings and made plans for the new day ahead.

Her dream had made her wakeful, as those in the O'Hare series usually did. Her bedside clock said twenty past one. She got up and went to the window, drawing back the curtains. It was a still starry cloudless night, the moon lighting up the bleak shape of Parke Castle on the far side of Lough Gill. Her room was at the back, next to her daughter's, for Brigid felt her 'visitors' should have the rooms with the sea view. Hers was the more easterly one so she had a better view of the red glow which by now was staining the sky a vivid angry orangey-red. Brigid stood and stared, seized by a strange foreboding. It looks as if Knockramore is on fire, she thought. No, surely not. The old lady died years ago. Old Mrs O'Hare, who was rumoured to have been a pyromaniac. The place is far too well run and well looked after now for any fire to break out.

Despite trying to reassure herself that all was well, Brigid returned to bed with a heavy heart and fell into a troubled, fitful sleep.

Knockramore was still steeped in memories.

Chapter Nineteen

Judith knocked softly on the door.

'Mrs O'Hare! May I come in? I've brought you a drink and your sleeping pills.'

A muffled voice came from the other side of the door.

'Yes, dear. Do come in.'

Judith put the tray down on the small table on the landing and opened the door. A strange scene met her eyes. Mrs O'Hare was gyrating slowly to soft music, wearing a pale turquoise nightie and a matching negligée, swathes of different toned turquoise scarves around her neck like Isadora Duncan. The room was lit entirely by candlelight.

'Oh, madam!' gasped Judith. 'You look beautiful and the whole room looks so lovely, but...'

Mrs O'Hare gave one of her increasingly manic-sounding laughs.

'Yes, I know, dear, you're afraid of a fire. But don't worry. I know how to take care of things now. And that was only a very small fire. Just a little accident.'

She took the proffered glass and pills from Judith. 'Thank you, dear. These should help me to sleep well.'

'Yes, they should,' replied Judith. 'But now I'm going to blow out all the candles.'

'All of them? Can't I just have one beside my bed?'

'No. I think you'll be much safer with a bedside electric light.'

Judith switched on the bedside light and walking around the room, she snuffed out all the candles.

'And get into bed fairly soon, won't you? Those pills are quite strong.'

'Yes, of course I will. Don't you worry. Good night, dear.' Mrs O'Hare gave another manic laugh.

'Good night. Sleep well.'

Judith closed the door and went to her own room.

'Oh, good! She's left the matches,' mumbled Mrs O'Hare, and going around the room, she relit three candles. She took her pills with a shot of brandy and resumed dancing, weaving and swaying gracefully to the soft seductive music, as the pills, coupled with the brandy, began to take effect. Sleep overcame her and she fell exhausted onto the bed, leaving the three candles burning. One of the candles fell onto the carpet, a flame slowly creeping along towards the curtains.

And still Mrs O'Hare slept...

Sean O'Hare drove along the narrow country lanes towards Knockramore. He had just left Killalee behind, grey and somnolent at half past midnight. They had all had such a jolly evening, he and Lindsay and the Monroes. It wasn't often that he and Lindsay spent an evening with friends. There were too many pressures at Knockramore to allow them much time for a social life. Colin was a generous host and Sean had had more to drink than was customary or prudent.

Time is running out, he thought dimly through his alcoholic haze. In three months crippled Roderick will be twenty-one and, crippled or not, stands to inherit not only Knockramore, but the vast fortune that goes with it. I will lose my present control over the estate; and therefore any further opportunity to place estate funds where I see fit. I know there's another will, he told himself. Unless Robert Brothers was lying? But Mr Brothers had never struck Sean as the sort of man who would lie. What did he have to gain by such a lie? On the other hand, did he stand to gain anything by telling the truth? He would never know now whether Mr Brothers was telling the truth or not; unless of course he could put his hand on the damn will himself. But as long as the will remained hidden, he could neither prove Mr Brothers' veracity or know whether or not he was, after all, a beneficiary.

There were two courses of action open to him. One was to find the other will, which he assumed must be somewhere in the private apartment. So it was only a question of tearing the place apart, even if it meant damaging some of the old panelling. It could all easily be restored at a later date.

The alternative course of action was to dispose of Roderick, who was living a great deal longer than Sean had bargained for, having narrowly survived the horrendous car accident he had so carefully engineered. The nurse was costing a great deal more than he bargained for too; and as for all the champagne! But that was more to placate his tiresome old mother, mad as a hatter and a pyromaniac to boot. She had to be kept well out of the way. He couldn't possibly have her mingling with the rich and important guests at Knockramore.

It was now a question of how to effect Roderick's demise. Another car crash just wouldn't do and whatever course of action he took he had to ensure it would look like an accident. He didn't want to end up inside for life for committing murder. The boy was sickly. In fact his quality of life was so poor that it would really be a kindness to end it. Incontinent, unable to walk, delicate stomach, no possibility of marriage, no sex ever. But how to do the deed? Poison? He had managed to amass some arsenic pills, but it would be almost impossible to get close enough to administer them. That damned Judith looked after the boy much too carefully – and his mad mother too. Shooting would be too noisy and would definitely look like murder. Smothering would be silent and very satisfying but would also look like murder and he would certainly be a prime suspect. In fact, with another suspicious death in the O'Hare family the police would probably reopen the file on the fatal car accident and he, Sean Thomas O'Hare, would be put away for life.

No, it would have to be something discreet. Something that could only look like an accident. A little fire perhaps? Just confined to the private wing?

Sean Thomas rounded the last corner of the drive and saw flames licking up the wall of the private apartment. He sat in his sleek BMW, watching the private wing of his ancestral home burn with a mixture of alarm and satisfaction. Alarm, because it would be most unfortunate if the whole house, guests and all, were to be devoured by flames. Satisfaction because, if only the west wing was destroyed then his scheme to engineer Roderick's death would come into effect without any effort whatsoever on his part; and it would have the additional bonus of incinerating his mother into the bargain. He wondered about his mother. Was it possible that she was the perpetrator of this little conflagration?

Had it been a accident or was it a harsh escape from the confinement he had imposed on her since her madness had become uncontrollable?

The fire was still contained, confined to the west wing. Fortunately the design of the house ensured it wouldn't yet spread to the main part of the building. The architect who designed it over two hundred years ago certainly knew a thing or two. The main part of the house, facing due north, was a large, three storey, almost square block with wings extending at either end, consisting of two storeys. The main central part was for the use of guests only. The east wing housed the staff and garaged the cars and the west wing contained offices and the O'Hare family's private living quarters.

Sean had to decide what action to take. Should he go into the main building and phone the fire brigade? This would almost certainly ensure the rescue of Roderick, the nurse and Mrs O'Hare; or should he let the fire burn for half an hour or so, giving it a chance to take hold and effectively dispose of his mother and his nephew? He gave an involuntary shudder. Death by burning would not be pleasant. Even the Elizabethan martyrs had found it hard to handle, but perhaps it was more merciful than indefinite incarceration, mad and crippled as they each were.

He decided to take the second option. He would drive into Killalee, or even Sligo Town, and phone the fire brigade from there. By then the fire would have well and truly taken hold of the private wing and the fire brigade would arrive in time to save the main part of the building.

Sean reversed the car and slid quietly down the drive towards the main entrance. It was ten minutes to one.

Mrs Brothers awoke with a start. Something was burning. Mrs Brothers was particularly sensitive to burning. Food was frequently burnt in the kitchen at Knockramore and she was partly responsible for financing the loss. She sat up in bed and glanced at her clock. Twenty minutes to one. Rather on the late side for one of the maids to be making themselves a toasted snack. Unless it was Ruth? When she had finally appeared to help with the dinner she had seemed unusually agitated. Perhaps she had gone for a late cycle ride and had returned feeling peckish? The young nowadays had formidable appetites, even the girls.

In fact, Ruth had seemed so upset that Mrs Brothers was sorely tempted to ask her how much she had actually discovered. Was it even possible – no, surely not, – that she might have stumbled upon the secret room and found Roderick, Judith and old Mrs O'Hare inside? But she doubted it. It was well and truly hidden. She had never found it herself. On her very rare visits to the secret room she always went round by the longer route, used by Mr and Mrs O'Hare and on occasional visits by the doctor, but forbidden to the guests. The secret panel was only for dramatic effect; part of the heritage of an old house, more like a priest's hole. And of course she hadn't told Ruth that Master Roderick actually lived in the house. Only that old Mrs O'Hare lived on her own in the private apartment. All she had told Ruth was that she believed there were old family documents secreted somewhere in a panel in the wall behind one of the portraits. Original documents that could help her with her research into the O'Hare family. There was no harm in that. And if the other will turned up, so much the better.

The smell of burning grew stronger. Mrs Brothers got out of bed and pulled on her dressing gown. She must find out what was burning. She slipped out of the side entrance of the staff wing. There was no point in raising the alarm just yet. No point in panicking the staff for nothing. Much better to find out if there really was a fire, then she could decide whether to sound the fire alarm or just quietly alert the fire brigade. She walked round to the front of the house, her feet, even in bedroom slippers, making a crunching sound on the gravel. From the far side of the house came a darting orange flame. My God! thought Mrs Brothers, there really is a fire! She quickened her pace as another orange flame darted out of old Mrs O'Hare's window and licked the curtain of Master Roderick's room next door. Mrs Brother's heart missed a beat. An accident – or not? And if it wasn't an accident was it the work of mad Mrs O'Hare or...?

At that moment the sleek BMW slid down the drive. In the light of another bright orange flame Mrs Brothers saw Sean O'Hare alone at the wheel. So it wasn't the old lady after all, thought Mrs Brothers, as she went into the house to phone the fire brigade.

Roderick groaned and tried to roll onto his side. There were times when he could manage a lateral movement quite well. He had always had complete control over the upper part of his body until the car accident, which had caused permanent injuries to some of his upper vertebrae. During the day, with the help and encouragement of Judith, he usually managed very well. The nights were the worst. He seemed to lose confidence on his own in the dark. Roderick sniffed. Funny smell. Like something burning. What could be burning in the middle of the night? Perhaps Judith was cooking herself a snack? Suddenly a tongue of orange flame licked its way through the open window and set one of the curtains alight. Within seconds it had travelled across the pelmet and the whole window was engulfed in a sheet of flame. Terrified, Roderick pulled himself up in the bed and switched on the bedside light. Now the wallpaper was on fire, peeling off in flaming chunks and falling onto the carpet, which smouldered at first, then started to burn with increasing intensity. The flames travelled along the carpet towards the bed, setting fire to a trailing blanket; creeping, vicious tongues of orange flame licking out towards him as he sat in bed watching in horror, unable to move, paralysed with fear.

'Jude! Jude! I'm burning! Come quickly! Come and save me! Judith! Please! Help me!'

Judith awoke with a start. She was a light sleeper, trained by her calling to respond to the needs of her patients, even while she slept. She smelt burning and heard Roderick's terrified cry for help. That mad Mrs O'Hare has done it again. She's trying to roast us all alive. She was out of bed in an instant, pulling on her dressing gown as she crossed the landing to Roderick's room which faced the drive on the north side of the building. As she opened his door the draught between the door and the open window fanned the flames even further, creating a blast furnace between the bed and the open window. It took Judith all her courage to enter the room. Opposite the door was a second window, mercifully closed, out of the range of the fire as yet, overlooking the drive. She pulled Roderick out of bed and dragged him, a dead weight, towards the window. She laid him on the floor and struggled to open the window from the bottom, staring down in terror at the small crowd which had gathered in the drive below.

Rhoisin was sleeping at Knockramore after a late night serving in the bar. Suddenly she awoke to the sound of the fire alarm, piercing, shrill, insistent; shrieking through the main building, terrifying the guests into instant panic, forcing the exhausted staff to abandon their slumbers. She got out of bed hastily, fumbling for her dressing gown and slippers, and went out into the staff hall. All the other staff were gathering; bleary eyed, yawning, grumbling, confused.

'What's up?'

'What is it?'

'What's going on?'

'What a dreadful din!'

'Can't someone turn that thing off!'

Mrs Brothers appeared in the doorway, looming large, calm and reassuring.

'I want you all to assemble in the main driveway so I can take a roll call. The private wing is on fire, but as long as the blaze doesn't cross the west courtyard there is no danger to anyone else in this building for the present. I called the fire brigade ten minutes ago so they should be here directly. Please follow me.'

And with that she led the way round to the front of the house where she read out all their names, ticking them off as they answered. To her relief everyone was present.

Further along the drive in front of the west wing the scene was quite different. As the guests poured out of the main building in disorder and panic, a sharp contrast to the staff's decorum, some were in tears, others screaming. Some were fully dressed, others wore night attire; many had tried to save their belongings. Disasters always attract the curious, often at great personal risk, and the higher the flames rose above the O'Hare's private wing the more the onlookers crowded round. By now both windows of old Mrs O'Hare's bedroom were engulfed in flames, leaping, crackling into the black night sky, vermillion and orange. The open window of Roderick's room was also ablaze and Judith, struggling to open the second window through which she prayed they would be able to escape, managed to throw it open just as Rhoisin and some of the other staff arrived on the scene. As Judith threw the window open a cheer went up from the swelling crowd below.

'Hurrah! Well done! Climb out! Jump! No wait! The fire brigade's arriving! They'll have a ladder!'

The heat in the room was intense. Now that a second window had been opened the draught fanned the flames into even greater activity. They crackled and roared, coming across the carpet like a devouring red sea to the only escape route now left. Judith struggled to get Roderick onto the windowsill. In her panic she somehow imagined that he would be able to stand up and jump off. But he was inert, a dead weight in her arms and all she could do was to get his arms over the edge. Roderick suddenly found an inner hidden strength. If his body had been healthy and normal he had no illusions that he would have been up and out of the window long ago, shinning down the drain pipe with Judith over his shoulder. But he was held prisoner in his own body, crippled, trapped by his deformity. Now he knew his number was up.

'Get out, Jude!' he screamed at her. 'Jump! Leave this hell hole and leave me with it! Go, before it's too late!'

Judith climbed onto the windowsill and looked down at the upturned faces of the people on the ground two floors below. People were screaming and cheering, shouting encouragement. She turned and looked back into the room, a burning inferno. Roderick was lying on the floor now, praying, calm and resigned.

'I can't, Rodders.'

'You must. You can't stay here.'

Judith jumped high into the air. It was like flying. She felt exhilarated, free. Then everything went black. She felt nothing. She had fallen, like a stone, to her death.

Rhoisin was looking up at the window. She was crying.

'Roderick! Roderick! Please someone rescue Roderick !'

As Judith's body landed in the drive three fire engines roared up, sirens wailing. The window from which she had jumped was now ablaze. In a last, final effort to survive, Roderick managed to pull himself onto the window sill. He saw Rhoisin's tear streaked face gazing up at him in horror. As the first fire engine drew up under the window his body was illuminated by a sheet of orange flame.

He waved down at Rhoisin.

'Goodbye, Rhoisin! Look after Judith!'

Then just as the firemen's ladder reached the window, he fell back, his hair alight and in a few moments his body was burnt to cinders.

Chapter Twenty

After witnessing the deaths of Roderick and Judith in such appalling circumstances Rhoisin went into total shock. She could neither eat, sleep nor speak to anyone for several days. It was bad enough to witness the death of any human being by whatever means. The death of the lollipop lady all those years ago was always at the back of her mind. Events such as dangerous driving, squealing tyres, police sirens, always jogged that painful childhood memory. But these last horrific deaths were a thousand times worse. After all, she knew the people. She had spent the whole afternoon with them, drinking champagne, listening to their stories; their sad tales of loneliness, disablement and imprisonment. She had learnt she had a brother, a real brother, who a few days ago was incinerated before her very eyes, burnt to death, by the scheming hand of their evil uncle. She had met her paternal grandmother, too: as mad as a hatter, but charming, elegant and often amusing. The firemen had discovered the charred remains of her body, unrecognisable, formally identified only because it was assumed that Mrs O'Hare had been sleeping in her own bedroom.

Rhoisin thought sadly of Judith, the heroic nurse, who could easily have walked away from the whole disaster unscathed. The fire had not yet touched the staircase when Judith had woken. Having smelt the fire and heard the crackle of the flames she could simply have left the private wing and walked down into the courtyard unharmed. Instead, she had presumably heard Roderick's cries for help and her unswerving answer to the call of duty had come before all thoughts of her own safety. So she too had met an agonising death in vain, but was still courageous enough to jump from a second floor window into a black void, only to crash to her death on the unyielding ground below.

Sean O'Hare, having chosen to leave his mother and nephew to burn to death, had driven off into the night, intending to phone the fire brigade at what he considered to be for him, the optimum moment. But the phone call was never made. Tired, somewhat overwrought and a great deal more inebriated than he had realised, Sean had fallen asleep at the wheel and had driven into a tree not very far from the spot where, eleven years ago, he had engineered the deaths of his own brother and sister-in-law.

The day following the fire Mrs Brothers realised that poor Rhoisin was in such deep shock that it would be best to get her away from Knockramore as soon as possible. So she arranged for her brother, who lived only an hour's drive away, to collect Rhoisin, along with Miread's battered bicycle, and take her back to Brigid Devlin's cottage in Killalee. Miread had left early that morning to return to Dublin and her job at the bank. She had turned down Dermot's proposal of marriage as any definite or imminent event, but managed to persuade Dermot that, as at present she had received no other firm offer, perhaps they should keep their options open for the moment.

Brigid had heard all about the fire. After all, it was visible for miles around. It was a splendid new talking point among the local residents and was reported in the press as far distant as Galway and Enniskillen. Brigid was not yet aware that Rhoisin had revealed her true identity to Mrs Brothers. However, she had read press reports of the horrific description of the deaths of the crippled Roderick O'Hare and his heroic nurse, Judith. The tabloids had spared no gruesome details, launching into a lurid description of poor Roderick's contorted features and his piercing screams of agonised terror as he slowly roasted to a cinder in the blazing inferno of his bedroom.

The tragic death of the brave nurse Judith also received much attention. The reports stressed how she could so easily have escaped unharmed, but her unstinting devotion to duty had led her to try and rescue her patient in vain, only to jump to her death and fall, completely shattered, into the driveway of her employers' home.

Brigid read all the press coverage with horror and the added fascination of one who knew the location of the tragedy and many of those involved. Her greatest sympathy went out to Ruth, as she still knew her, for having been a witness to such tragic events. As Miread had returned to Dublin, Eamon had gone on a week's fishing holiday and her 'visitors' were very few in number, Brigid was able to devote all her time and energy in administering exclusively to Rhoisin's needs. She still had the strongest suspicions that Rhoisin was another of Thomas O'Hare's offspring, but the poor girl was so distraught by the appalling events she had just witnessed that it would have been extremely insensitive to start asking any questions.

Instead she tried to tempt Rhoisin's appetite by offering her especially delicious morsels. But finding after a day and a half that the girl wasn't responding to her best treatment, she suggested it would perhaps be better if Rhoisin returned to London. Rhoisin thought about this proposal for a few moments.

'Yes, Mrs Devlin, I think you're right. I'll go and make the arrangements.'

'Would you like to phone your family?' suggested Brigid. 'You can do it from here free of charge.'

Rhoisin was most grateful.

'Thank you very much.'

She telephoned Stephen. She had been thinking of doing so for a couple of days. She expected he would be out but she knew he had an answering machine so she could leave a message. He was in.

'Hello. It's Rhoisin. I'm coming back tomorrow. I've decided to fly.'

'Good idea! I'll meet you at the airport. What time's the plane?'

'I haven't booked it yet.'

'Right. Call me when you have, or leave a message on the machine if I'm out and I'll be there to meet you.'

'Thank you.'

'Everything all right?'

'Yes, fine.'

'See you tomorrow.'

'Yes. Bye.'

The easiest and quickest route was to take the train from Killalee to Dublin and fly directly to London from there. Now she had made up her mind to return to London, Rhoisin was in no mood to hang around any longer. As she hadn't been able to find her father, her mission was in some sense incomplete. Even so she had indisputably established the fact that she was indeed Thomas O'Hare's daughter. She had also fulfilled her ambition to see where her father had lived and where she might have been brought up. She had unravelled her full identity; discovered her Irish half, hidden for twenty-two years. She had also found and then lost, within a few hours, her crippled brother; a loss that for someone who longed for a sibling as much as Rhoisin always had, came as a particularly cruel blow. She had run the full gamut of emotions and was beginning to long for more familiar surroundings. She had had enough of the silence and remoteness of Killalee. She was weary of the limited social life that The Laughing Goat and The Sheaf and Sickle Hotel had to offer. She was sick of the country, the seemingly vast expanse of open space, green fields, grey sky, grey dry stone walls. And the weather above all! Never a day passed without rain. Not a decent, substantial downpour to clear the air and disperse the clouds, but endless, constant drizzle falling from a sombre, leaden grey sky. No wonder the Irish drank so much whiskey! Rhoisin felt she might join them if she stayed much longer.

But there remained Knockramore. Her father's home. It could have been her birthplace. It was elegant, magical and quite beautiful. She wasn't unduly worried by the damage done to the private wing. It was all interior damage. The walls were still intact and the ravages of the fire could easily be rectified in time. She was sure it was a listed building and the restorations might even qualify for a government grant. Knockramore. Even the name had an evocative ring. Would she ever see it again? She stopped herself from being sentimental. She was really looking forward to returning to London; to the noise, bustle and excitement she had missed so much.

Then there was Stephen, who would meet her at the airport...

Rhoisin had to spend another night in Killalee. There was no flight available from Dublin to London until mid-afternoon of the next day, so she left early the following morning. Mrs Devlin insisted on giving her a lift to the station. It was another grey morning with light, drizzling rain. Mrs Devlin bade her a fond farewell as she boarded the train. The route lay along the side of Lough Gill, a shimmering light grey in the rain as the sun tried to break through the cloud. As the train passed the end of the Knockramore golf course, sloping down towards the edge of the lake, the sun shone briefly, forming a rainbow over Knockramore, still hidden by the trees. There it is! thought Rhoisin excitedly. Knockramore beyond the rainbow!

Rhoisin stared out of the tiny aeroplane window at the brilliant blue sky. They were thirty thousand feet up over the Irish Sea, or perhaps already over Wales. She looked at the solid bank of fluffy white clouds below them, like a sea of cotton-wool. She had never been in an aeroplane. Before the journey she had been extremely apprehensive, but now she was enjoying it. She had expected to feel cramped, constrained, or even claustrophobic, but instead she felt liberated, weightless, as if she were flying under her own power.

'It was such a beautiful place! That wonderful house! So symmetrical and elegant. It must have been Georgian, or even Queen Anne. And the magnificent grounds, too. The ancient trees, the immaculate golf course sloping down towards the lake. I'd hate to think I'd never see it again.'

Rhoisin looked sadly across the table at Stephen.

'Knockramore,' he replied thoughtfully. 'Knockramore beyond the rainbow.'

He reached out and took her hand.

'I'd like to see it too. Maybe we should book that holiday sometime when things have settled down a bit. At least Mrs O'Hare won't think you've come about the post of chambermaid.'

Rhoisin laughed. 'We'll be among the smart guests next time.'

'We certainly shall. The smartest. And I'm looking forward to trying one of the landlord's special cheese and pickle sandwiches at The Laughing Goat.'

'I dare you! I bet you wouldn't eat it when you see how it's made.'

She was looking better, thought Stephen. Poor girl: what an ordeal she's been through. He looked round for the waiter to ask for the bill. He had taken her again to Justino's in the Liverpool Road, hoping the ambiance and good food would help her to relax. He hailed a taxi outside the restaurant to take them the short distance to Almeida Street. He could see she was exhausted. Once in the hall he took her in his arms and kissed her tenderly.

'I've made up the bed in the spare room,' he said, 'though if you prefer...'

She smiled gratefully. 'I think I need a good night's sleep.'

Stephen took her arm, full of understanding, and guided her upstairs. She needed to sleep, to rest, to heal.

Chapter Twenty-One

The small private chapel at Knockramore was packed for the funerals of Sean, Roderick, and old Mrs O'Hare. Mrs Brothers was surprised to see so many people. Mr Sean, as he was still referred to, despite his attempt to be known as Tom, had always been extremely unpopular with the locals. They thought of him as mean; a schemer and a cheat and were of the opinion that Mr Sean was rich enough not to need to behave in such a despicable manner. Most people suspected he had been responsible for the terrible accident that had killed nice Mr Tom and his delicate, pious wife. But they agreed, as the police had found no firm evidence to pin on Mr Sean, it was more prudent not to make any private accusations. It was odd, though, that Mr Sean should meet a similar death so close to the spot where his brother and sister-in-law had met theirs. A strange kind of justice.

And then poor Mr Roderick! Local sympathy had gone out to him after the accident. Only nine years old! And born a cripple. Never to lead a normal boy's life. It was known he had survived sitting in the back of the car. It was known too that he had ended up in an even worse state than he had been in before the accident and everyone assumed he was being looked after in a proper hospital for the severely disabled in Dublin, or even somewhere in England. Everyone knew there was plenty of O'Hare money available to give the poor boy the very best medical care. Then the news broke that he had been burnt to death. That was shocking enough in itself, but to discover he had been imprisoned at Knockramore by Mr Sean, his own uncle! Well, it just didn't bear thinking about. Incarcerated then incinerated.

And what about the poor old lady! Ninety-two and as mad as a hatter. As she hadn't been seen around the neighbourhood for years everyone assumed she had died naturally of old age. Then a few years back it was rumoured there had been a little fire at Knockramore. Fortunately not much damage had been done, but it was enough to bring it to the attention of the press. Another rumour went around that a pyromaniac was living in the house. Maybe it was old Mrs O'Hare herself, whom nobody had seen for years, perhaps bedridden, unable to go out.

Only she, Mrs Brothers, had known the full truth about old Mrs O'Hare and poor Master Roderick. She did have a lot on her conscience. She crossed herself and prayed for guidance and forgiveness. Well it was all out now, so she could go to confession and make a clean breast of it at last.

Then there was the nurse, Judith. No one except her had known of Judith's existence at Knockramore. As the reason for her being there was a secret, so too must her presence also be kept secret. Mrs Brothers was over-whelmed with guilt. She wondered now, in retrospect, how she had managed to bear such a heavy burden for all those years.

Judith was not being buried at Knockramore. Only members of the O'Hare family were laid to rest in the private cemetery. After the gruesome formalities had been completed, Judith's family had collected the body from the morgue in Killalee and made their own funeral arrangements.

The cortège was filing out of the chapel. Twelve pall bearers, four to a coffin, bearing the grisly, charred and mangled remains of the last of the O'Hares to their final resting place in the damp chilly cemetery. The only O'Hare still to bear the name was Lindsay. Shrouded in black, she carried herself bravely and with great dignity as she followed the three coffins out of the chapel for burial in the drizzling rain outside.

The forensic experts spent several days searching through the charred remains of the west wing at Knockramore. It wasn't just a question of finding out how the fire had started. The insurance assessors had been trying to estimate how much the restoration of the building would cost and they were, of course, most anxious to prevent a similar disaster ever happening again. On preliminary investigation it appeared the fire could have started in old Mrs O'Hare's room. She was known to have been of unsound mind and also to have a fondness for candlelight.

All the staff and guests were painstakingly interviewed by the police, one by one. Even Rhoisin was called to the police station in Killalee on the eve of her departure, much against the wishes of Mrs Brothers, who was most anxious to protect poor Rhoisin from any further stress. But when the police found out Rhoisin was almost certainly the illegitimate daughter of Thomas O'Hare, they immediately classed her as a prime suspect and warned her that if they did not come up with satisfactory answers they could insist she be recalled to Killalee at some future date.

Mrs Brothers, feeling that as Sean O'Hare was now dead and buried there was no point in stirring cold ashes, had originally decided to say nothing about seeing him in his car in the drive just as the fire was beginning to take hold. But as the police enquiries threw the net wider, the forensic experts carried off more and more sacks of ashes and the insurance assessors measured every nook and cranny of the west wing, she felt she should come clean. After all, she had enough on her conscience already. Her explanation seemed to satisfy the police and it was suggested that Sean O'Hare had started the fire himself in order to claim the insurance money.

Brigid Devlin spent the day after Rhoisin's departure spring cleaning the bedrooms. With Miread and Rhoisin gone, Eamon still away on a fishing trip and no 'visitors' expected till the following Saturday, Brigid began to feel the house was rather empty. By the evening she was feeling bereft and downright lonely so she decided to make one of her rare outings and treat herself to steak and chips and a pint of stout in The Laughing Goat. She had ensconced herself at her favourite table in a corner with her plate piled high and her glass brimming over, when who should she see looming large in the doorway but her old friend Mary Brothers. Feeling in need of a companion to chat to she called over to Mary to join her and within minutes the two good ladies had their heads together in such conspiratorial fashion that it would have been a brave person who would have dared to interrupt.

Mary filled Brigid in on almost everything she didn't know so far. They both agreed they had suspected quite early on that Rhoisin Hobbs might have had some connection with the O'Hare family. It seemed a tenuous and unlikely story that a well-educated young English girl should choose to do research into an obscure, wealthy landowning family in a remote part of the West of Ireland. Ironically, Brigid had not realised it was she who had put the idea into Rhoisin's head in the first place.

On her part, Mary realised she had to tread with extreme caution throughout. She had not seen Brigid for some considerable time, and although about fifteen years younger than she was herself, Mary was distressed to find how much Brigid had aged since their last meeting. Being so much older, Mary remembered only too clearly the whole sad story of Brigid's wild and passionate affair with Tom O'Hare, which was the talk of Killalee at the time. There were many who said that pretty lively Brigid Sheehan was just the right sort of person to inject new life into the O'Hare family. Rumour had it there was so much inbreeding in the family, (well-connected, moneyed Catholics being scarce on the ground in that part of the world) that the blood was thinning to such an extent that madness and deformity were on the increase in the O'Hare family.

Some people said at the time that Brigid Sheehan was only interested in the money; others said she was only in it for the sex. Many approved; some did not.

'Sure, Thomas O'Hare will just cast her off like an old coat when he's done with her. 'An O'Hare will never marry a peasant. They're all such snobs.'

Which was exactly what happened. Only Brigid was pregnant into the bargain.

So Mary Brothers knew that Miread Devlin was Thomas O'Hare's child. And she knew that Brigid knew she knew. So they both knew Thomas O'Hare had at least one healthy, wholesome, illegitimate offspring she felt she must be particularly sensitive and careful.

But she said nothing at all about Thomas O'Hare's will.

What Mary Brothers didn't know was that very afternoon the forensic experts had discovered a securely fastened metal box under the charred floorboards of the drawing room in the west wing. It was taken to the police station, forced open and found to contain many historical and legal documents. The whole box was dispatched without delay to the O'Hare's family solicitors in Dublin, Meagan, Keogh and Geoghan.

It was a matter of several months before the documents were sorted out and the relevant people traced.

Chapter Twenty-Two

It was a chilly March day. The wind whipped along Baggot Street in sharp piercing gusts making Miread Devlin feel she was living in the Arctic wastes of Siberia rather than in the supposedly temperate climate of Dublin's fair city. And only yesterday the sun was out for about half an hour, making the good burghers of the town feel their meteorological lot was not so bad after all. Miread pulled up her coat collar and tightened her scarf around her neck. Days like this made her want to plan her next escape to a sun-drenched region as soon as possible. Since her marvellous holiday in Turkey last September she counted the days and the pounds until she could make another similar trip to another equally warm and exotic land. Unfortunately she couldn't take another holiday for a while yet. Miread had recently changed jobs. After five and a half years in the bank she was just sick of it all. The argumentative, ungrateful customers, especially those on the phone, the mountains of mail to go through and, above all, the hierarchy among the employees. She had actually been to see the manager about the chance of further promotion but he had merely said, rather caustically she thought:

'Miss Devlin, although the bank ranks you highly as being among one of its most trusted and respected employees, you must understand that not being a university graduate, you cannot take your place, as you otherwise certainly would have done, among the high-flyers in the fast lane. I deeply regret to have to inform you that the bank is unable to offer you any further promotion.'

A week later Miread gave in her notice and left at the end of the month.

She walked past The Shelbourne Hotel, imposing, elegant, the pavement in front usually cluttered in the tourist season with a posse of wealthy Americans visiting the Emerald Isle 'in search of their roots.' But today there was no one. Even the livery attired hall porter remained just inside the large revolving door. Miread hesitated at the top of Kildare Street. She couldn't decide whether to walk down past Mansion House, the handsome Georgian building, housing the offices of the Lord Mayor of Dublin, where many banquets were held. Instead she crossed the street, and deciding to stay on Stephen's Green, she took the next turning down Dawson Street, to the small boutique selling elegant, expensive clothes on the corner of Anne Street, where she now worked.

Miread had left Killalee the day after the fire so she was spared all the gory press coverage of how two unfortunate people were burnt to death and a third was killed in a panic jump from a second floor window of a stately home. If she had been in Killalee at the time she would no doubt have devoured the tabloids with as much relish as all the other inhabitants, for there is nothing like a scandal or a tragedy to whet the appetite. But as Miread wasn't there she had no idea of any of the details of what had taken place. She knew there had been a fire. She had seen it with her own eyes. But as she had never been to Knockramore, nor met any of the residents, the fact that three of them had perished in a fire made little impression. She had heard of the O'Hares of course. You couldn't live in Killalee and not have heard of them, but to Miread Devlin the O'Hare family were just remote, wealthy people who had never had any direct bearing on her life. And by the time she returned to Killalee over two months later for a weekend visit to her mother, the fire at Knockramore, although by no means forgotten, was no longer a main talking point.

Miread enjoyed her new job at the boutique. The manageress was a jolly, friendly woman in her early thirties who promised to take Miread into partnership if she continued to show her present flair for organisation. Miread's skill with figures was a great help in running a business, so both she and her boss were fairly optimistic about her future prospects.

She had a new boyfriend called Gerry, who worked as an errand boy in a solicitor's office. He was talking about taking articles and becoming a solicitor's clerk. To Miread that was fairly unimportant. To her what mattered was that he had enough money, quite lot of which he spent on her, and more importantly, he was really splendid in bed. In fact, they were at it most nights; at her place, his place, just after work, late in the evening after a meal; during the night and in the early morning on the occasions when they managed to spend the nights together. In fact, Miread's cup of happiness was full to overflowing and if it weren't for her feelings of guilt about her mother, she saw no reason why she should ever visit dreary Killalee again.

Miread sat in the waiting room of Meagan, Keogh and Geoghan, Solicitors, totally mystified and increasingly curious. Three days ago she had received a letter which ran:

Meagan, Keogh and Geoghan, Solicitors,
17, Fitzwilliam Square, Dublin 2, Ireland.
22 October 1976

'Dear Miss Devlin,
It is with great pleasure that we write to inform you that we have a matter of great import to impart. We therefore beg you to make an appointment to visit us at your earliest convenience.
Yours truly, Sean Geoghan.'

'Mr Geoghan will see you now, Miss Devlin.'

Miread followed the pert little secretary; wearing a skirt so short it barely covered her bottom, heels so high she could hardly walk, with an enormous ladder down the back of her left leg. She was shown into a very large room, perfectly proportioned, with a high ceiling and a magnificent view over Fitzwilliam Square. Mr Geoghan, small, sandy haired, with thick spectacles, got up to greet her.

'Good morning, Miss Devlin. As I intimated in my letter I have some important news to impart. But first I must ask if you are the daughter of Brigid Devlin, née Sheehan, at present residing at Rose Cottage, Killalee, County Sligo?'

'Yes, I am,' replied Miread, surprised.

'Good,' said Mr Geoghan. 'Are you aware that you are not, in fact, the daughter of Mr Seamus Devlin, deceased, but the daughter of Mr Thomas Liam O'Hare, also deceased?'

Miread gasped and felt a hot rush of blood to her face.

'I am sorry, Miss Devlin. I see you were not aware of this fact and I apologise for having unwittingly upset you. But this has been substantiated by your mother.'

'My mother!'

'Yes, Miss Devlin. Please allow me to explain. The O'Hare family have been clients of Meagan, Keogh and Geoghan for several generations. It has always been their custom to make their wills here in this office with our advice and guidance. We therefore possess a copy of the will which we can then execute with reasonable ease after the death of the testator. But apparently, in your father's case, this did not happen. For reasons known to him alone, which may come to light at a future date, your father decided to make a new will by himself, without any legal advice, which has superseded any other will already in our possession. Fortunately for you, your father was a man of great knowledge and presence of mind. The will is correctly signed, dated and witnessed so everything is in perfect order.

'I now propose to read to you your father's will.

'*I, Thomas Liam O'Hare, being of sound mind, do make my will this 21st day of June, 1958. I here request that on my death my entire property be divided as follows: fifty per cent of my estate shall go to my legitimate son, Roderick Thomas O'Hare, when he reaches the age of twenty-one. Until that time the estate shall be managed by my brother, Sean O'Hare, who shall inherit nothing when Roderick attains the age of twenty-one. The rest of my property shall be divided equally between my two children born out of wedlock when they reach the age of twenty-one. The first one being the child of Linda Hobbs, residing at the time of conception at 119, Lonsdale Road, Kilburn, London NW2; the second one being the daughter of Brigid Devlin, née Sheehan, residing at the time of conception at 16, Fox Lane, Killalee, County Sligo. If my son Roderick should not reach the age of twenty-one, I then request that my entire property be equally divided between the two last named.'*

Mr Geoghan put down the will and looked directly at Miread.

'It so happens your half-brother did not reach the age of twenty-one. It appears that he perished in a fire at the O'Hare family home.'

Miread caught her breath. The truth was now beginning to dawn.

'So the entire estate of Knockramore, Killalee, plus a considerable amount of money, estimated conservatively at ten million pounds after tax, is to be divided between you and your half-sister, Rhoisin Hobbs. May I congratulate you, Miss Devlin, and apologise for the delay in imparting this information but I am sure you appreciate the amount of detective work involved.'

And Mr Geoghan got up, went round the table and solemnly shook her hand.

Miread was stunned. Five million quid! And a half share in this place – Knockramore? She had never been there but she could imagine it.

So Seamus Devlin wasn't her father after all. Well, she did have her suspicions. It was a relief too. It meant that idiot, orange-haired Eamon was only her half-brother. But her mother! Imagine never telling her who her real father was! What was she going to say to her mother about it all? She wouldn't be able to stay away from Killalee so much now. But would she? Or would she have to live in this Knockramore place? She would go and check it out, anyhow. It could be OK with five million quid to live on. And what on earth would Gerry think?

And then she had this half-sister, Rhoisin Hobbs. Maybe she would want to live in Knockramore too. And what was she like? There was a great deal to work out, a lot to think about. She had heard it said that having money brought responsibility. Well, soon she was going to find out.

Miread stood up and extended her hand.

'Thank you, Mr Geoghan. Goodbye.'

'Goodbye, Miss Devlin. We'll be in touch. My secretary will see you out.'

Chapter Twenty-Three

It took Rhoisin several months to recover from her ordeal. She slept badly and had terrible recurring nightmares, re-enacting the scene of the fire and her first and last meeting with Roderick and her grandmother. The fire scenes were particularly grisly: Roderick's face in close up, contorted in agony and fear. Judith flying into the air, a ball of flame, screaming, hitting the ground with a tremendous thud and bursting open in an explosion of blood and entrails. She dreamed of how her grandmother had suffered too. Rhoisin saw her dancing, as she had seen her dancing that afternoon, daft as a brush, cackling with mad laughter, drunk on champagne, slowly gyrating in her turquoise dress to soft, sensuous music, oblivious to the orangey-red flames licking up her legs.

Then Rhoisin woke up screaming, in a pool of sweat.

Stephen was extremely worried. He realised she was going through post trauma, a condition which can, at its worst, have a permanently damaging effect. He urged her to seek counselling but Rhoisin wouldn't hear of it.

'It'll be much worse if I have to talk about it all over again to some mad shrink. And it wouldn't stop there either. He would want to know all about my childhood; they always do, about the rape and everything. I'd be seeing him for years and I'd end up a total wreck. Anyway, I haven't got the money.'

Money's no object, thought Stephen. She would probably get it on the National Health Service. But he said nothing. In the end time would hopefully work its usual miracles.

It wasn't just the shock of the fire and witnessing the violent deaths of three human beings that was so upsetting. After all, the scene had been watched by many other people as well, and who knows how much anguish was being suffered by Mrs Brothers, Moira, Peggy and all the others at this very moment? There were times when Rhoisin had a strong urge to return to Knockramore to see how everyone else was faring. But something stopped her. She probably realised, intuitively, that it would be impossible for her at the moment to take on the extra burden of anyone else's grief.

The feeling of loss was Rhoisin's greatest problem. The horror had been bad enough but it was the loss of her brother and grandmother whom she had known only a few hours which was sometimes too hard to bear. There was her father too. Now she knew who her father was, but she would never know him, meet him, talk to him, feel him; for he was dead too. She had found and lost her family in the shortest imaginable space of time and she was again alone in the world. Then she would wait till she was alone and cry inconsolably. Gradually they became healing tears and slowly she managed to get herself together and somehow face the world and different challenges.

Stephen was extremely supportive. She stayed in his house for several weeks, sleeping in the spare room. He was affectionate, often taking her in his arms, but it was more of a brotherly embrace. He didn't try to kiss her or make any other suggestion of a sexual nature. At first she didn't think about it, then she did start to think about it, wondering whether she should do something or whether he was getting his oats elsewhere. For the moment she was grateful for his support. She had a lot to work through and unlike her half sister Miread, whose existence she was barely aware of, sex was low on her list.

By the beginning of September Rhoisin was beginning to feel the need for her own space. She had been staying in Stephen's house for five weeks and now wanted her own independence and the opportunity to regain her own identity. This feeling of the need for freedom coincided with the good news that she had a new job. A proper job at last, befitting someone with her qualifications. She was a research assistant for the BBC. So she moved back to the old flat in Kilburn where she had lived all her life; back to all the childhood memories and her life with Linda and Jim.

Jim. With so many other troubles on her mind Rhoisin had hardly given Jim a thought, but now back at the old stomping ground, his image began to haunt her. She thought she saw him lurking in doorways; she imagined him hiding under manhole covers. But she was enjoying her new job; she was seeing Stephen on the same basis as before and life seemed to be taking an upward turn.

Then one day she opened a newspaper and there on the inside page was Jim's photograph leering back at her. Even in the black and white photograph he seemed to have an orange glow. She read the report underneath.

'Jim Banks, aged 47, previously married to Charlene Burrows, marriage dissolved in 1965, was yesterday sentenced to twenty years imprisonment for rape at

Snaresbrook Crown Court, East London. Banks, who admitted 33 offences, has a history of rape with violence, especially against small girls. The offence for which he was caught was a particularly nasty one involving the rape of a ten-year-old girl on a caravan site in Margate. Banks owned a static caravan on the site and used it as a base for his unpleasant sexual attacks on small children, boys as well as girls. It appears that Banks, who started out as an ordinary rapist, later developed into a sadist of the first order. In this particular case the little girl was bound and gagged, burnt with...'

Rhoisin felt sick. She put the paper down. She tried to erase the scene from her mind. The hot August day. Alone with Jim in the caravan. 'Have you enjoyed your holiday?' Stroking her leg higher and higher... Rhoisin wanted to scream. She felt the pain again. She went through the trauma for the little girl. But it was over now. Jim was in prison. Twenty years. Let's hope he'll get twenty years. Perhaps the other prisoners will kill him? That happens. Even among the criminal fraternity child rapists were pretty unpopular. Rhoisin just sat for a while. Then she realised she had to get a move on if she wasn't going to be late for work. Suddenly she felt liberated; safe and free. It was all over. No more Jim lurking in corners, ready to pounce, to rape her. She knew Jim would never come out of prison. She could now get on with her life.

That evening she showed the news cutting to Stephen. They had just returned from dinner at Justino's and Stephen had poured two large brandies. They were sitting on the sofa with Stephen's arm around her. Stephen read the cutting in silence trying not to show how shocked he was.

'I'm free now,' said Rhoisin calmly. 'That brute has been put away for twenty years. Hopefully he'll never come out.'

'Yes,' said Stephen, his admiration for Rhoisin's stoic fortitude knowing no bounds. His arm around her tightened, their mouths met. And then, Jim and the brandies forgotten they made love on the floor in front of the sofa; passionate, complete love with no holds barred.

Rhoisin was indeed free at last.

At the beginning of November Rhoisin received a letter from Brent council offering her alternative accommodation. She went to see it: a spanking new flat in a terrace of newly restored Victorian houses, light and airy and much more conveniently situated to shops and public transport than where she was at present. She was delighted and accepted the council's offer at once. She told Stephen about it in great excitement and was absolutely amazed by his reaction.

'I'm pleased, of course, if that's what you really want. But if you're prepared to go through all the inconvenience of moving why don't you move in with me?'

'Move in with you?' She was stunned.

Stephen laughed. 'I don't know why you're so surprised. It's not that unusual.'

'No.'

Stephen looked at his watch. 'Let's discuss it over a bite of lunch'.

Stephen paused outside a jewellers in the Burlington Arcade, just off Piccadilly and inspected the elegant goods, exquisitely displayed. He wandered slowly along the covered arcade, studying the merchandise and thinking about Rhoisin.

He had realised for some time he was in love with her. Since Christmas in fact, when she had spent a week staying with him at his parents' house. That was the test, he thought ruefully, the test which many of his other lady friends had sadly failed. On the whole Mr and Mrs Piper did not take kindly to their son's lady friends. As he grew older he began to feel a little more at ease with his parents, his father in particular. They would have long discussions about politics, religion, history and the books he had read. Sex was hardly ever mentioned, and never in front of his mother. He remembered one evening in his father's study; he had just gone up to Oxford and was feeling particularly confident and optimistic about life. He had recently lost his virginity to an older woman, one of his tutors, and a whole new world had opened up. He wondered, he still wondered, if his father had guessed.

'Never get a woman into trouble, my boy. It could compromise you, ruin your life. Always take the appropriate precautions.'

'Yes, Father. Of course I will. I'll always be very careful.' He had felt embarrassed and changed the subject as soon as possible.

He remembered the first time he had brought a girl home. He expected separate rooms of course, but he had been a little surprised at his mother's attitude towards Caroline, the daughter of an eminent surgeon and absolutely out of the top drawer. His mother made it quite clear that a woman's place was in the home, preferably in the kitchen, but definitely, absolutely not on a university campus. Caroline took a dim view of this and an argument had ensued. Stephen was relieved when the weekend was over.

His father said: 'Nice girl, Caroline. Maybe a little bit too forthright.'

His mother sniffed: 'Much too modern for me.'

It was some time before Stephen had invited another girl for the weekend.

But there had always been some feeling of tension. Stephen was always aware that his parents had disapproved of his choice. Until Rhoisin arrived, with her wide-set grey eyes, pale skin and demure, shy smile. Stephen felt his parents really took to Rhoisin in a way they had not taken to any of his other girlfriends. On the other hand, he wasn't choosing a wife to please his parents. But it would certainly make life easier if they liked and approved of her.

He thought of Rhoisin from his point of view: intelligent, sensitive, understanding and appreciative of all the artistic interests that meant so much to him. Pretty as a picture and at last good in bed. Now she had laid the ghost of all her sexual repressions she had become a wonderfully free, erotic creature. He went into the third shop along the arcade and purchased a large expensive diamond ring.

Rhoisin slit the long thick envelope with a kitchen knife. She didn't receive much mail and this letter struck her as being unusually weighty and official. She turned the envelope over before extracting the contents. On the back was printed: Meagan, Keogh and Geoghan, Solicitors, Dublin, in embossed, thick black lettering. How extraordinary! she thought.

She drew out the contents: a heavy official looking document on thick paper, folded lengthways with a seal on top; also a covering letter on slightly thinner paper with the full address at the top. She sat down and started to read.

Meagan, Keogh and Geoghan, Solicitors,
17, Fitzwilliam Square, Dublin 2, Ireland.
3 November 1976

'*Dear Miss Hobbs,*
It is with great pleasure that we enclose a copy of your late father's will. In order that probate be effected without delay we would ask you to call at our London branch at your earliest convenience, taking with you your birth certificate for formal identification. The name of the London branch is Grieves, Shadbolt and Grieves, 110, Chancery Lane, London WC2.
'*Your obedient servant, Sean Geoghan.*'

Completely stunned, Rhoisin sat down and read the copy of her father's will. She read through the will again. She couldn't believe it. It was like winning the National Lottery. She had won a prize in the lottery of life: she, Rhoisin Hobbs. It was incredible! Things like that happened to other people, not to her. She was a millionaire! She couldn't grasp it all. The implications were enormous. What did millionaires do? Did they have to work, or did they just invest their money and live on the proceeds? Where was the money? Was it already invested or had it just been discovered in a tin box under the floorboards? And Knockramore! Knockramore beyond the rainbow! She owned half of Knockramore with her half-sister, Miread Devlin. She had guessed that Miread was her half-sister when she had recognised a family likeness in the portrait in the private sitting room. But to share Knockramore with this girl! She had only met her once. What did she think of it all? Mrs Devlin's daughter who worked in a bank in Dublin. Would they live there together and run it as a hotel? Would they need to run it as a hotel with five million quid each? Could she actually live there? Beautiful as it all was it was extremely remote and Killalee was pretty dead. And after all, she was a Londoner born and bred. Her brain was in a whirl.

And what about Stephen? What would he think? What did he think of her anyway? He had wanted her to move in with him: 'To save all the inconvenience of moving', he said, when she had told him that Brent Council had offered her another flat. She had resisted it and moved into her new flat. She wanted her own space. Time to think, to breathe on her own. Even so, she spent most weekends with Stephen, either in Almeida Street or in a cosy country inn. He hadn't yet mentioned marriage. That depressed her. Whenever she thought about it her old lack of self-confidence came flooding back. She wasn't good enough for him; she wasn't sufficiently upper crust. She had grown up in a council flat in Kilburn, born out of wedlock to a working class mother, who had worked partly as a courtesan.

Whereas Stephen...!

Memories of Christmas with his parents came flooding back. The well-appointed house near Petworth in leafy Sussex, in the stockbroker belt, just within commuting distance of London. The house with its mock Tudor beams, 'a desirable detached residence set in its own grounds.' The five double bedrooms and three elegant reception rooms. A small, book-lined study, where Mr Piper, a senior partner in a prominent firm of solicitors in the City, often worked into the small hours.

But something about them puzzled Rhoisin. They were charming, kindly, well-educated and most welcoming but somehow she couldn't connect them with Stephen at all. It wasn't just their appearance, which didn't resemble Stephen in the slightest. Stephen was tall, willowy, almost gaunt. Mr and Mrs Piper were both short. Mrs Piper was on the plump side. Well-corseted under her elegant little silk dresses, she could even be described as dumpy. Her carefully groomed hair had a delicate blue rinse to soften the grey. Her face, though scarcely lined, had a slightly puffy look. Her ankles bulged slightly over the expensive-looking shoes.

Mr Piper, sandy haired with piercing pale blue eyes, was hardly any taller than his wife. He wore very thick glasses which constantly slid down his nose. He had over-large hands and feet, which rather made him resemble a penguin or a porpoise.

Rhoisin also noticed a lack of mental and emotional communication between them and Stephen which is usually present in nearly all close families. It was as if the invisible thread that binds the family, the thread that creates the family, had been broken. Or perhaps had never existed in the first place?

She wasn't surprised when she and Stephen had been shown to separate bedrooms. She had somehow expected it. Stephen would wait until his father had gone up to bed, till the voices had ceased and the light was out and he would creep silently into her room and slide into the enormous double bed beside her. Even if she were already asleep he would stroke her flat stomach, her smooth pale skin. She would wake, moaning softly as he caressed her breasts, tonguing, then suckling her nipples, letting his free hand slide between her legs, feeling for her soft private place that was now his too. And she would feel his excitement as he grew hard and they came together in the darkness.

It was a happy time. The days were cold, crisp, sunny and full of laughter. The nights were warm, dark, velvety and erotic. They couldn't keep away from each other. But still Stephen hadn't mentioned marriage.

Rhoisin hadn't yet been able to take time off from work to visit Grieves, Shadbolt and Grieves in Chancery Lane. It might have to wait till Monday. Meanwhile, today was Friday, 15 March, the anniversary of her first proper meeting with Stephen. They were going to celebrate it by meeting for lunch at their usual coffee bar. The real celebration would to be this evening when they would dine in style at the Ivy.

She couldn't wait to tell him her news! She was a millionaire! But hang on a minute! Perhaps he *would* marry her now. Marry her for her money rather than for what she really was. Rhoisin decided she would say nothing for a day or two. She would just enjoy her secret, keep it to herself at least until she had had time to see the solicitors on Monday.

The tube rattled to a halt just before Camden Town station and they sat in the tunnel for a good ten minutes. She looked at her watch in dismay. She was fifteen minutes late. Bloody Northern Line. The worst in London. They called it the Misery Line. She got out at Leicester Square, rushed up the steps two at a time, hoping that Stephen would forgive her for being late. He liked people to be punctual. When she reached the street crowds were milling around the entrance to the Underground Station sheltering from the rain, which was bucketing down. Rhoisin felt around for the umbrella she usually carried in her large floppy handbag, but it was nowhere to be found.

Damn it! she thought. I'm going to arrive drenched. I'm going to look like a drowned rat. Briefly she contemplated waiting for a little until the worst of the rain had stopped. She glanced again at her watch. Too risky, she thought ruefully. I'm twenty minutes late already. She walked out of the station and turned the corner towards Leicester Square. She was the only person in the street. Everyone else was taking cover from the torrential downpour. It was barely five minutes from the station entrance to the coffee bar but by the time she arrived Rhoisin was soaked to the skin. She literally dripped with water. The coffee bar was crowded and smoky, just as it had been on her first chance meeting with Stephen. Rhoisin stood in the doorway and looked around for him. She could barely see through the pall of smoke. He looked up, saw her and smiled. He got up from the table, immaculately dressed as always, wearing well-tailored navy trousers, freshly laundered shirt with a cravat casually tucked into the open neck. His jacket was draped over the free chair. He squeezed his way past the other lunchers, huddled round the closely packed tables. He reached the door as Rhoisin struggled out of her soaking wet coat, sending showers of raindrops over the people sitting nearby. Stephen took her coat and kissed her, laughing when he saw the state she was in.

'My goodness! You're soaked to the skin! Maybe we should go the pub instead and have a brandy.'

He guided her to the tiny table in the corner. He had already ordered the sandwiches, egg mayonnaise in granary bread, the filling oozing out onto the paper napkin. As they sat down, Rhoisin's wet hair dripped onto her sandwich.

On the table was a small box. Stephen took her hand and gave it to her.

'I have a special present for you,' he said.

Chapter Twenty-Four

Lindsay O'Hare returned to Knockramore during the afternoon the day after the fire, in complete ignorance of the previous night's horrific events. By then the police had found her husband's body in the car on the Boyle road but had removed all traces of the accident which had taken place on the very road she had just travelled. She was informed of the fire and the tragic deaths in truly appalling circumstances of old Mrs O'Hare, young Roderick and Judith, the nurse. The dreadful news was almost more than she could take in. Distraught to find her home burnt to a cinder and herself widowed into the bargain she took to her bed, leaving the entire running of Knockramore and the care of the guests to Mrs Brothers.

Four days later Mrs O'Hare finally managed to face being interviewed by the police. She told them that she and her husband, Sean, had been invited to lunch by friends who lived locally. Later, during the afternoon, it was suggested they stay the night. She confirmed Sean had decided against spending the night away, feeling his responsibilities lay at Knockramore. By then the police had already come to the conclusion that Sean was killed in a car accident on his return journey to Knockramore. And as no one except Mrs Brothers had seen Sean's car in the driveway as the fire was taking hold, the police made no further investigations into the matter. They were now fairly well assured that Sean had started the fire himself to claim the insurance money.

The fire had totally destroyed the secret apartment and also badly damaged the private rooms where Mr and Mrs O'Hare lived. So for the foreseeable future Lindsay O'Hare was forced to sleep either in the main hotel wing or in the staff quarters. As the hotel was full she had no option but to bunk down in the east wing with the staff.

In the days following the fire, the staff at Knockramore showed great courage and resourcefulness. Although they had all witnessed the horrific events at first hand, they were persuaded by Mrs Brothers that life must go on and it was their duty to keep Knockramore running. As it was the high summer season, there were many guests from England and the United States and the bookings were full until mid-October. Realising there was no one capable of taking charge except herself, Mrs Brothers was up at 5.00 am and on the go until well past midnight. She had to run the kitchen, supervise the serving in the dining room, make sure the bar was running smoothly and in addition, ensure that all the bedrooms were properly cleaned. At fifty-nine years old she found the work a heavy burden and just prayed that she could get through it all until Mrs O'Hare had sufficiently recovered to take over. Fortunately for Mrs Brothers, Lindsay O'Hare found some inner strength and in just two weeks after the fire she took charge herself of running Knockramore, albeit in a rather subdued manner.

Going about her usual duties running the Knockramore Country House, Lindsay O'Hare began to think about her future. Now her husband, Sean, his mother mad Mrs O'Hare and his disabled nephew Roderick were all dead, who would inherit the Knockramore estate? Of course there was a will. Sean would have made a will leaving the estate to her in event of his death, especially as he was fifteen years her senior. She decided to make an appointment with the family solicitors, Meagan, Keogh and Geoghan, in Dublin.

'Mrs Brothers, I have to go to Dublin to see the solicitors about the will.' Mrs O'Hare explained to her housekeeper, beaming confidently.

'The will. Yes, of course, madam.' Obviously Mr Sean must have left a more recent will than Mr Tom's, leaving everything to his wife.

Lindsay O'Hare sat on a hard high backed chair in the solicitors' elegant Georgian waiting room. Like Miread a few weeks earlier, she followed the pert little secretary in her short tight skirt into Mr Geoghan's office overlooking Fitzwilliam Square.

'Mrs O'Hare, how do you do? Please take a seat. May I offer my condolences on the death of your husband.' Mr Geoghan's tone was unctuous and rather patronising.

'Thank you.' Lindsay O'Hare sat down, smiling confidently.

'I've come to ask you about my husband's will.'

'Your husband's will? I'm afraid we don't have a copy of your husband's will. Perhaps he left it in a secure place at Knockramore? I have been told forensics are making a thorough search of the badly damaged part of the house. Very sad about the terrible fire. But I'm sure something will turn up and we'll let you know in due course.'

Six weeks later Lindsay received a letter from Mr Geoghan.

'Dear Mrs O'Hare, Please come and see me at the above office at your earliest convenience.

Your obedient servant, Sean Geoghan.'

Once more back in the solicitors' elegant Georgian waiting room, Lindsay O'Hare sat on a hard high-backed chair, waiting for the pert little secretary to show her into Mr Geoghan's office. Once more he got up as she entered the room, shook her hand solemnly and offered his condolences.

'So my husband's will has surfaced at last,' said Lindsay pleasantly.

'Your husband's will? I'm sorry to say your husband didn't leave a will, Mrs O'Hare.'

'No will? How extraordinary! I always thought he was very well organised and good at planning ahead. So who is going to inherit the Knockramore estate?'

'I didn't say there wasn't a will. I said your husband didn't leave a will. There is another will drawn up by your late brother-in-law, Thomas O'Hare. I understand that Thomas O'Hare and his wife perished in a road accident about eleven years ago, shortly after the will was drawn up, but were survived by their disabled son.'

Lindsay had a hollow feeling in the pit of her stomach. Road accidents appeared to be a recurring disaster in her life.

'Twenty years or so before Thomas O'Hare made his will, Liam O'Hare, his father and your late husband's father, made a will leaving the entire Knockramore estate to his elder son, Thomas O'Hare. For some reason best known to himself, he cut your husband out of his will altogether. So your husband had nothing, absolutely nothing, to leave to you.'

Lindsay O'Hare was stunned. It was the very last thing she had expected.

'You mean, I get nothing? After eight years of marriage?'

'It appears so.'

'Is there no other will? A later one?'

'As far as I am aware your husband made a very thorough search of Knockramore in the hope of finding a will leaving the estate to him.'

'But he found nothing?'

'As far as I am aware of, no. As solicitors to the O'Hare family for many generations we would certainly have been informed if any other will had been found. As I understand it, the search still continues in the section of the house which was so badly destroyed by the fire.

'I see. Could I... could I contest this will?'

'On what grounds?'

'That as Sean O'Hare's wife, no provision of any kind has been made for me?'

'I'm sorry, Mrs O'Hare, but you fail to understand that this will was not drawn up by your husband. It is his brother's will, made eleven years ago, three years before you and your husband were married. Your husband would have been well advised to make his own will after his marriage to you; but so far records indicate that he did not do so. I am extremely sorry about this but there is nothing I can do about it.'

'Am... am I allowed to know the contents of my brother-in-law's will?'

Mr Geoghan looked grave. 'I'm afraid that is not possible. A will is a confidential document and the contents can only be revealed to the beneficiaries.

Lindsay was shaking. 'But what shall I live on? I have no money.'

'No money at all? No bank account?'

'It was my husband's bank account.'

'A joint account?'

'No. Just in his name. Most of the money went back into the estate.'

'I see. Have you received any bank statements since your husband's death?'

'No. Nothing.'

'Which is your bank, Mrs O'Hare?'

'The Bank of Ireland, Baggot Street Branch.'

Mr Geoghan reached for the telephone. 'Get me the Bank of Ireland, Baggot Street Branch, please, Tracey.'

Lindsay O'Hare faced the bank manager across his desk in the small cramped office on the first floor of the Baggot Street Branch.

'Mrs O'Hare, how can I help?'

'I was wondering if it would be possible for me to know how much money there is in the account of my late husband, Sean O'Hare.'

The bank manager's eyebrows shot up. 'Sean O'Hare? Deceased?'

'Yes. My husband died two months ago.'

'My condolences, Mrs O'Hare.' The manager picked up the telephone. 'Please bring me the account details of Sean O'Hare, please, Liam.'

'Do you have ID, Mrs O'Hare?'

'ID?'

'Passport, driving license, even an envelope with your address on it?'

Lindsay shook her head.

'In that case... I'm not sure.... Oh! Thank you Liam,' to the office boy who handed him a folder.

Lindsay watched in silence and trepidation as the bank manager went slowly through her husband's bank statements. He finally looked up.

'This account belonged to Sean O'Hare of Knockramore, Killalee, Co Sligo. Was that your husband's address, Mrs O'Hare?'

'Yes. And also my address.'

'Well, I regret to say that your husband's personal account has been frozen. But there is a separate account with available funds to run Knockramore Country House.'

Chapter Twenty-Five

Feeling tired and stiff after the journey from Dublin, Miread climbed down slowly off the coach. Killalee again. How was she going to cope with four days in Killalee? Her heart sank as she slowly made her way to her mother's whitewashed rose-covered cottage. Brigid was delighted to have her daughter back to stay with her, even if it was only for four days. Without knowing it, Miread had chosen a period when her mother had no 'visitors' and the extra good news was that her half-brother, Eamon, was away on holiday. Mother and daughter would be able to have long uninterrupted chats: to clear the air, thought Miread ruefully.

Miread helped her mother to clear away breakfast, then poured them both second cups of tea. She didn't know how much her mother already knew so it was difficult to know where to start. She decided on the oblique approach.

'So, Mam, tell me about the fire at Knockramore. It must be about two months ago now. I think I left Killalee the day after the fire.'

'Indeed and I think you did.' Brigid was also unsure about how much her daughter knew. 'The police aren't sure whether the fire was a terrible accident or whether it was started deliberately by Sean O'Hare to claim the insurance money.'

'And did he get the insurance money?' Miread thought she would test her mother a little.

'Indeed he did not. Sure he was killed on the Boyle Road. On the exact same spot where it's rumoured he set up the accident that killed his brother, Tom and his wife eleven years earlier. It's said his disabled son survived and was living in a hospital in Dublin. But then it turned out that he was living at Knockramore the whole time, hidden away. No one seems to know who inherited the Knockramore estate. It seems logical it would go to Sean O'Hare's wife, Lindsay. Though Mary Brothers, the housekeeper up there, told me Lindsay O'Hare is back working at Knockramore, like she used to in the old days when her husband was alive.'

'Mam, I have something to tell you.' Miread was feeling distinctly nervous. She had no idea how her mother was going to react to the news that she knew she was the illegitimate daughter of Thomas O'Hare.

'Yes, darling. And what would that be?'

Miread decided to start with Eamon.

'Mam, have you ever thought that Eamon and I are rather different?'

'You mean with him having red hair an' all and not being too bright?

'Well, yes. Did you ever think that perhaps we had different fathers?'

The truth slowly began to dawn on Brigid. Miread knew that Seumas Devlin was not her father. Did she know her real father was Thomas O'Hare?

She said quite sharply. 'What are you trying to infer, young Miread?'

'Mam, I'm not inferring anything. I now know the truth. I'm the illegitimate daughter of Thomas O'Hare.'

Hearing her daughter say the words out loud gave Brigid an even bigger shock than she was prepared for.

'And who gave you that amazing bit of news?'

'The O'Hare's solicitors. Thomas O'Hare left half the Knockramore estate to his legitimate son Roderick, and the other half to be divided between me and my half-sister, Rhoisin Hobbs. But as Roderick perished in that terrible fire the estate will now be divided between Rhoisin and me.'

Brigid was afraid she was going to faint.

'Mam, I've invited Gerry to stay. He'll arrive on Friday afternoon. I hope that's OK. He's coming by car so we can drive over and take a look at Knockramore.'

'Knockramore! Your inheritance. Your estate. I still can't get my head round it.'

Miread gave her mother a hug. 'Don't try to, Mam. Just let it all wash over you. You'll get used to it in the end and you won't have to take in any more visitors.'

'No, I suppose not. I never thought about that. But what'll I do all day living here all on my own with just Eamon for company?'

'Don't worry. We'll sort something out. Now, which room do you want Gerry to have? Can he have the big double next door to me?'

Brigid gave her daughter a knowing look. 'Well, I don't see why not.'

Gerry arrived around four o'clock on Friday afternoon, driving a bright red two-seater sports car with the hood down. Hearing the car, Miread rushed out to greet him. They exchanged a long embrace and a passionate kiss.

Brigid followed her daughter slowly outside and waited to be introduced.

'Mam, this is Gerry.'

Brigid extended her hand. 'Nice to meet you, Gerry.'

'Me too, Mrs Devlin.'

Brigid liked what she saw: a tall slimly-built young man in his early twenties, well turned out in a blazer, open-necked shirt and well-pressed trousers. He had an abundance of fair curly hair and laughing blue eyes.

'Let me take your bag.'

'No, of course not. I wouldn't dream of letting a lady carry my bag.'

Miread laughed. 'I told you! She's treating you like one of her lodgers.'

'Tea,' said Brigid firmly, feeling it would break the ice.

As soon as Mrs Devlin was safely in bed, Gerry slipped into Miread's room and slid into her bed. They cuddled up close as he stroked and caressed her, and starved of sex as they both were, they enjoyed a prolonged and passionate sexual orgy.

'Gerry and I'll be out for lunch, Mam.'

'Out? Sure and where are you going out for lunch?'

'To Knockramore. I've booked a table for one o'clock.'

Brigid's eyes widened. 'Lunch at Knockramore? Well, you'll have plenty to tell me when you get home.'

Just after midday she waved them off, standing by the front door until the bright red two-seater sports car turned the corner. Smart young lad, she thought, to be able to afford a car like that. Smartly dressed, too. Miread and Gerry agreed that they should dress up for such an important occasion. Gerry wore a suit and tie and Miread wore a floaty summer dress with a well-cut jacket. The drive to Knockramore took barely fifteen minutes, but Miread wanted to have a good look round before they went into lunch.

The road was winding and undulating, like a switch back. On top of the last hill Gerry involuntarily stopped the car so they could both gaze down at the view below. Miread gasped with amazement at the beauty of it all: the smooth waters of Lough Gill with Parke Castle in the distance, the grey dry stone walls and the scudding white cirrus clouds.

'It's beautiful!' she cried. 'I never imagined anything quite so beautiful.'

'And you've lived most of your life in Killalee and you've never been here?' Now it was Gerry's turn to be amazed.

'No. What would be the point? Simple people like Mam and me didn't go to posh places like Knockramore.'

'Well, you're going there now.' Gerry let the clutch out and they sailed down the hill the as sun came out.

They arrived at the impressive wrought iron gates on which there was a bell with a sign above saying: PLEASE RING. Miread got out of the car, rang the bell and in a few moments the gates opened as if by magic and they drove through as the gates closed behind them. Driving along the gently curving drive, bordered on either side by well-established rhododendrons, they rounded the last bend and stopped to admire the magnificent golf course; the greens short and smooth like billiard tables. Parking the car in the designated area at the side of the east wing, they walked round to the front to inspect the house: Georgian, impressive, and extremely elegant.

One wing was badly charred, the windows boarded up. That's where the fire broke out, thought Miread.

They walked up a long flight of steps, through a magnificent double front door into the hallway, panelled in dark oak. On the marble tiled floor was an elegant antique table on which stood a hand bell with a notice: PLEASE RING. Miread rang the bell and a maid in a black and white uniform appeared immediately, almost as if she had been hiding behind the curtains.

'Good afternoon, madam. Good afternoon, sir. Do you have a reservation?'

'Yes,' said Miread. 'We certainly do.'

The maid picked up a book off the table and opened it. 'And the name please?'

'Devlin.'

'Just for lunch, Mrs Devlin?'

'Just lunch.'

'And would you care for a drink in the bar to give you an appetite?'

Miread looked at Gerry, who nodded.

'Yes, that would be lovely.'

Miread and Gerry followed the maid along a corridor to the bar at the back of the house. They settled themselves at the table with the most advantageous view of the golf course and ordered two glasses of white wine.

A little later they were seated in the spacious dining room, the tables well spaced, with a view of the walled garden. They had just finished their main course when a well-dressed lady came up to their table.

'Everything all right, sir? How have you enjoyed your meal so far?'

'The meal so far is excellent, thank you,' replied Gerry in a warm friendly tone.

'And you, madam? Are you enjoying the meal too?'

Miread looked up and flashed the lady one of her dazzling smiles. 'Thank you so much. It's all quite delicious.'

The lady gave a little gasp and murmuring: 'I am pleased,' she moved on to the next table. She's the image of Ruth Hobson, thought Lindsay O'Hare. I wonder what happened to pretty little Ruth?

'Mam, will you come with us to the Laughing Goat for lunch?'

'Lunch at the Laughing Goat?' Brigid sounded surprised. 'But you had lunch out yesterday at Knockramore.'

'We're on holiday, Mrs Devlin,' said Gerry laughing.

'That's what young people do on holiday, Mam.'

'I think you two would be far better off lunching on your own. Whether it's at Knockramore or the Laughing Goat, I'd just be in your way. Go off and enjoy yourselves. I can have a restful afternoon before I cook your last supper for you here.'

'The last supper!' Miread laughed. 'Sounds as if you think we won't be returning to Killalee.'

'Oh, I've no doubt about that now that you're an heiress an' all. You'll need to return to Knockramore at some stage to sort things out.'

Miread gave her mother a hug, 'OK, Mam. We'll take you at your word but I want Gerry to see all the sights of Killalee.'

Miread and Gerry walked slowly through the little town, arm in arm, looking at the shabby houses with peeling paint, the front gardens filled with rubbish.

'Well, what do you think of Killalee?' asked Miread.

Gerry didn't want to offend her. 'Do you like it?'

'Good God, no. You know I can't stand the place. I told you that when we first met. I dread returning here but I have to because of Mam.'

'You've another reason to return now that you've inherited half of Knockramore. What are you planning to do with it?'

'Quite honestly, I don't know. Keep running it as a hotel? Engage a manager? I couldn't live in it, beautiful as it is.'

'Have you heard anything from your half-sister. What's her name?'

'Rhoisin.'

'Pretty name.'

'Pretty girl.'

'So you've met her?'

'Only once, very briefly. She was staying at Mam's. I only spoke to her for about five minutes.'

'Perhaps you should get in touch and devise a plan.'

'Perhaps we should. Well, here's the Laughing Goat. What do you think of the sign? I think it's comical but perhaps a little evil.'

Gerry looked up at the sign, swinging gently in the breeze, its body in profile, the head face on, the expression rather menacing, as if daring people to enter its premises over which it had some evil control.

'I agree. I think it's evil. What's the food like?'

'No better or worse than the food anywhere else in Killalee, except Knockramore, of course.'

'That was quite exceptional.'

Gerry held the door open for Miread and she went inside. The landlord looked up as she entered. 'Well I never! Miread Devlin has returned to Killalee. And how long do we have the pleasure of your company, Miread?'

Miread felt irritated by the landlord's jocular manner. 'I'm leaving tomorrow,' she said shortly.

'And where are the lucky people to expect you tomorrow?'

'Dublin.'

'Oh, Dublin. We've gone posh now, have we, living in a capital city?'

'May we have two menus, please?'

'Two menus, an' all!'

'One for my friend.'

The landlord noticed Gerry standing behind Miread. He picked up two greasy dog-eared menus from behind the bar and passed them to Miread. Miread gave one to Gerry and moved away from the bar so they could discuss their selection out of the landlord's earshot. The choice was short and simple: three different sandwiches, shepherd's pie or sausage and mash.

'What'll you have?' asked Miread.

'Bacon and egg sandwich.'

'Me too.' Miread went up to the bar. 'Two bacon and egg sandwiches, please.'

'Sorry, love. No eggs. The lodgers have ate them all.'

'No eggs, Gerry.'

Gerry joined Miread at the bar. 'I'll have ham and cheese.'

Miread eyed the landlord. 'Two ham and cheese.'

'Right, love. And what'll you have to wash it down?'

'Two glasses of white wine,' said Gerry.

'But I can't open a whole bottle just for two glasses!'

'We'll have the bottle then,' said Gerry recklessly.

There were only half a dozen or so customers in the pub, all elderly men. Miread and Gerry found a table in a corner away from the other drinkers and furthest from the bar. It was covered in crumbs and cigarette ends.

'I see what you mean,' said Gerry.

'I'll ask the landlord to clean it off.'

'No, I will.' Gerry went up to the bar. 'Could you wipe our table down before you bring the sandwiches, please?'

'You could have chosen a clean table.'

'We like that one.' Gerry was beginning to wish he had booked lunch at Knockramore. The landlord wiped the table over and plonked down the bottle of wine, already opened. No tasting the wine at the Laughing Goat. The sandwiches arrived and they both bit in cautiously.

'OK?' asked Miread.

'It'll do. I'm already looking forward to your Mam's last supper.'

A young man came into the pub, went up to the bar and ordered a pint.

'Oh, hello, Dermot,' said the landlord. He leant over the bar and said in a confidential tone: 'Your old girlfriend, Miread Devlin, is over there. Looks like she's got a new young man.'

Dermot Malone looked over in the direction in which the landlord was pointing. Miread! His Miread! He had asked her to marry him less than a year ago. She had turned him down saying she wasn't ready for marriage and now it looked as if she had hitched up with someone else. He wasn't sure whether to let sleeping dogs lie and find a seat in the opposite corner of the pub, or go across and say hello. He decided on the second option. He picked up his foaming pint and took it across to the far table where Miread and Gerry were deep in conversation.

He put his pint down on the table beside the half empty bottle of wine.

'Hello, Miread! How're you doing?'

Miread looked up, startled.

'Dermot! Fancy running into you again in the Laughing Goat.'

Chapter Twenty-Six

Since Stephen's proposal of marriage Rhoisin had thought of nothing else. It was on 15 March, the anniversary of their first real meeting, that Stephen gave her a box containing a huge glittering diamond ring and asked her to marry him. She was going to marry Stephen and become Mrs Stephen Piper! She was so happy that Knockramore and her inheritance barely crossed her mind. The terrible fire that had destroyed her new family she had barely known for a few hours was becoming a dim memory: still horrendous and sometimes painful, but slowly the pain was lessening. Of course she had no idea what was happening at Knockramore. She didn't realise that Lindsay O'Hare had not inherited what she considered to be hers by right. She didn't know either that Lindsay O'Hare was unaware she was her niece, Tom O'Hare's illegitimate daughter; or that she and her half-sister, Miread Devlin had inherited the Knockramore estate. At the moment Knockramore was very far away: on the other side of Ireland: a good day's journey. There would be plenty of time to think about Knockramore once she had settled down to married life.

Drawing up the guest list for the wedding made Rhoisin realise how few people she knew. She had no close friends. Her only real friend was Julie, and as far as Rhoisin was aware, Julie was still in Australia. She contemplated inviting two of the girls she worked with in the BBC research department but decided against it. She had only known them a few weeks. A wedding was too intimate an occasion to invite girls she had known such a short time. The wedding took place at the Registry Office in Islington's handsome Town Hall on 7 May 1977, Rhoisin's twenty-third birthday. Stephen's parents were there, looking even smaller and older than when Rhoisin had last seen them at Christmas. They each gave Rhoisin a quick peck on the cheek.

'We are so happy for you, dear.'

'It's good to see Stephen fixed up at last.'

Stephen's partner came: tall, with a deep plummy voice, dressed in a man's suit. Three of his clients were there too: actresses beautifully attired in expensive designer clothes. Rhoisin was relieved she more or less came up to their standard in her ivory Armani trouser suit. She had spent a week searching for the appropriate outfit and was pleased with her choice. Stephen, in a dark grey suit and spotted bow tie, thought his wife-to-be looked stunningly beautiful.

Auntie Liz and Uncle Jack had made the trip down from Leeds for the day to support Rhoisin on her wedding day. They were amazed and delighted when she told them all the good news on the phone the day after Stephen had proposed.

'I'm delighted, Rhoisin, love. It'll be great to see you married off to such an important young man.'

Rhoisin wasn't sure why they thought Stephen was important. 'He's just a theatrical agent, Auntie Liz.'

'But that's important, isn't it?'

And at thirty-eight he's not that young either, thought Rhoisin. But soon he'll be my husband and I'm very grateful and very happy.

The news about her inheritance stunned her aunt and uncle.

'You've inherited half an estate in the West of Ireland?' said Uncle Jack, incredulously. 'And five million quid into the bargain? We'll have to keep in touch,' he joked. 'Good thing we met up!'

After the ceremony Stephen and Rhoisin took a white Rolls Royce the short distance to Justino's in the Liverpool Road, while their eight guests followed them in a cab.

Their honeymoon was spent in New York. As one of London's foremost theatrical agents, Stephen visited to New York regularly to see plays on Broadway and hopefully pick up new clients. They spent ten days staying in a fully serviced apartment overlooking Central Park. Stephen enormously enjoyed showing his attractive new wife around New York. By now Rhoisin had acquired such poise and sex appeal that heads turned when she entered a restaurant or even boarded a bus. Stephen had booked tickets for all New York's top entertainments. They went to the opera at the Metropolitan Opera House and an orchestral concert at the Carnegie Hall. They did two Broadway musicals and two theatres. They took a helicopter ride and a dinner cruise on the Hudson River. They rode on several tourist buses, exploring the length and breadth of Manhattan, from Harlem in the north to Wall Street in the south. They took a ferry to Ellis Island, where their Irish forebears were said to have landed and helped to found New York. They visited the Metropolitan Museum of Fine Art and the Museum of Modern Art. Although a Londoner born and bred, Rhoisin was totally overwhelmed by the vitality and electric energy of New York.

'It is truly the city that never sleeps,' she said.

Near the end of their visit they were standing in Times Square at the point where Broadway and Seventh Avenue merge.

'And this is Times Square,' explained Stephen.

'Where?' asked Rhoisin.

'Right here.'

'But where's the Square?'

'What do you mean exactly?'

'Well, it's not square, like Trafalgar Square, or Bloomsbury Square. All London's Squares are square. Times Square is not only not square, but it doesn't seem to have a beginning or end either.'

Stephen roared with laughter and gave her a great big hug. 'Oh, my darling! You're enchanting. It's the New Yorker's version of a non-square Square.'

They arrived back at No 10 Almeida Street to an enormous pile of mail, so large it was difficult to open the front door. With the help of some good strong coffee – they had both found the coffee in New York rather lacking in strength and taste – they got stuck in to opening the mail. They divided it into appropriate piles: Stephen's pile; Rhoisin's pile, to be answered sooner rather than later. Then there was the pile advertising operas, concerts, and theatres; and finally the pile to go immediately into the bin.

In Rhoisin's pile was an official looking letter from Dublin on expensive cream paper which she seemed to recognise.

Meagan, Keogh and Geoghan,
17, Fitzwilliam Square, Dublin 2
22 March 1977

Dear Miss Hobbs,
I would be pleased if you would call at our London Branch of solicitors, Grieves, Shadbolt & Grieves at 110, Chancery Lane, London, WC2 at your earliest convenience.
Your obedient servant, Sean Geoghan.

As the letter was written nearly two months ago, Rhoisin realised she should get a move on and make an appointment within the next few days.

Rhoisin sat in the waiting room in Chancery Lane of the Solicitors, Grieves, Shadbolt and Grieves. After about ten minutes a tall thin man in his early fifties appeared, wearing a dark grey pin-striped suit.

'Miss Hobbs? I'm Roger Grieves. How do you do?'

He led the way to a spacious office on the first floor overlooking the narrow end of Chancery Lane.

'I must apologise for the delay in making the appointment,' said Rhoisin. 'You see, I've recently married and no longer live at the address to which the letter was sent. I suppose Royal Mail took their time about forwarding the letter.'

Roger Grieves smiled as he opened the file in front of him on the desk. 'May I ask your married name, Mrs...?

'Piper. My husband is Stephen Piper and the address is No 10 Almeida Street, Islington, London N1.'

'Not far from here?'

'No. Not far at all.'

'Well, the reason for your visit is quite simple: or perhaps not so simple, depending how you look at it. Our Dublin partners, Meagan, Keogh and Geoghan, have contacted us in respect of your substantial inheritance in the West of Ireland. To be more precise, Mrs Piper, you and your half-sister, Miread Devlin have each inherited a half share in the considerable estate of your late father, Mr Thomas O'Hare at Knockramore, Killalee, County Sligo.'

Rhoisin nodded.

'I don't know if this was expected or ...'

'Most unexpected.'

'Just so. Did you know of this Knockramore estate before you inherited it?'

'Just a few months before. A year ago I went to Killalee in search of my father. It appears my late mother, Linda Hobbs, had a brief fling with Thomas O'Hare, of which I was the unwanted result on Thomas O'Hare's side.'

'I see.'

'It appears also that Thomas O'Hare fathered my half-sister with a lady living locally. It seems that some years later he wanted to make amends for his rather... shall I say... loose behaviour by leaving his property to his two illegitimate offspring.'

'And you have only been aware of all this within the last year?'

'Yes. That's correct.'

'Do you know, or have you heard of, a lady named Lindsay O'Hare?'

'Yes. When I went to Killalee last year Lindsay O'Hare was married to my uncle, Sean O'Hare and managing his home, Knockramore, as a Country House Hotel.'

Rhoisin couldn't understand why Mr Grieves didn't have all this information at his fingertips. 'You didn't know all this?'

Mr Grieves shook his head. 'No. No idea.'

Rhoisin was puzzled and began to think Lindsay O'Hare was all or part of the reason for her visit to Mr Grieves.

'You might like to read this letter, Mrs Piper.

The letter was headed:

Meagan, Keogh and Geoghan,
17, Fitzwilliam Square, Dublin 2
11 January 1977

Dear Roger,
I am writing on behalf of one of my clients, Mrs Lindsay O'Hare, widow of Mr Sean O'Hare, Knockramore, Killalee Co Sligo. Mrs O'Hare is naturally most distressed to discover that on the death of her husband in a road accident last August, she has inherited nothing from his estate. In fact, as you may remember, Sean O'Hare left no will at all. The only will in existence is the one drawn up eleven years earlier by his brother, Thomas, also deceased, leaving the estate to be divided between his two daughters born out of wedlock, Rhoisin Hobbs and Miread Devlin.

Mrs Lindsay O'Hare is so far unaware of who has inherited what she thought was her husband's estate. As confidentiality prevents me from revealing the identity of the beneficiaries, I ask you in good faith to inform Miss Hobbs of this unfortunate situation and perhaps suggest that either she or Miss Devlin would inform Mrs O'Hare of this rather delicate matter.

I hope you and the family are keeping well.

With best regards, Sean.

Rhoisin handed over the letter. 'I see. I was beginning to wonder what the reason for my visit was.'

'And now you know.'

'Simple?'

'No. Not simple.'

'Mrs Piper, have you ever met your half sister, Miread Devlin?'

'Once. Very briefly when I visited Killalee last summer. I was staying at her mother's house. She runs a B&B. I only spoke to her for about five minutes.'

'Were you aware she might be your half-sister. Did you have any sisterly feelings towards her?'

'At the time: none at all.'

'May I suggest you should get in touch with Miss Devlin?'

'Yes, I think it would be a very good idea.'

'I'll give you her address and telephone number.'

In mid-July Rhoisin and Stephen flew to Dublin and spent two nights in the Shelbourne Hotel on St. Stephen's Green. Stephen said he would like to see a little bit of Dublin before they drove all the way across Ireland to Knockramore.

Rhoisin laughed as they lunched in the hotel grill room.

'Do you know, this is almost the exact anniversary of my first visit to Ireland in search of my father. And it wasn't at all like this.'

'Such a lot has happened in a year, hasn't it, darling? Tell me about your last visit to Dublin.'

'I travelled by train to Liverpool and took the boat, arriving in Dublin very early in the morning. I struggled across the city to the station for the West of Ireland for the ten thirty am train. But I was so exhausted after the ghastly boat trip in a cabin for four people that I fell asleep in the waiting room and missed it. The next train, a very slow one, was at four o'clock so I didn't arrive in Killalee until after eight pm. I was quite shattered, but I was lucky enough to find Mrs Devlin's cottage, where I took a room.'

'Your half sister, Miread's mother?'

'Yes. She was a lovely person. The room was lovely too.'

'And you met Miread?'

'Yes, but only for about five minutes.'

'And you had no idea she was your half-sister?'

'No idea.'

'No little family feeling?'

'Absolutely none.'

'Are you looking forward to meeting her again?'

'I can't say, really. I suppose I'm feeling a bit... apprehensive, you might say.'

'Of course. Most understandable. Where are you planning to meet her? At Knockramore, or at Mrs Devlin's cottage?'

'Oh, at Mrs Devlin's cottage. It's an environment we're both familiar with. I think Knockramore would be much too overwhelming.'

'I'm sure you're right. Though I must say I can't wait to see Knockramore.'

'Well, you won't have to wait long. We'll be there tomorrow evening in time for dinner. I must say I'm looking forward to being among the guests instead of one of the staff.'

The following day Stephen drove the hired car across Ireland. They both agreed the scenery in the middle of the country left much to be desired. It was flat and dull with a great deal of small cottages which had been left to fall down while the owners built new ones next door. Although the new ones seemed hardly an improvement on the original ones. There were no fields and hardly any agriculture or domestic animals.

'It's just a great big bog, really,' remarked Rhoisin, a little disappointed. 'Sligo has some good scenery, though. You'll see.'

Once they had driven across the border into County Sligo the scenery showed a dramatic improvement and when they reached the shores of Lough Gill it was quite stunning. They stopped at the brow of the last hill, just as Miread and Gerry had done less than three weeks before and gazed down at the beautiful scene: the smooth waters of Lough Gill with Parke Castle in the distance, the grey dry stone walls and the fluffy white clouds.

'Wow!' exclaimed Stephen. 'The view is quite special. And to think, if Thomas O'Hare had done the decent thing and married your mother, you might have been brought up here.'

'Yes, I know. It's a sobering thought. That's exactly what went through my mind when I stood here with Miread's battered bicycle.'

'She lent you her bicycle?'

'Her mother did.'

'So you arrived at Knockramore on a bicycle!'

'No. Not exactly. I hid it in some bushes and walked in.'

Stephen laughed, put the car into gear and they sailed down the hill. As the sun came out through the drizzling rain, forming a rainbow, Stephen said: 'we're off to Knockramore beyond the rainbow.'

A pert little maid in a black and white uniform showed them up to their bedroom. She cast a puzzled glance at Rhoisin but said nothing.

'Your luggage will be up shortly, sir – madam.'

'Thank you.'

Rhoisin looked round the room trying to remember if she had been paid to clean it only a year ago. It all looked vaguely familiar. Stephen had booked one of the best rooms. After all, his new wife now owed half the property so half the cost would be repaid. He went to the window and marvelled again at the stunning view. This time the golf course was in the foreground, greens immaculately kept, the eighteen holes undulating away towards Lough Gill in the distance.

Rhoisin studied the items laid out on the antique dressing table: a set of sliver hairbrushes, comb and hand mirror, a Wedgwood ashtray, a paper knife and a bowl of flowers. Propped up against the central mirror was a letter addressed to her. Slitting it open with the paper knife she sat down in one of the comfortable armchairs to read it.

16, Fox Lane, Killalee, Co: Sligo
7 July 1977

Dear Rhoisin,

Welcome to Knockramore! I hope my letter will await your arrival. I am so looking forward to meeting you as we have such a lot to discuss. May I suggest we meet here, at my mother's house. It's familiar ground to both of us which will hopefully help to reduce any inhibitions either of us may have. Perhaps you could come about four o'clock this coming Saturday, 13 July. Would this suit you?

Much as I am looking forward to meeting your husband, Stephen, I think it would be best if our first meeting was just between the two of us. Perhaps Stephen could drop you off here and then take a stroll around Killalee? Then we could meet him later at the Laughing Goat, say about six o'clock? The pub car park is straight on from here and then first right. If there is any problem about this arrangement just give me a call on 7482 0933.

With warmest regards,
Your sister Miread.

A sob rose up in Rhoisin's throat as she read the letter. Then she passed it over to Stephen.

They spent the following day exploring the delights of Knockramore. After an excellent full Irish breakfast with scrambled egg and smoked salmon, hot buttered scones and soda bread, they were so replete they wondered if they would be able to manage lunch. At the reception desk Stephen booked a round of golf and they set off on a long walk around Lough Gill hoping to restore their appetites. After a light lunch, 'how sensible to have a choice of salads at lunch time,' Stephen remarked, they went on their separate ways for a couple of hours: Stephen to play golf; Rhoisin to explore more of Knockramore and hopefully look up Mrs Brothers. She wondered if she might even run into Mrs O'Hare.

Rhoisin walked up the main staircase, her hand on the smooth shiny mahogany rail she had polished so assiduously last year. Arriving in the Long Gallery, she began to study the family portraits with increasing interest. Next to a rather unattractive country scene was the door to the private apartment. Just a year ago she had been requested by Mrs O'Hare to clean the private apartment on a day she and her husband were going out to lunch. That was the day she had found the secret panel behind the portrait of a rather handsome gentleman wearing a Charles II style wig. And the secret panel had led to the hidden suite of rooms where she had discovered her long lost brother, crippled Roderick, and his mad grandmother, ninety-two-year-old Mrs O'Hare.

She turned the handle to the door of the private apartment, but it was locked. At that moment she saw a familiar female figure at the far end of the Long Gallery, watching her intently. She turned away and glanced at her watch. It was three o'clock, the 'dead' time in the kitchen quarters, a time when Mrs Brothers even tried to take a little nap in her armchair at the far end by the back door. It was the ideal time to seek out Mrs Brothers; to try and tease out more information about Lindsay O'Hare.

She retraced her steps down the wide staircase, again stroking the mahogany stair rail, unaware she was being followed. She crossed the wide hall, passing the empty dining room, where a servant was nonchalantly sweeping, dusting and tidying up for the evening meal. As she approached the door to the kitchen quarters, she experienced a slight shock of remembrance. This was the very spot where she had first almost bumped into Sean O'Hare as she carried a pile of heavy plates from the dining room to the kitchen. Sean O'Hare: the man she supposed was her father, but who had turned out in the end to be her wicked uncle. Well, he had got his just desserts.

She went through the swing door to the servery, a space containing a sink and cupboards, before the kitchen area was reached. Her stalker was now almost on top of her and as she turned the handle of the kitchen door, she felt a hand on her arm.

'I'm sorry, madam, but the kitchen is out of bounds to guests.'

Turning round, Rhoisin looked straight into the eyes of Lindsay O'Hare.

'Ruth! It is you! Have you come back to spy on me again?'

'Well, n… no. Of course not. I'm here on a holiday with my husband. I was just looking round for old times sake.'

Chapter Twenty-Seven

Rhoisin decided not to tell Stephen about her chance meeting with Mrs O'Hare. There was nothing he do about the accusation she was spying on Mrs O'Hare. Come to think of it, if their roles were reversed: if she were Mrs O'Hare, she might think she was being spied on too. Tomorrow she was meeting Miread, her half-sister. She would tell Miread all about being shadowed by Mrs O'Hare. Hopefully Miread would come up with a solution and then, once Mrs O'Hare knew that she and Miread had inherited the Knockramore estate, she would see things in a different light. But what that light might be Rhoisin couldn't rightly image at the moment.

After her little confrontation with Mrs O'Hare Rhoisin didn't feel up to chatting to Mrs Brothers. Having been reprimanded by the manager of the hotel, no less, it didn't seem appropriate to go hob-nobbing with the kitchen staff. She considered going for a swim in the heated indoor pool: not an activity that had been available to her a year ago in her post as a mere chambermaid. But suddenly she felt overwhelmed with tiredness, so she went up to the room, undressed, fell into bed and went fast asleep. She was still asleep when Stephen returned from his game of golf over two hours later.

As etiquette required at Knockramore Country House, Rhoisin and Stephen joined the other guests for a pre-dinner drink in the over-furnished drawing room. Small groups of guests were already there, chatting to each other, American accents predominating. After the compulsory drink, and afraid that Mrs O'Hare would come in at any moment and start her reprimands, Rhoisin led the way to a table for two in the furthest corner of the dining room. Stephen, always happy to follow wherever his wife led, was delighted to find their table had an excellent view of the golf course. And having played golf with three Americans all afternoon, he was more than happy to chat exclusively to his lovely new wife. During dinner Rhoisin continued to keep a weather eye out for the reappearance of Mrs O'Hare, but unbeknown to her, on Friday and Saturday nights Mrs O'Hare was on duty in the bar. The bar was open every evening to non-residents, a custom Lindsay O'Hare disliked intensely. On Fridays and Saturdays the drinkers could become rowdy and as the sole manager of the hotel since the death of her husband, Lindsay O'Hare felt she should be in charge on those two days in case any problems should arise.

Dinner was well-cooked, well-served and leisurely so it was after ten o'clock before they finished and Stephen suggested a night cap in the bar.

'Great idea,' said Rhoisin, leading the way. At the entrance to the bar she stopped dead in her tracks, causing Stephen to bump into her. There, serving drinks behind the counter was Lindsay O'Hare. She happened to look up just at that moment and saw Rhoisin in the doorway. Totally unnerved, she dropped a glass on the floor where it smashed into tiny pieces, shards flying everywhere. There was dead silence as one of the waiters swept up the pieces. White faced, Rhoisin made her way towards the staircase. Stephen caught up with her.

'You OK? You seem upset.'

Rhoisin took the stairs two at a time. Unlocking the door of their room, Stephen held it open for her. Rhoisin sat down on the end of the bed, shaking.

'My darling! What is it? What's upset you so much?'

'The lady at the bar. She's Uncle Sean's widow, the manager of Knockramore. She thinks I'm spying on her and she doesn't know I have inherited half of the estate.'

The following afternoon, promptly at four o'clock, Stephen drew the car to a halt outside Brigid Devlin's whitewashed rose-covered cottage. As he got out of the car to open the door for Rhoisin, a slim young lady of about Rhoisin's age came down the garden path. She looked so like Rhoisin that Stephen's heart missed a beat. When they met so briefly a year ago how could they have not known they were sisters? As Rhoisin stepped out of the passenger seat Miread came up and gave her a hug.

'Rhoisin? This is great. I'm Miread.' Seeing Stephen, she extended her hand. 'I'm Miread Devlin. You must be Stephen. I hope you're not upset I'm not inviting you in right away. But I'm sure you understand we have a great deal to discuss. Shall we meet up at the Laughing Goat in about two hours?'

'Of course. That's perfect.'

Watching the two girls walk up the garden path arm in arm, Stephen felt a lump rising in his throat. He got back hastily into the car and drove on down the road. He remembered to turn right just in time and found the car park by the side of the Laughing Goat. Looking up at the pub sign now hanging slightly crooked, swinging and creaking in the slight breeze, he thought the expression on the goat's face was rather menacing, almost evil. Following Rhoisin's suggestion he decided to take a walk through the town. After all, his wife owned half of an important estate in the area: it could only be a good idea to see how the land lay. Ever since Rhoisin's return from Killalee just a year ago, after her fruitless search for her father, Stephen had been curious to experience the town at first hand. Rhoisin had obviously fallen in love with Knockramore, the place that might have been her ancestral home if fate had deemed otherwise. But she hadn't thought much of Killalee.

'A leaden grey dump,' was how she had described it. 'Grey houses with front gardens filled with rubbish. Those poor sods who have to live in Killalee.'

'They probably don't know anywhere else,' Stephen had replied. 'They might even think they're well off.'

So now Stephen was going to experience Killalee at first hand. Following the sign for 'Town Centre', he walked down what he supposed was the main street towards the sea at the far end. The two-storey Victorian houses were not unattractive but they were certainly grey and rather neglected-looking. The paint on most of them needed renewing and many of the front gardens were piled with rubbish. There were a few shops displaying goods that wouldn't sell in a car boot sale in southeast England. It was a sad place, no doubt about it. He walked on to the end of the town and stood by the edge of the sea, an Atlantic inlet that curved its way past Sligo Town and beyond. In the other direction was Lough Gill, a freshwater inland lake: a fisherman's paradise. Straining his eyes he thought he could make out a castle, also leaden grey. Beyond the castle was a swathe of trees which hid Knockramore. Knockramore: his wife's new country estate. How often would they come here? he wondered. How long would they stay? At least Knockramore itself had a great deal to offer. He wondered how Rhoisin and her newly found half-sister were getting on. Had they made any decision about the tyrannical-sounding Mrs O'Hare who had accused Rhoisin of spying on her? Mrs O'Hare, who obviously thought the Knockramore estate should be hers and didn't yet know that it never would be.

Although it was mid-July, a chill wind blew up and Stephen turned up his coat collar. A coat in July! He should have been wearing shorts and sandals. That was the crux of the problem: the weather. The scenery was attractive; in places quite stunning. With the sea on one side and an expanse of lake on the other, it should surely be possible to turn Killalee and the surrounding area into a tourists' paradise. But this was no paradise, by any stretch of the imagination and there were certainly no tourists. He was the only person in sight. Then the clouds thickened, darkened and increased their speed; the heavens opened and the rain came down. Time to return to the pub, he thought.

Stephen arrived at the Laughing Goat soaking wet, and attempting to shake off the excess moisture on the doormat, he sent raindrops cascading all over the nearby tables and chairs. Feeling the sudden draught, the landlord looked up.

'It must be raining. You've made me chairs and tables all wet.'

'Yes. I am sorry, but they'll dry off.'

'People dry off too.'

'Yes. I'm sorry.' Stephen considered leaving and sitting outside in the car, but realised he would have to come into the pub at some point to meet Rhoisin and Miread. He laid his coat on one of the wet chairs and walked up to the bar.

'A glass of red wine, please.'

'A glass of red wine! Sure and we don't serve wine by the glass. Who would finish the bottle?'

'D... don't other people in Killalee drink wine?'

'No. That's for sure and they don't. I'd have to finish the bottle all on me own and that mightn't be so good for business. I can offer you stout, bitter or a whiskey. I've got both the Irish whiskeys: Powers and Jameson's. The Powers is Catholic and the Jameson's is Protestant.'

Stephen was surprised. 'Catholic and Protestant whiskey? Is it usual in Ireland to have whiskey with a religious flavour?'

'Oh, it is, certainly. Ireland is a country with a strong religious bias. Religion comes into everything in Ireland: especially in the North.'

Stephen wasn't sure that he wanted to enter into a religious discussion with a total stranger. 'I'll have a whiskey, please: the Catholic one.'

'Right you are, sir. Neat, water or soda, sir?'

'A little water, please.

The landlord mixed the drink and handed it over. 'What part of England are yous from?'

'London.'

'London?' The landlord's eyes widened. 'I believe London's very large and very noisy. It must be hard to find any peace and quiet in London.'

'Well, there are little oases...' Stephen regretted his choice of words.

'Oases? Like in the desert?'

'Well, not quite.'

Stephen took a sip of whiskey and looked around the pub. It was completely empty.

'Not very busy for a Saturday,' he ventured.

'Ah, but it's still early on. We'll fill up later.'

'Oh, good.'

'Would you like a sandwich to help steady your drink?'

A sandwich! The thought hadn't occurred to him.

'Do you do egg mayonnaise?'

'Funny you should ask for egg mayonnaise. There was a young lady from London in here about a year ago and she asked for egg mayonnaise. Maybe it's a London thing, egg mayonnaise.'

The Leicester Square sandwich bar flashed through Stephen's mind's eye: egg mayonnaise oozing out of the thick succulent sandwich, translucent, palely yellow… And the waitress intoning dully: 'White bread, rye bread, granary bread, French bread, pitta-bread, Nan-bread or pumpernickel…'

'Yes, why not? What sort of bread do you have?'

'Not much choice, I'm afraid. Mother's Pride sliced white is all I do have. But I don't have no more eggs. The lodgers eat them all up at breakfast. But I can do you a cheese and pickle.'

Rhoisin's description of the construction of the cheese and pickle sandwich flashed through Stephen's mind. It seemed to involve a great deal of nose wiping and other rather unsavoury activities.

'No, thanks. I think I'll just stick to the Catholic whiskey.'

'That'll be two pounds fifty, please.'

Stephen handed over a fiver, picked up his change and took his whiskey to the farthest seat away from the bar.

He looked at his watch: ten past five. Nearly an hour before the arrival of Rhoisin and Miread. He wasn't accustomed to waiting for people. He was more accustomed to people waiting for him. It was a curious situation. Neither he nor Rhoisin knew exactly how things would turn out. No one seemed to be in control of anything, not even the lawyers. The person who was least in control was Stephen himself. Although not a control freak as such, he did prefer to know what direction events were taking. As far as he could ascertain the situation surrounding the Knockramore estate didn't seem to have any direction at all.

The whiskey measure was generous; probably double that of a measure in London. Stephen lay back with his head against the wall and fell fast asleep.

Just before six o'clock Rhoisin and Miread came into the Laughing Goat. Looking around for Stephen, Rhoisin burst out laughing when she saw he was fast asleep. She came over and sat beside him.

'Wakey, wakey, darling. We've arrived. Miread is here.'

Miread went up to the bar. 'Hello, Mike.'

'Oh, hello, Miread. So you've graced us with another visit. That another new boyfriend?' he nodded towards Stephen.

'No. He's just a friend. My sister's husband.'

'Your *sister's* husband. I didn't know you had a sister.'

'Nor did I. She just showed up.'

'Well, I never. And what'll you have?'

'Two port and lemon, please.'

'So you have a sister?'

Mike couldn't wait to impart the news to his Saturday night customers later this evening.

258

Chapter Twenty-Eight

By half past midnight on Saturday, when she had closed the bar and supervised the clearing up, Lindsay O'Hare was completely exhausted. On that particular Saturday she was more than usually stressed out. She was haunted by the presence of Ruth Hobson. Only a year ago Ruth had been merely a chambermaid at Knockramore Country House. Now it appeared she was a guest. Why had Ruth returned to Knockramore? And how could she find out? She dragged herself off to bed in her as yet temporary quarters and slept badly.

Lindsay O'Hare slept late and left Knockramore around midday to lunch with her friends, Colin and Alison Monroe. Colin and Alison had been good friends over the last eight years and Lindsay was looking forward to her visit.

'But who *has* inherited Knockramore?' enquired Alison over the delicious homemade lemon mousse.

'No one seems to know,' replied Lindsay.

'But that's absurd,' protested Colin, helping himself to a generous second portion. 'Didn't Sean leave a will?'

'Apparently not.'

'How extraordinary! He always seemed so well organised.'

'Exactly. That's what I thought.'

'Isn't there a will at all then?'

'Yes. Apparently my deceased brother-in-law made a will shortly before he was killed in a car accident.'

'Oh, the accident,' said Alison. 'I remember the accident quite well, although it was at least eleven years ago. Quite a while before your arrival on the O'Hare scene, Lindsay.'

'Yes. Sean told me about the accident. He said Roderick, his nephew, survived but was badly injured and being well looked after in a spinal injury unit in Dublin. I did think it odd that he perished in that dreadful fire along with his grandmother and his nurse.'

'Didn't you know Roderick and his grandmother were living at Knockramore?'

'No. I had no idea.'

'Isn't that rather strange? After all, you were virtually running the hotel on your own. Someone must have sent meals up to them. And you didn't know anything about it?'

'With hindsight I do think it's extraordinary I never suspected anything. It occurred to me after the fire. I would have asked Sean about it, of course, but then he was killed in a car crash.'

'Two brothers, each killed in a different car crash. A strange coincidence.'

Colin felt he should change the subject. 'You mentioned a few moments ago that your brother-in-law left a will. Do you know what's in the will?'

'No. Not yet. Wills are confidential, so my lawyer tells me. Only the beneficiaries are permitted to know the contents.'

'But surely, as the only surviving O'Hare, you should be allowed to see your brother-in-law's will?'

'Apparently not. But I do intend to press the issue further. There's another strange thing I haven't mentioned.

A year ago I engaged a chambermaid called Ruth Hobson. The odd thing about Ruth was that she didn't seem the sort of girl to apply for a job as a chambermaid. She was too well-bred and far too intelligent. One day I found her poking around, examining the paintings in the Long Gallery as if she was looking for something. She was staying in the house on the night of the fire. Well, she's come back to Knockramore as a guest and her presence gives me an uneasy feeling.'

Alison laughed. 'I think you're just a bit overwrought, Lindsay. You're not having it easy at the moment: that's quite plain to see. Why don't you stay overnight? The room's all made up. Then we can have a nice boozy dinner and you can drive back in the morning.'

Lindsay O'Hare was sorely tempted by Alison's suggestion. 'I'd love to, but Monday is Mrs Brother's day off so I have to be up early to supervise breakfast.'

'And Mrs Brothers is…?'

'The cook/housekeeper: the bedrock of Knockramore.'

Colin and Alison managed to persuade Lindsay to stay for a light supper.

'We won't have too much to drink,' promised Colin.

It was 9.30 and not quite dark as Lindsay left the Monroe's house on the twenty minute drive back to Knockramore. Tomorrow will be another heavy day, she thought as she prepared for bed. Mrs Brothers' day off always increased her workload.

'I'll take a couple of sleeping pills,' she said to herself. 'Then I'll be sure of a good night's rest.'

She went into the bathroom and looked in the medicine chest. She seemed to be out of the sleeping pills her doctor had prescribed after the fire. However, there were more bottles in the cupboard she hadn't noticed before. Some of them bore Sean's name rather than hers. But sleeping pills are sleeping pills, she thought. It won't make any difference whether they have been prescribed for Sean or for me. She selected a bottle exactly similar to the one that was empty. The label said: *'Mr Sean O'Hare: one or two to be taken at night.'* To be on the safe side she took two and chased them down with a large tot of whiskey, which she always kept in the bedside table for these sort of emergencies. Climbing thankfully into bed, she turned off the light and fell asleep almost immediately.

Lindsay never woke up. She died in her sleep.

There was great consternation at Knockramore when it was discovered that Lindsay O'Hare had died. Only the staff were informed. It was deemed unnecessary to inform the guests. After all, if the manager of a well-known and renowned country house hotel dies in her bed, the same misfortune might befall any of the guests. In her early forties and in the peak of health Lindsay O'Hare appeared a most unlikely victim of sudden death.

The post mortem revealed some sinister and unexpected information: a large amount of arsenic was found in Mrs O'Hare's stomach. All the medicine bottles in the bathroom cabinet were thoroughly checked and several of those with Sean O'Hare's name on were found to contain poison. It was assumed Sean O'Hare was either planning to end his own life or that of someone else. The discovery of traces of arsenic in Lindsay O'Hare's stomach indicated that she might have been poisoned.

But who would want to poison Lindsay O'Hare?

The police were called in and everyone at Knockramore was interviewed. They called in the staff first and then all the guests, one by one. Mrs Brothers gave the longest statement. She told the police all she knew about the wills: the one she had witnessed and the one that had never existed. She told the police that Thomas O'Hare had bequeathed the Knockramore estate to his two daughters, Rhoisin Hobbs and her half-sister, Miread Devlin, both born out of wedlock, which had resulted in Lindsay O'Hare inheriting nothing. She told them that on Sunday, the last day that Mrs O'Hare was seen alive, she had gone to have lunch with friends, Colin and Alison Monroe who lived locally. She didn't mention Ruth Hobson. She didn't think it was necessary.

The police sergeant went to visit Mr and Mrs Monroe.

'Mr Monroe? Good afternoon. I'm Police Sergent Murphy. I'm investigating the very sudden and unfortunate death of Mrs Lindsay O'Hare.'

'Oh, no! Lindsay's dead! Surely not?' Alison Munroe covered her mouth in horror. 'I can't believe it! She was here just a few days ago. She seemed quite well.'

'So I've been informed by several witnesses at the Knockramore Hotel.'

'So, what happened? How did she die?' Colin went over to sit by his wife on the sofa and took her hand.

'She died in her sleep last week. On the night of Sunday and Monday shortly after her visit to you here.'

'Do you know the cause?'

'The post mortem has found there were considerable traces of arsenic in her stomach.'

'*Arsenic!* You mean... someone tried to poison her?'

'That is a possibility. We cannot rule out anything at this stage.'

'How simply dreadful!' Alison was shaking so much that Colin put his arm around her.

'Have you any inkling who that person might be, Sergeant?'

'Again, not at this stage. May I ask how long you have known Lindsay O'Hare?'

'At least eight years. We met her shortly before she married Sean O'Hare.'

'And how well did you know her?'

'Oh, quite well, really. Not that we saw her or Sean very often. They were both extremely busy running the Knockramore estate, which I'm sure you know is quite a considerable one.'

'Yes, of course. As the last people to see Mrs O'Hare alive I'm sure you understand that your testimony is crucially important,' said Sergeant Murphy, a notebook poised on his knee. 'Would you be able to describe her state of mind? Was she in a good frame of mind? Did she seem happy or was she anxious?'

Colin looked thoughtful. Alison sat immobile, clutching her husband's hand tightly.

'I couldn't say Lindsay seemed happy,' said Colin. 'Her greatest concern was that she had inherited nothing at all. It appears her deceased husband left no will...'

Sergeant Murphy nodded. This confirmed what Mrs Brothers had told him earlier, but he said nothing to Mr and Mrs Monroe.

'Something else also seemed to upset her.'

'Yes?'

'She thought she was being spied on by one of the guests.'

'Spied on by a guest?' Sergeant Murphy made more notes. 'Do you know the name of the guest?'

'A young lady called Ruth Hobson. A year ago Mrs O'Hare engaged her as a chambermaid at Knockramore. She happened to be there when the terrible fire broke out. And then, according to Lindsay, Ruth Hobson came back to stay in the hotel as a guest.'

'Ruth Hobson.' Sergeant Murphy wrote the name on his notepad. ' Thank you, Mr Monroe. That will be all for the moment. I'll see myself out.'

Sergeant Murphy drove back to Knockramore and asked to see the hotel register. He went through every entry for the last three weeks but found no one named Ruth Hobson. It didn't occur to him to interview Mrs Brothers once again. Mrs Brothers had already given her testimony and Sergeant Murphy was fully satisfied. Finally, the police decided to reopen the file on the events that had taken place on the night of the fire just over a year ago.

As she was not on the staff at Knockramore, nor had she been staying there as a guest, Miread was not interviewed by the police. She heard the news a week later when she popped into the Laughing Goat before returning to Dublin. The pub was agog with the revelations. As soon as he saw her coming through the door, Mike, the landlord, called her over to the bar.

'Miread! Have you heard the latest news from Knockramore?'

'No. What is it?'

'Lindsay O'Hare is dead.'

'Dead? Lindsay O'Hare? How did she die? Another car crash? Not another fire?'

'No, Neither of those. She died asleep in her bed. Arsenic was found in her stomach. They say she was poisoned.'

'Good God!'

In the evening Miread phoned Rhoisin in London.

'Hi, Rhoisin! It's Miread here. I've got some rather grisly news. Mrs O'Hare died in her bed last week. The post mortem found traces of arsenic in her stomach. The police think she might have been poisoned!'

On the fateful Monday morning Rhoisin and Stephen had left Knockramore before Lindsay O'Hare's body was discovered. They were on their way to Dublin in their hired car to catch the plane for their return journey to London as the news broke of Lindsay O'Hare's death. Miread's phone call was the first they had heard of it. Rhoisin was stunned.

'Mrs O'Hare is dead! Any suspects?'

'Not yet.'

'Well, I'm sorry, of course. But it simplifies our problem, doesn't it? Now we don't have to work out how to tell her it's us who have inherited Knockramore.'

'And we don't have to explain that we were planning to give her a generous subsistence allowance. She might have found it very embarrassing.'

'Keep me posted about the funeral arrangements.'

'Of course.'

It was slowly beginning to dawn on Miread that her life had changed completely. However, looking at herself close up in the mirror she didn't think her appearance had changed too much. Perhaps a few bags under the eyes? And those little lines at the side. What had caused them? Not laughing, that was for sure.

Her financial circumstances had completely changed for the better. Mr Geoghan had set up a new account for her in the Baggot Street Branch of the Bank of Ireland. The same bank where she had toiled away for five and a half years, mainly dealing with customers' complaints. It was an odd feeling to make an appointment with her old boss to discuss the intricacies of managing her substantial amount of money: money most people would only dream about: money she had no idea existed until six months ago.

As the secretary showed Miread into the small office where she had had her last meeting with Mr Doyle, her old boss, just over a year ago, he got up to greet her.

'Congratulations on your newly acquired fortune, Miss Devlin. Your life has certainly taken a change for the better since our last meeting.'

'Yes, it certainly has.' Miread thought of the last meeting. 'Miss Devlin, as you are not a university graduate, the bank regrets it is unable to offer you any further promotion.'

She beamed across at Mr Doyle, wondering if the same thought was crossing his mind too.

'So Mr Geoghan has set up a handsome monthly payment to go into this account, Miss Devlin. Will you want to keep your old personal account open?'

Miread thought for a moment. 'I don't really think there's much point. Do you?'

'I wouldn't have thought so. Are you... er... are you still in employment?'

'Well, no, actually. I gave up my job last week. I've enrolled at UCD to read for a law degree, starting in the autumn.'

Mr Doyle's eyebrows shot up. 'A law course! So you're planning to be a lawyer!'

'Well, I'll start off by doing the course. It's a four year course, so I'll see how it goes.'

'Of course.' Mr Doyle stood up and extended his hand. 'Well, goodbye, Miss Devlin. I'm delighted about your happy news all round and if there's anything I can do, just let me know.'

'Thank you, Mr Doyle.'

'You see, dear, I've just turned sixty and I'm really not up to running Knockramore any longer.'

Mrs Brothers gave Miread a long hard look. Goodness! She and Ruth were like peas in a pod! How could they not have realised at their first meeting that they were sisters? Well, half-sisters, but still sisters for all that.

Miread smiled warmly. She had enormous respect for Mrs Brothers and all she had done for Knockramore over more than forty years.

'I know Mrs B. I do understand and I really can't thank you enough for all your excellent hard work. Of course a manager will have to be found to run this huge place, sooner rather than later. How do I go about finding one?'

'Well dear, you could advertise in all the papers. The Dublin ones would probably be best. You mightn't get the right type of person if you were to restrict yourself to the *Sligo Herald*. Sligo's a bit of a small town, if you follow me.'

Miread nodded. 'A good idea.'

'Another possibility is to go to one of those recruiting agencies; by which I don't mean the Job Centre. I don't think you'd find the right type of person at the Job Centre. But go up to Dublin, dear. You enjoy Dublin, don't you? Your Mam always said how happy you were in Dublin: that you found Killalee too quiet altogether.'

'Well, I suppose Killalee's not too bad. But, yes, I much prefer Dublin.'

Miread returned to Dublin and scoured the recruiting agencies. Within a week she had found a young couple in their early thirties, well-qualified in hotel management, who were delighted at the prospect of running a hotel as prestigious as the Knockramore Country House.

And Mrs Brothers agreed to stay on as long as it was necessary to help the new managers find their feet.

When Lindsay O'Hare's body was finally released for burial in late October, Miread realised the funeral arrangements would be her responsibility. Although not an O'Hare actually in name, she and Rhoisin were, in effect, the last remaining descendants of the O'Hare family who had lived at Knockramore for over four hundred years. It was not a responsibility to be undertaken lightly.

Miread was now dividing her time between Dublin and Killalee. Although it was no longer necessary for her to have a job, Dublin provided the stimulus and excitement in her life. Killalee supplied the hard work. In Dublin there was Gerry, warm, energetic, amusing and marvellous in bed. If she was away for more than a week from Dublin and Gerry, Miread became randy and irritable. Although she and Gerry had discussed marriage in a general way, Gerry had made no formal proposal. He was working insanely hard to become an articled clerk of the court. He would be qualified in a few weeks, so Miread just lived on in hope.

In Killalee there was her mother, Brigid and her inane, repulsive half-brother, Eamon. Miread couldn't decide whether she was protecting her mother more from loneliness or the embarrassment of having spawned such a hideous son.

Then there was the Knockramore estate. Miread felt far less emotionally tied to Knockramore than Rhoisin. Rhoisin still had fantasies about how her life would have been if she had been brought up in Knockramore. Miread completely understood Rhoisin's more intense feelings. After all, she had lost her mother recently and had never had any siblings until the brief discovery of Roderick. But Miread was of a much more pragmatic disposition and saw Knockramore as a practical challenge. The house was run as a prestigious hotel with a fine reputation and she felt it was now largely up to her that this reputation was maintained and the hotel run to the highest standard. Although immeasurably grateful to loyal, hard-working Mrs Brothers, whom she had generously pensioned off, Miread felt it was now time to engage a highly qualified chef of international standing to supply more cachet. On her next visit to Dublin she called in at the recruiting agency, where she had engaged the couple who were now successfully managing Knockramore. She engaged a chef on a month's trial, which meant she was required to dine in the restaurant quite frequently, an event which her mother thoroughly enjoyed.

When she stayed in Killalee there were almost daily visits to Knockramore so a car was now essential. Miread purchased a silver four-seater BMW, which was soon recognisable to everyone in the neighbourhood as she shot around from Sligo Town to Knockramore and back to Killalee.

Miread discussed the funeral arrangements with her mother.

'I think the private chapel at Knockramore is too small for the funeral. I'd like to invite all the residents of Killalee to pay their respects to the last named member of the O'Hare family and perhaps hold the wakes at the Laughing Goat. What do you think, Mam?'

'It sounds a very good idea to me.'

Miread went to see the parish priest in Killalee.

'Of course, Miread. I think that's a splendid idea. Let me look at the appointments book. Now... let me see. How about Friday 3 November? Say midday. Does that give you enough time to arrange all the food for the wakes?'

'That's great, Father. Thanks a lot.'

'Let me know if you need anything, Miread. You're a great girl to organise all this.'

Miread smiled wanly. 'Someone has to do it, Father.'

Father Ignatius didn't know about her inheritance. Practically no one in Killalee knew about it. That was the whole point of inviting the whole neighbourhood to the funeral. She was going to give a speech, a eulogy she would call it, informing everyone of what had happened.

Next she called in to see Mike at the Laughing Goat.

'Mike, would you be prepared to hold the wakes for Lindsay O'Hare at the Laughing Goat? All expenses would be covered, of course.'

'The wakes here? Sure and that would be great. And when would you be wanting it?'

'Friday 3 November. It's only five days away. Can you manage that?'

'It depends on what you would be wanting. The usual stout and bitter? A few bottles of whiskey?'

'Yes. And could you order some wine?'

'Wine? I don't know a great deal about wine, young Miread. Sure not many of the people around here do drink wine.'

'OK,' said Miread shortly. 'I'll arrange the wine. Now we'll need food. It'll be lunch time. They shouldn't drink without something to eat. What can you offer, Mike?'

'Sandwiches? There's me cheese an' pickle. That always goes down well with the locals.'

Rhoisin's unsavoury description of Mike's cheese and pickle sandwich flashed through Miread's mind's eye.

'I was thinking more of canapés… and perhaps some cheese on sticks and vol-au-vents?'

'Miread, I'm not a French chef. I'm just a simple publican. Since you've gone to live in Dublin your ideas have got a bit too ambitious for these parts. Listen, you arrange your canapés and I'll just offer up what I've got here in the premises.'

Miread tried not to feel annoyed.

'OK, Mike. I'll order the food in Sligo Town and have it sent over. Thanks for lending the pub, anyway.'

Miread drove to Sligo Town, parked in the car park near the centre and went to the post office. She looked up 'caterers' in the Yellow Pages and made a few phone calls. One sounded quite promising.

'I'll be round in ten minutes.'

Miread placed a substantial order for 'finger food', as they called it, paid a 50% deposit and arranged for it to be delivered to the Laughing Goat in Killalee on Friday 3 November around 10.00 am.

'The Laughing Goat? Are you serious?' asked the callow youth who had taken the order. 'I've never heard of a pub called the Laughing Goat.'

'I'm serious, I'm not laughing.' Miread was tempted to say: 'like a goat.' That's what the pub is called.'

'Well, I never. We'll see to all that for you, Miss Devlin.'

Miread went next door to the off license and asked to see their wine list. With a little thought she ordered one dozen bottles of Côtes du Rhône and a dozen of Orvieto Classico.

'Please deliver it to the Laughing Goat in Killalee before next Friday. The landlord is expecting it. He'll sign for it.'

The middle-aged assistant wrote down the address without batting an eyelid. 'Certainly, madam.'

Miread paid for the wine and drove back to Killalee for lunch.

'I'm home, Mam! All done. Mission accomplished.'

With all the arrangements in place for Lindsay O'Hare's funeral and several days to spare before it actually took place, Miread drove up to Dublin. She wanted to see Gerry and as she had nothing suitable to wear for the funeral, she needed to do a bit of shopping in Grafton Street. She needed an outfit that was both smart and sober. In Brown Thomas she found the perfect solution: a well-cut charcoal grey trouser suit, which she planned to lighten up a little with a light coloured sweater and matching scarf. An expensive pair of black Ferragamo shoes and matching handbag completed her outfit.

She called Gerry on the phone the night before her departure.

'I'll book a nice restaurant,' he said over the phone. 'I've got a surprise present for you.'

'That'll be nice,' said Miread, her heart thumping a little. I wonder what that'll be, she thought.

The restaurant Gerry had booked was a newly opened French restaurant in a mews off Baggot Street. Gerry wore and suit and tie. Miread looked especially lovely in a cream dress with a black jacket. She had taken special care with her make up, the mascara accentuating her sparkling grey eyes. As they sat down at the table Gerry placed a small box in front of her.

'Your special present, darling. I hope you will marry me. I love you very much.'

Gerry drove Miread down to Killalee in her four-seater BMW. They realised they might need the extra space to ferry Miread's mother to the private burial at Knockramore cemetery. As soon as they arrived at Brigid Devlin's cottage Miread gave her mother a big hug. 'Mam, Gerry and I are engaged to be married.'

Mrs Devlin beamed. 'It's just what I've been hoping for. I know you'll both be very happy.'

The day of Lindsay O'Hare's funeral on Friday 3 November dawned grey and cloudy with the light drizzling rain so typical of the West of Ireland. Why does it so often rain on funerals? thought Miread. Isn't it bad enough having to bury the dead without rain into the bargain?

Brigid accompanied Miread and Gerry down to the Killalee parish church. The funeral car was outside the church, the door open at the back, the coffin fully visible, four pall bearers waiting to carry it inside. Father Ignatius shook Miread's hand.

'You're a grand girl, Miread. You've a full congregation to welcome you and I'm sure everything will go smoothly. You've planned it all well enough.'

Miread led the way up the aisle followed by Brigid and Gerry. Her smart new Ferragamo handbag hung loosely over her shoulder containing the carefully written copy of her eulogy. She and Father Ignatius had drawn up the order of service together. It was agreed he would invite her up to the lectern at the appropriate moment and introduce her to the congregation.

As the last verse of the hymn died away, Miread walked slowly up to the chancel steps, clutching her script.

'Perhaps not everybody present knows Miread Devlin, who was born and bred in these parts...' He looked across at her and smiled. 'Just when you're ready, Miread.'

Miread opened her script, her hands shaking slightly.

'A funeral is always a sad occasion, especially if it is for a young or even a middle aged person. Lindsay O'Hare was only forty-two when she died in her sleep nearly four months ago. Thorough police investigations have failed to confirm whether the arsenic found in her stomach was taken by her own hand or placed within reach by someone else. Lindsay O'Hare was widowed just a year earlier so she may have been suffering from depression. It is not well known in Killalee that Lindsay O'Hare inherited nothing from the Knockramore estate due to the fact that her late husband, Sean O'Hare, did not leave a will. The only known will was the one left by

Sean's brother, Thomas, who died in a road accident a few months after making the will. I only discovered after Sean O'Hare's death that I, and my half-sister, Rhoisin are the daughters of Thomas O'Hare, born out of wedlock. And to make amends for the fact that he did not do the decent thing in marrying our mothers, Thomas O'Hare left his entire estate to be divided between me and my sister, Rhoisin.'

A gasp went up from the congregation and everyone started to chat. Father Ignatius held up his hand for silence. 'Please let Miread finish.'

'So although Lindsay O'Hare is the last person to bear the O'Hare name at present, Rhoisin and I are now established as the joint owners of Knockramore. After the service I hope you will all go along to the Laughing Goat, where Mike and I have laid on refreshments.'

Clapping and cheering broke out as Miread returned to her front pew.

At the end of the service the congregation filed out of the church and crowded round Miread.

'Congratulations, Miread!'

Whoever would have thought…!'

'I had no idea…'

The congratulations continued for a good fifteen minutes, everyone milling around. Finally Father Ignatius persuaded everyone to continue chatting in the Laughing Goat.

'There is one more practical matter to effect,' he explained. 'The body of Lindsay O'Hare must be taken to the burial ground at Knockramore and interred in the private cemetery. Miread, Gerry, Brigid, Mary and I will join you all in the Laughing Goat as soon as we can.'

With that Father Ignatius opened the door of the funeral car for Miread and waited as her mother and Mrs Brothers climbed in after her. The car took them straight to the cemetery at Knockramore where the sombre little group stood around the freshly dug grave. They watched as the coffin was carefully lowered into the hole and Father Ignatius intoned prayers for the dead. As he sprinkled holy water over the coffin, the grave digger heaped in the earth. The sad little ceremony took less than ten minutes and in less than half an hour the small group was back at the Laughing Goat.

Here the mood was quite different and in total contrast to the sombre atmosphere in the cemetery. Drinks had been served, food was being passed round and all the mourners were laughing and joking. The hilarity struck Miread as almost obscene. However, she thought, few of the people in Killalee had ever met Lindsay O'Hare and no one had known her well. Come to think of it, although she was considered to be the chief mourner, she had never met Lindsay O'Hare either. She had taken on the role partly on behalf of Rhoisin, who had known Lindsay O'Hare, but most of all because, although she didn't carry the O'Hare name, she was definitely a member of the family.

Chapter Twenty-Nine

Rhoisin threw up after breakfast. Then she went back to bed and slept for two hours. Feeling better, she ate a light lunch and took a bus to Regent's Park, hoping the fresh air would make her feel better. It was a sultry day in mid-September with a hazy sunshine caused by the heavy traffic pollution of a large and great city.

After a gentle hour's stroll Rhoisin took the bus back to Upper Street and walked the short distance to Almeida Street. Stephen was away in New York. He had asked her to come along too, but Rhoisin was beginning to tire of the hectic pace of New York. She preferred London, in places also hectic but with many quiet parks and squares, almost totally absent in New York .

The following morning she was sick again after breakfast. A thought occurred to her: could I be pregnant? The natural product of lovemaking and being married. She made an appointment to see her doctor.

'Yes. Your symptoms certainly make it sound as if you are pregnant.' The doctor handed Rhoisin a bottle. 'The toilet is next door. Just leave the urine sample at the appointment desk on your way out. We'll let you know, Mrs Piper.'

And that was that. Short and sweet, thought Rhoisin. However, it's not her baby who might be on the way: it's mine.

She spent a gentle quiet day pottering around the house and before retiring early to bed she phoned Miread.

'Hi, Miread! It's me. Rhoisin. I've got some great news. I think I'm pregnant!'

'That's marvellous! Congratulations, Roosh!'

'I knew you'd be delighted. The O'Hare dynasty will continue. The less good news is that I'm as sick as a dog every morning and totally exhausted all the time. My doctor says this is quite normal. It's the price that women pay to society for the privilege of giving birth.'

'He didn't say that. Surely not.'

'Yes, *she* did, which I think makes it even worse.'

'Maybe you should change your doctor.'

'Not as easy as it sounds over here. We have something called the National Health Service. The standard of care depends on your postcode.'

'Oh, I see,' said Miread; but she didn't.

Although excited at the prospect at the birth of her first baby, Rhoisin was feeling a little bit out on a limb. She discovered that being a research assistant at the BBC wasn't all it was cracked up to be, so she had given up her job two weeks ago. OK, she was working for the prestigious BBC: that was great cachet and would look good on her CV; but was it going to lead anywhere? And where was her CV going to lead her? She had made a good career start with a 2-1 in History from London University. Then after her boring stint selling tickets at the Duke of York's Theatre she had made the big decision to go to the West of Ireland in search of her father. And what a strange and upsetting experience that had been! To be reunited with her long lost brother for the first time only to lose him in that terrible fire.

VALERIE HANSARD

Then to discover her father had died in an accident eleven years earlier. And finally, to meet for the first time her half sister, Miread, and be given the news that they had inherited the Knockramore estate between them.

All that money! Rhoisin had never had much money – ever. Now it was pouring into the new bank account that Roger Grieves had set up for her at Coutts Bank in The Strand. What should she do with all the money? There must surely be something useful she could do with it. Should she do a course? Open a new business? One evening she broached the subject to Stephen.

'I've got all this money, darling, just pouring into my Coutts bank account.'

Stephen laughed. 'I think that's great.'

'It is of course. But what am I going to do with it?

'Why, spend it. What else does one do with money.'

'But what on? I've got everything I want. I don't need more clothes. I hardly go anywhere except to the theatre with you. We've got this lovely house and soon it'll be mortgage free.'

'That's fantastic: to have a house free of a mortgage in one of Islington's most sought-after streets.'

'Yes, I know. It's wonderful. But it still doesn't solve my problem.'

Stephen came over and sat beside her on the sofa and put his arm around her.

'What's your problem?'

'I don't seem to have any direction in life. No real purpose.'

Stephen's arm tightened around her shoulder. 'You've got me.'

'Yes, I know.' Rhoisin snuggled close to him. 'But you're so self-contained. You just get on with your life

280

and your job marshalling actresses into better roles. You can do all that without me.'

'I hope you don't feel entirely left out of my life. We live in the same house, eat at the same table and share the same bed. I think you are a perfect wife.'

'Well, I'm glad. Perhaps I'm expecting too much from life. Maybe I'm being greedy.'

'Greedy? Why greedy? You've hardly touched your inheritance, except to pay off my mortgage. Then there's the baby on the way. Aren't you looking forward to the birth of the baby?'

'Oh, very much. I think it's the waiting that's getting me down.'

The following day Miread telephoned.

'Hi, Roosh! It's me, Miread. How're you doing?'

'I'm OK. The morning sickness has stopped and the baby's beginning to show. But...'

'But what?'

'I'm bored, Miread. I don't seem to have enough to do to keep me occupied. I gave up my job in the BBC research department because it was boring and it wasn't going anywhere. Now I rather regret it.'

'Ah!'

'You're so lucky. You've got your degree course to work for.'

'But you did a degree course when you were far younger than I am now. I'm what's called a 'mature student' at the age of twenty-four! Sure, I'll be twenty-eight before I'm qualified. Perhaps you should do a course in something. Get some brochures and get stuck into something after Christmas. You've still got nearly six months before the arrival of the baby. I hope you're looking forward to it?'

'Oh, yes. It's the waiting that's getting me down.'

'Listen, Rhoisin. I'm going to come and visit you. My term ends on 8 December. How if I come and stay with you for a few days before Christmas?'

Rhoisin was more delighted than she thought she would be to see her sister again. Miread was full of energy and enthusiasm: qualities Rhoisin now realised she sadly lacked. On Miread's first evening Stephen was, as usual, out at the theatre so Rhoisin booked a table at the Almeida Restaurant.

'It's just across the road,' she explained to Miread. 'And it has the added advantage of being one of the better restaurants in Islington.'

They both dressed quite smartly. 'Of course it's not mandatory,' said Rhoisin. 'You know what it's like nowadays: people dine in really smart restaurants in torn jeans and trainers. But the Almeida is a restaurant where you don't look too out of place if you're well dressed.'

'I know you like this table, Mrs Piper,' said the manager as he showed them to one of the best tables in a corner. 'And you won't be disturbed too much by the other diners, I hope.'

They ordered their food and before it arrived Miread started straight into Rhoisin's problems.

'You're bored, Roosh? Yes? That's what you said on the phone. Why are you bored? You should be up and running and having a go at everything. You've got the money to do exactly what you want. We both have.'

Rhoisin sighed. 'Yes I know. Perhaps it's having all the money that makes me... well, a bit lethargic.'

'Could be the pregnancy. Your growing another person. That must be quite tiring.'

'It's partly the pregnancy. But I was lethargic before I became pregnant. I just don't seem to have enough to do.'

'Despite nurturing another human being?'

'It appears so.'

'What about Stephen? Have you told him?'

'Yes, I have.'

'Has he come with any suggestions?'

'Not really. He's so engrossed in his own work. He's out all day meeting prospective film and theatre stars and then watching them act in the theatre most evenings.'

'Do you go with him to the theatre?'

'Yes, But not to everything. Some of the plays are dreadful and then Stephen comes home in a right bad mood.'

'So you feel a bit detached from Stephen's work.'

'Very detached.'

'How about Stephen's parents? Do you get on well with them?'

'We hardly ever see them. Strange you should ask about them, but the few times I've met them I don't feel they have any connection with Stephen at all.'

'What do you mean exactly?'

'Well, I know it sounds weird, but I have difficulty in believing they are really his parents.'

'You mean, you think Stephen may have been adopted?'

'I don't know. I've never asked him.'

'It sounds as if Stephen and you are living different lives.'

'Yes, perhaps we do some of the time.'

'What about friends? Do you have many friends in London?'

There was a heavy pause. 'You'll hardly believe this, Miread, but I have no friends in London .'

'None?'

'No. Not any more. I had Julie but she emigrated to Australia a couple of years ago.'

'But that's awful – to have no friends.' Miread was quite shocked. 'But at school and at uni, didn't you bring friends home and go for sleep-overs at each others' houses?'

Rhoisin sighed. 'There's something I haven't told you, Miread. My mother never allowed me to bring friends home to the flat.'

'Why?'

'Well, it was because of all the people she had coming and going. Men. You see, my mum was a courtesan.'

Miread gasped. 'A courtesan! And you knew all about it?'

'No. I knew nothing about it until after her death. Then I found all her letters. That's how I found out about my father – our father.'

Poor Rhoisin, thought Miread. She's had such a mixed up life she still can't get things sorted out. I'll have to come up with a plan: something she can get her teeth into and put a bit of sparkle back into her life. And Stephen doesn't seem to be as involved as he should be in his young wife's life.

Miread spent four days staying with Rhoisin and Stephen at Number 10 Almeida Street. She and Rhoisin painted the town red. They went on shopping trips to Harrods and Harvey Nicks, visited the National Gallery and took in two musicals: a quite different kind of theatrical entertainment to the ones Stephen patronised.

By the time Miread left Rhoisin was exhausted but in a much happier frame of mind.

Miread tried to persuade Rhoisin to visit Killalee for Christmas.

'I'd love to, but it's not possible. We have to spend Christmas with Stephen's parents in their mock Tudor home in the stockbroker belt.'

Miread laughed. 'Good luck!'

After Christmas, on Miread's suggestion, Rhoisin enrolled on a course at an adult education centre in Covent Garden. In the very comprehensive brochure there were so many courses to choose from that she found it difficult to make up her mind.

'How about Italian?' suggested Stephen. 'I speak a little bit of French, so if you can pick up a bit of Italian, we'll have two foreign languages between us.

'Isn't that a bit over optimistic? All I can say in Italian is 'good morning' and 'goodbye.'

'You'll soon pick up a bit more.' Stephen was already dialling the phone number of one of his soon-to-be stars.

The Italian class was a great success and Rhoisin enjoyed it immensely. She discovered she had an aptitude for foreign languages she had so far been unaware of. She found memorising the vocabulary quite easy; getting to grips with the grammar was a challenge and her pronunciation was the best in the class. She devoted hours to the set homework and bought an Italian daily newspaper. But best of all, she made a friend.

She had selected a morning course, starting at 11.00 am. She felt at her freshest in the morning and it meant also that her evenings were free to accompany Stephen to the theatre. Although Stephen would have liked his lovely wife to be with him most evenings and to dine afterwards in theatrical restaurants such as The Ivy and Rules, Rhoisin found many of the plays either too gloomy or downright boring. And as for dining out: by the time she had survived three hours of watching people caper around on the stage in totally unbelievable situations, she was more than ready for bed.

At the first class Rhoisin was dismayed to discover how elderly the other students were. In fact, it would have been kind to call them middle aged. As the college was called an adult education college, it could be expected that some of the students were mature, but not elderly. There were those who were hard of hearing and others with poor memories. There were students who had either lost their homework or had forgotten to do it; there were those who had lost not only their text book, but their entire work file. However, due to the enthusiasm and excellent organisation of the tutor, the class was a great success and much enjoyed by everyone.

As was the norm, Rhoisin was eighteen when she had started her history degree at London University, and as far as she could gather, all the other students were in the same age group. Looking back at her university days, she failed to understand why she hadn't made any friends. She could hardly blame it all on her mother's unusual profession. It must have had something to do with her; perhaps her lack of empathy towards others. But by the second week everything changed. Rhoisin was already seated when a young lady of about her age came into the classroom. The seat next to Rhoisin was vacant and the young lady sat down and introduced herself.

'I'm Vicki Davies,' she said, extending her hand and flashing a warm smile.

Rhoisin was startled. None of the other students had introduced themselves.

'I'm Rhoisin Piper.'

'Rhoisin? That's unusual.'

'Yes. It's Irish. My father was Irish.' She remembered saying this to Stephen the first time they met, long before she had tracked down her father's ancestry. But this time she knew it to be true.

After the class Vicki suggested they have lunch together and led the way to a cosy attractive-looking Italian restaurant in Bow Street, just opposite the Royal Opera House.

'The college is pretty well placed for lunching and shopping,' said Vicki gaily, as they perused the menu. 'Wine?'

'Well, just a small glass. I'm expecting a baby.'

'So am I! When is yours due?'

'The 10 June.'

'Mine's due the 10 July!'

Rhoisin and Vicki bonded immediately and became close friends. Rhoisin's life was changed for ever. Maybe it was because she had neither a father nor a sibling as a child that she had found it difficult to strike up relationships. Now her problems appeared to be over.

Between the Italian class and her blossoming new found friendship with Vicki, Rhoisin found the days just flew by. She realised, as did the tutor and all the other students, that due to the arrival of the baby, she would be unable to finish the term. Nevertheless, she made every effort to attend each class, travelling to and from the college by taxi for the last two lessons. Luckily, Islington is only fifteen or twenty minutes from Covent Garden by car. The class was on a Wednesday. There were only four more left and Rhoisin knew she would be unable to attend the last three. Unfortunately her waters broke during the night on Tuesday and the following day Rhoisin went into labour a whole week early. It wasn't just the Italian class that suffered. Stephen had carefully arranged his plans so that he would be free for two weeks, starting on 10 June. He wasn't prepared for an early birth.

However, by Wednesday 3 June the baby seemed well on the way. As Rhoisin struggled with her birthing practise routine that had been drilled into her at the natural childbirth classes, Stephen spent two hours on the phone cancelling all his appointments. As he put the phone down, Rhoisin picked it up and dialled 999 for the ambulance.

The ambulance deposited Rhoisin, now squirming and moaning with pain, at St Bartholomew's Hospital in Smithfield. Accompanied by a very anxious Stephen, she was taken straight to the labour ward on a trolley, where she spent a miserable and agonising length of time in labour. Stephen was constantly by her side, appalled at his wife's suffering, stroking her face, her arms, holding her hand and passing her a damp sponge to suck. After twenty hours had passed and there had been little progress in the arrival of the baby, the midwife called in the consultant obstetrician. Immediately assessing the situation, the consultant spoke quietly and with authority to Stephen.

'I'm sorry, Mr Piper, but your baby is in serious difficulties. I shall have to ask you to leave the delivery room while I perform an emergency caesarean section on you wife.'

The following day Stephen put a announcement in the 'birth' columns of both *The Times* and *The Irish Times*.

Stephen and Rhoisin Piper, of 10 Almeida Street, Islington London N1, are delighted to announce the birth of their baby, Thomas Liam O'Hare Piper, weighing 7 lbs and 9 ounces, on 4 June 1978.

Before he went to visit Rhoisin in hospital in the afternoon, he spent two hours on the telephone informing friends and colleagues of the most happy event. The first person he called was Rhoisin's sister, Miread.

Rhoisin spent a week in hospital. She had suffered a haemorrhage and was very unwell. In spite of her delicate condition she managed, with the expert help of the hospital staff, to establish breast-feeding, an experience she found both comforting and rewarding. The day after she arrived home in Almeida Street, Miread appeared bearing gifts of flowers, chocolates, champagne and a huge parcel of baby clothes. She had booked a room in a nearby hotel so she wouldn't impose on Stephen's hospitality and always phoned in advance before visiting Rhoisin, so as not to interfere with feeding time or the mother's essential naps.

Miread was relieved to see that the bond between Rhoisin and Stephen had become much closer. Stephen cancelled all his engagements for the next few weeks. He did the shopping, cooking, washing-up, used the washing machine with great expertise and ministered to Rhoisin's every need. He adored the baby and even took his turn at nappy changing. Hopefully Rhoisin's life has now taken a turn for the better, thought Miread.

Miread planned the date of her wedding with extreme care. She had to arrange it around her law course at university, and although the long holidays gave her plenty of choice, she also had to consider Gerry's new job. He had passed his articles with flying colours and was now a clerk of the court at the Central Criminal Court in Dublin. So at least both their holidays coincided. Just as she had done for Lindsay O'Hare's funeral, she wanted to invite everyone in Killalee, both to the church service and the lavish reception she planned to host at Knockramore afterwards. Knockramore was, of course, at its busiest during the summer months, so it would seem kinder to her French chef, Marcel Dubois, to hold the reception a little bit out of season. But above all she wanted her sister, Rhoisin, not only to attend but to be the matron of honour.

Rhoisin's recovery from her emergency caesarean section took a full six weeks. By the third week of July she was able to leave the house on her own, with her baby in its pram, and do a little shopping of a not too strenuous nature along Upper Street. September seemed the optimum time, so Miread decided to try for Saturday 3 September, exactly ten month's after Lindsay O'Hare's funeral.

She called Rhoisin.

'I'm trying to work out a suitable wedding date, Roosh. Do you think you can come over to Ireland for my wedding on 3 September?'

'I don't see why not. I'm improving every day and little Tom is going from strength to strength. He weighs 9 lbs 6 ozs now.'

'That's great! I'm delighted! I'll go for 3 September, then.'

Miread decided she would wear the full wedding dress with veil and all the extras. She had an ivory dress designed and hand-made by a well-known designer in Dublin. She left Rhoisin free to choose her own design and colour, as long as she approved of it.

Rhoisin, Stephen and baby Tom flew to Dublin, spending a night at the Shelbourne Hotel. As before, Stephen drove across Ireland in a hired car, his glowingly lovely wife beside him and his baby son, now almost three months old, fast asleep in his carry-cot on the back seat. Arriving at Knockramore, where Stephen had booked the best suite with a magnificent view over the golf course, Miread was there to welcome them warmly.

The following day the little church in Killalee was packed with wellwishers. Everyone had made a great effort for the occasion; even the roadsweeper and the butcher's errand boy no longer dressed as they usually did, so there must have been someone who had helped them to select a reasonably respectable looking outfit. Father Ignatius wore his most elaborately decorated surplus and all the choirboys had new gowns. Miread had asked Stephen to give her away. Having no father, she felt that this intimate and important ritual should be performed by a member of the family.

Gerry waited for his bride at the altar, turning round expectantly every few minutes. At his side stood Rhoisin, pale, very slim, wearing an elegant midnight blue dress. At last the congregation rose as Stephen guided his sister-in-law-to-be up the aisle to the altar rail. Heavily veiled and looking quite stunning in her off-the-shoulder long ivory dress, Miread was feeling extremely nervous.

Handing the ring over to Gerry at the appropriate moment, Stephen's heart stopped as Miread lifted up her veil and he saw the two sisters, so alike, standing side by side.

At the end of the service the organist played an energetic voluntary as the bride and groom led the way down the aisle into the bright sunshine outside. Here a whole fleet of coaches was standing by to carry the guests off to the sumptuous reception at Knockramore Country House. In the splendid setting of the ancestral home, everyone let their hair down as they ate, drank and danced the night away.

Chapter Thirty

Brigid Devlin had formed the habit of having supper at the Laughing Goat at least once a week. She had no guilty feelings of being extravagant. Thanks to Miread's handsome inheritance she no longer had to take in any more 'visitors.' Miread saw she was well provided for, so she was now comfortably off. Miread had helped her to open a bank account in Sligo Town and bought her a small practical car so she could visit Sligo, Knockramore, or any other places of local interest that took her fancy. In order to avoid the raucous crowds that often gathered in the pub on Fridays and Saturdays, Brigid restricted her visits to the middle of the week.

On that particular Wednesday the Laughing Goat was unusually quiet. In fact it was almost empty. Brigid sat down at a table by the window in the corner furthest away from the bar and waited for Mike to bring her the menu.

'Evening, Brigid. And what can I get you? Your usual?'

'I'll have a look at the menu, please Mike. And you can bring me a pint of stout at the same time.'

As Mike was pulling the pint an older lady in came into the pub. Brigid looked up and saw her friend, Mary Brothers, standing uncertainly in the doorway. Brigid waved and half got up.

'Mary! Hello! Come and join me.'

Mary came over and sat down at the table.

'I didn't want to force myself on you,' said Mary. 'I thought you might be after a bit of peace and quiet.'

Brigid laughed. 'Sure me whole life is peace and quiet now.'

'Yes, I was wondering how you would be coping, all on your own, like, with Miread married in Dublin and Eamon away at college. Don't you feel lonesome at all?'

'Oh, it's not so bad. It's a big change in life to have me daughter married. But my Miread is ever so good to me. She's set me up a nice a little pension so I don't have to take in any more 'visitors.' Although some of them were good company an' all, they were real hard work. I was always up at half past six in the morning, so as to have enough time to get all the breakfasts. Then there were the rooms to clean and the beds to make. Some of the lodgers wanted lunch as well as breakfast and dinner, so there was always a lot of shopping and cooking to do. But you know all about cooking, Mary. You've done a lot of it in your life.'

'Sure an' I have; and that's the truth. But I was cooking in a big kitchen in a posh hotel with plenty of help. Though I must confess some of those girls hired by Mrs O'Hare were quite useless.'

'I can imagine.'

'Poor Mrs O'Hare.'

'Yes, indeed,' agreed Brigid. 'Did the police ever find out why she died of poisoning? Was it an accident, do you think, or did someone actually poison her.'

'I have my theory.'

'Tell me your theory, Mary.'

At that moment Mike arrived to take their orders. Mary shut up like a clam and ordered steak and chips and a pint of stout.

'I'll have the same,' said Brigid.

Mary moved her chair closer to her friend. 'I won't spill the beans 'til Mike's done serving us. I don't want my poison theories to be entertaining the customers in the Laughing Goat for ever and a day. Tell me about Eamon and I'll get back to my theories once Mike's out of the way.'

'Well, it's all down to my Miread, of course.'

'Clever Miread.'

'Oh, yes. Most definitely. Miread's studying at university in Dublin.'

'So she told me herself.'

'She did, did she? Well, she probably told you she's planning to be a lawyer an' all.'

'Yes, she did mention the law.'

'So she said to me, Miread said: "Mam, now that I've got the chance to go to university with the money from Knockramore, why doesn't Eamon enrol at a college?" I thought that was a grand idea, entirely, so Eamon went off and enrolled at the college in Sligo Town to study hotel management. That was Miread's idea, of course. She thought he could get in some practise at Knockramore to help him along. But poor old Eamon, he wasn't up to the course at all. It's as if his poor brain isn't all there. Maybe he has a slipped chromosome or something. Is that what they call it?'

'Something like that.'

'Or perhaps he has several what's slipped. In any case, he wasn't up to the hotel management, so now he's on the painting and decorating course, which is suiting him just great. Miread said it was no harm he couldn't do the hotel management. She said he was probably better suited to the painting after all. And of course there's a lot of painting to do at Knockramore.'

'Of course there is. That's just great, Brigid. I'm very pleased that Eamon has found a useful purpose in his life.'

'Oh, yes. He's much happier waving his paint brush than he was shoving all that luggage around at the Sheaf and Sickle. And doing the nights as well.'

Mike arrived with the two plates of steaming hot food and the two ladies tucked in, too absorbed in eating to make much conversation. Finally, Mary broke the silence.

'Your Miread's been right good to me too, Brigid. That girl's a real star.'

'She is an' all.'

'She set me up with a nice little pension and a small flat in Knockramore. It's in a part of the private wing where Mr and Mrs O'Hare used to live. But you wouldn't know, she's had it done up that nicely. And she said to me the other day: "You know Mrs B, if you get tired of living here at Knockramore I can always find you a little place in Killalee. I'm keeping my eye out just in case." And of course I've still got my little car so I can buzz around the place and go into Sligo Town. I went into Fermanagh the other day, across the border...'

'Into Northern Ireland?'

'Indeed. Northern Ireland.'

'And was there any border control?'

'Well, yes. There were security guards standing on high platforms, looking all around and waving guns.'

'That must have been very frightening. Did they stop you?'

'Yes, of course. I had to get out of me car and they searched the whole thing very thoroughly. They took everything out of the boot and waved a kind of black stick underneath the whole car.'

'Did they say anything?'

'Yes. They were quite friendly, really. They said I didn't look the sort of person to have any IRA connections.'

'And what made you go there, in the first place?'

'I suppose I was curious. The 'Troubles,' as they're always called, started in 1969, didn't they? That's eight years ago. I wanted to see Northern Ireland for meself. Especially as it's not so far away from County Sligo. You just drive through the narrow bit of County Leitrim and you're there'

'And what was it like once you were in? Is it very different to here?'

'Not a lot different, really. The pillar boxes are red, and of course the notes have different pictures on them. They all have pictures of the Queen. She looks a very nice lady.'

'And when you came back across the border did the guards stop you again?'

'No, they didn't. They just waved and called: "Bye now. See you soon." '

'That was quite an experience. Would you go again?'

'I don't see why not. Maybe you'd join me, Brigid? They say it's much cheaper to shop in the North.'

'Well, now. That's worth thinking about, that is.'

Mike came up to take the plates away. 'Can I get you ladies something else?'

Mary looked enquiringly at Brigid who shook her head.

'Not watching your figure, are you?'

'Not at the moment, but I may have to soon.'

Mike collected up the plates. 'I'll leave you to think about it for a while.'

Just at that moment two young couples wearing rucksacks came into the pub. Good, thought Mary, they'll keep Mike occupied for a while and the noise of their conversation will make it more difficult for him to eavesdrop on ours.

'So what's your poison theory, Mary. Do you think someone deliberately poisoned Lindsay O'Hare?'

'No. I think it was an accident. But it was an accident waiting to happen.'

'And what makes you say that?'

'Well, we have to go back quite a bit to young Mr Roderick and the car accident.'

'The accident over eleven years ago?'

'Yes. The accident on the Boyle Road that killed Thomas O'Hare and his wife. You see, it was intended that Mr Roderick should also have died. But because he was sitting in the back of the car he escaped with his life, but he suffered the most terrible injuries; really awful injuries. I saw them with my own eyes.'

'You saw little Roderick O'Hare after the accident? I thought he was sent to a hospital for spinal injuries in Dublin.'

'He was for a while; but not for nearly long enough. His uncle, Sean O'Hare, got tired of paying the huge medical bills so he had him brought back to Knockramore far too soon. And then, so no one would know Mr Roderick was in the house, he locked him up in a secret wing that no one was allowed to enter. No one that is, except Mr Sean himself and the doctor, when necessary and' – she paused for dramatic effect – 'myself.'

'You, Mary! You knew Roderick O'Hare was locked up in that place long before the terrible fire broke out!'

'I did.'

'And why didn't you go to the police?'

'There wouldn't have been any point. Mr Roderick couldn't look after himself. He was wheelchair bound and depended entirely on his uncle financially. His grandmother, mad Mrs O'Hare, was locked up along with him as well as the nurse, Judith, who jumped to her death at the time of the fire.'

'I heard that. A terrible thing.'

'And then there was the will.'

'Thomas O'Hare's will?'

'Yes. Robert and I were the two witnesses.'

Brigid gasped. 'You knew about Thomas O'Hare's will all the time! You knew Miread and Rhoisin were going to inherit the Knockramore estate on the death of Sean and Roderick O'Hare?'

She took a long draught of stout and stared hard at Mary. 'Goodness, gracious me, but you bore a heavy secret for a long time.'

'I did. But a will is confidential. So because of the will, I couldn't go to the police.'

'Yes, I see.'

'But knowing the contents of the will made me realise Sean O'Hare would do his utmost to bump off Mr Roderick before he attained the age of twenty-one. Of course no one expected him to live that long. No one expected him to survive the car accident, but with the great medical advances we have now and the excellent nursing care supplied by Judith, Mr Roderick defied all predictions. But, believe you me, Brigid, Sean O'Hare did his utmost to do away with Mr Roderick; because he was sure that on Roderick's death Knockramore would be his. I'm convinced Sean O'Hare set up the car accident. The brakes were said to be faulty and the garage was blamed. But then it turned out the car hadn't been in the garage, or any garage, for over six months. It's my bet that Sean O'Hare tampered with the brakes. And then, in case the accident didn't work, there was the poison. My guess is that he stored up the arsenic tablets to poison Thomas, Thomas's wife and Roderick. Then when there was only Roderick left, the pills could be given to him.'

'And the fire? Do you think Sean O'Hare started it, or was it old mad Mrs O'Hare?'

'I'm not sure about that. Mrs O'Hare was known to have been a pyromaniac. She started a couple of little fires, easy enough to put out. She may have started the big one or it could have been Sean O'Hare.' She paused again. 'You see, I saw his car in the drive on the night of the fire, just as it was taking hold. He might have started it and then driven off to his death in the car.'

'Do the police know you saw Sean O'Hare's car in the drive?'

'They do. But it doesn't prove it was him who started the fire, does it? And now he's dead, does it matter?'

'I suppose not. And did you suspect that Rhoisin, Ruth, as we knew her, was Thomas O'Hare's daughter?'

'I had an idea she might be. She reminded me so much of your Miread: same fine features and the laughing grey eyes. There's a portrait in the Long Gallery at Knockramore of Liam O'Hare, Thomas and Sean's father, that I look at sometimes. The expression has quite a resemblance to Rhoisin and Miread.'

'And does Miread have any idea you knew about Thomas O'Hare's will all along?'

'No. None at all.'

'Will you ever tell her?'

'What would be the point? She got her father's inheritance; along with her sister. There's no more to be said.'

'It's extraordinary, isn't it, what an impact Knockramore has had on both our lives. Yours above all, as you worked there for over forty years and gave it your all. And now my daughter has inherited half of it! There are times when I still can't take it all in.'

'I'm sure. Me as well; especially with the lovely flat and pension I've got.'

'And now there's Rhoisin's little boy to look forward to. Thomas Liam O'Hare. She's even put O'Hare into his name.'

'Yes. He'll be an O'Hare. I wonder if he will ever go and live at Knockramore?'

'Well, we'll never know, will we?'

'Knockramore, beyond the rainbow.'

'Well, Mary, thank you for confiding all your theories and secrets in me. I'll keep them all safe, don't you worry.'

'Oh, I'm not in the least worried. And if it does come out, sure it wouldn't matter, would it? I think after all that talking, I rather fancy an ice cream.'

'Me too,' said Brigid, waving across the room to get Mike's attention.

www.ingramcontent.com/pod-product-compliance
Lightning Source LLC
Chambersburg PA
CBHW031553240626
47153CB00002B/494